more . . .

P9-CFL-430

"Muller packs plot, personality, and lots of life's messiness into the continuing saga of the San Francisco private investigator . . . Highly recommended."

"Her cases continue to be complex and chilling . . . This book is a good one."

"McCone remains one of the most popular of hard-boiled female private eyes . . . You don't have to be a card-carrying McCone fan, however, to appreciate the tightness of plot and wealth of intriguing background in her latest adventure."

"*Dead Midnight* is superb, above and beyond Muller's past work . . . Muller is one in a million, and so is McCone."

"A fun who-done-it for those readers who want a story line faster than a world class 100-yard dash."

LISTEN TO THE SILENCE

MARCIA MULLER

THE DANGEROUS HOUR

WARNER BOOKS

NEW YORK   BOSTON

Copyright © 2004 by Pronzini-Muller Family Trust
Excerpt from *Cape Perdido* copyright © 2004 by Pronzini-Muller Family Trust
All rights reserved. No part of this book may be reproduced in any form or by any electronic or mechanical means, including information storage and retrieval systems, without permission in writing from the publisher, except by a reviewer who may quote brief passages in a review.

Cover art and design by Tony Greco

The Mysterious Press name and logo are registered trademarks of Warner Books.

Warner Books

Time Warner Book Group
1271 Avenue of the Americas, New York, NY 10020
Visit our Web site at www.twbookmark.com

Printed in the United States of America

Originally published in hardcover by Mysterious Press
First Paperback Printing: June 2005

10 9 8 7 6 5 4 3 2 1

In memory of Sara Ann Freed,
dear friend, and editor for twenty-one years

A number of people have volunteered their time and expertise during the writing of this novel. Many thanks to:

Melissa Meith, director and chief administrative judge, Office of Administrative Services, California Department of Consumer Affairs, who not only provided legal insight, but suggested the subject matter.

Kathleen Hamilton, director, Department of Consumer Affairs.

Sherrie Moffet-Bell, deputy chief, Bureau of Security and Administrative Services, Department of Consumer Affairs.

Michael G. Gomez, chief, Division of Investigation, Department of Consumer Affairs.

Linda Robertson, attorney-at-law.

Eileen Hirst, San Francisco County Sheriff's Department.

Paul Cummins, San Francisco District Attorney's Office.

And, of course, Bill Pronzini, who is always there for me.

THE
DANGEROUS
HOUR

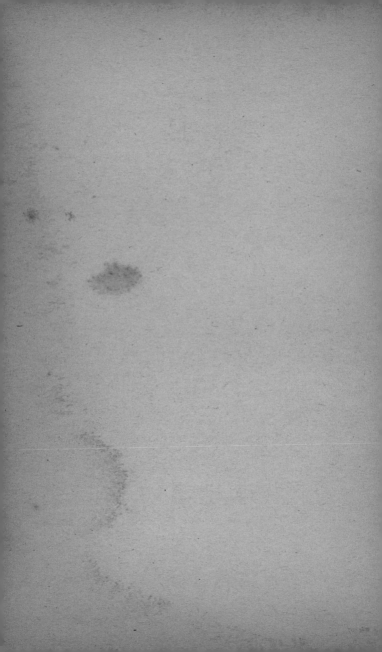

Friday

•

JULY 11

I dropped the legal pad full of notes on my office desk, went to the high, arching window that overlooked San Francisco Bay, and waved exuberantly at the pilot of a passing tugboat. He stared, probably thinking me demented, then waved back.

The reason for my impulsive gesture was that I'd just come from a midafternoon meeting with my entire staff in our newly refurbished conference room—a let-the-phones-go-on-the-machine, everybody-must-attend gathering, during which we'd discussed McCone Investigations' present healthy state and bright future prospects. When the session broke up, the others were as high-spirited as I.

During the past two years our business had tripled. Last year we'd taken over all the offices fronting on the north-side second-story catwalk at Pier 24½. My nephew, Mick Savage, now headed up our new computer forensics department and was about to hire another specialist in that area. His live-in love, Charlotte Keim, was overwhelmed with her financial investigations—locating hidden assets, tracing employees who had absconded with company funds, exposing other corporate wrongdoing—and I'd authorized her to begin interviewing for two assistants. Craig Morland, a former FBI agent, was invaluable on governmental affairs, as well as a damn good man in the field; and my newest hire, Julia Rafael, had shaped up into a fine all-around operative. I didn't see any reason why either wouldn't eventually supervise his or her own department. Of course, my office manager, Ted Smalley, had yet to settle on an assistant who lived up to his exacting standards of efficiency—so many had passed through his office that I'd stopped trying to remember their last names—but I had no doubt that in time the individual whom he called "a paragon of the paper clips" would appear, résumé in hand.

Not a bad situation for a woman who once worked out of a converted closet at a poverty law firm.

Still, sometimes I missed those days when my generation had held the firm conviction that we could change the world. Which was why the ratty old armchair where I'd done some of my best thinking inside that closet now sat under my schefflera plant by the window of this spacious office at the pier—covered, of course, by a tasteful handwoven throw. I flopped into it to savor my professional good fortune.

I'd basked in the afterglow of the meeting for only a few minutes, while conveniently ignoring a couple of personal issues that had been nagging at me, when the phone buzzed. I went to the desk and picked up.

Ted. "You'd better get out here fast!"

Something wrong. Really wrong. So much for basking.

I dropped the receiver into the cradle. As I hurried onto

the catwalk, I heard the words ". . . silent. Anything you say can and will be used against you in a court of law."

Two men near the top of the stairway. Plainclothes police officers; I recognized one. He stood poised to assist as his partner struggled with Julia Rafael, attempting to handcuff her. She bent over, kicking backward at his shins, trying to break his grasp. Beyond them Ted and Mick stood, looking confused and helpless.

"You have the right to speak to an attorney . . ."

Confusion gripped me, too. "What the hell's going on here?" I demanded.

Before either man could reply, Julia screamed, "Help me, Shar! I didn't do anything!" Then the fight went out of her, and she collapsed, nearly taking down the officer.

He steadied himself, went on, "And to have an attorney present . . ."

He finished Mirandizing Julia and yanked her upright by the cuffs. She cried out in pain, and I warned, "Careful. You've got witnesses."

He ignored me.

I turned to the other officer. August Williams, an inspector on the SFPD Fraud detail. On several occasions I'd supplied him with leads that I'd stumbled across. "What's the charge, Augie?" I asked.

"Ms. Rafael has been accused of grand theft," he replied. "Specifically, stealing and making purchases with a MasterCard belonging to—"

"I'll take her downstairs," his partner said.

I looked at Julia. Now she stood erect, dwarfing the arresting officer by some two inches. Her severe features were stony, her dark eyes blank. She didn't meet my eyes.

She'd been in this situation before, as a juvenile, and knew the drill.

I said, "Go with him, Jules. I'll call Glenn Solomon."

At my mention of the city's top criminal-defense attorney, the inspector who was ushering Julia toward the stairway paused, then glared at me. Great—a hard case, one of the types that the department was attracting, and eventually having to discipline, in increasing numbers. Thank God he was partnered with Williams, an even-tempered and by-the-book cop.

As his partner ushered Julia down the stairway, I touched Williams's arm. "Augie," I said, "make him go easy."

He nodded, his jaw set.

"As you started to say," I added, "a MasterCard belonging to . . . ?"

He looked down at me—a big, handsome man with rich brown skin, close-cropped gray hair, and concerned eyes that were pouched from lack of sleep. For a good cop, sleep is always in short supply.

"A credit card belonging to Supervisor Alex Aguilar. He alleges she stole it from his wallet after he rejected her sexual advances last month, and has used it to run up over five thousand dollars' worth of purchases."

Alex Aguilar. Founder and director of Trabajo por Todos—Work for All—a Mission-district job-training program designed to bring the city's disadvantaged Hispanics into the mainstream. Two-term member of the city's board of supervisors. Rumored to be positioning himself to become our first Hispanic mayor.

Alex Aguilar—our former client. He'd hired us to investigate a series of thefts from the job-training center. I'd assigned Julia, since she was my only Hispanic operative. When I called Aguilar after she'd brought the investigation to a satisfactory conclusion, he said he was pleased and would recommend our services to others.

Now he was accusing her of grand theft.

"I don't believe it," I said.

Williams shrugged. "I'm sorry, Sharon, but there's more. I have a warrant to search any part of your offices that Ms. Rafael has access to."

I took the document he held out as a pair of uniformed officers came up the stairway. It specified packages and merchandise from Amazon.com, Lands' End, J. Jill, Coldwater Creek, Sundance, Nordstrom, Bloomingdale's, and The Peruvian Connection, as well as a MasterCard in the name of A. Aguilar.

The warrant was in order.

"Go ahead and search," I said.

I accompanied Williams and his men to the office Julia shared with Craig Morland. Craig wasn't there, and neither were any of the items listed on the warrant. When they finished, Augie asked, "What other areas does she have access to?"

"All of them. I trust my employees and don't restrict them."

But was I wrong to put my trust in Julia? Given her history?

I pushed the doubts aside and added, "We'll start with my own office."

After Williams and the uniforms had left empty-handed, I said to Ted, "Get Glenn Solomon on the phone for me, please."

Ted hesitated, looking at Mick, who had remained on the catwalk with him. "May we speak privately?"

"Of course."

We went inside his office, and he shut the door. "You didn't tell them about the mail room," he said.

". . . It slipped my mind."

"Nothing like that slips your mind. You deliberately didn't tell them. Does that mean you think Jules is guilty?"

"I don't know what to think. They must have some pretty compelling evidence, to walk in here and arrest her without first asking her to come in for questioning."

Ted crossed his arms, leaning against his desk, and shook his shaggy mane of gray-black hair. He'd been growing it long—always the prelude to some change in fashion statement—and it was at the unruly stage. "I can't believe you don't have more faith in her. After all, you hired her in spite of her juvenile record. You're the one who keeps praising her for the way she's turned her life around."

His implied accusation made me feel small, disloyal to an employee who had, up until now, given me no reason to doubt her. But doubt still nagged at me. Ted saw I was conflicted and let me off the hook. "I'll get Glenn on the phone now."

"Thanks. And then will you please print me out a copy of the Aguilar file?"

I went back to my office and flopped onto my desk chair, numb. All the good feelings I'd been reveling in were gone now. Once again life had reminded me that things are never as secure as they seem. That none of us is immune to the sudden, vicious blow that can descend at any time and place.

Ted put Glenn through a few minutes later.

"This is bad news, my friend," he said when I finished explaining the situation.

"You don't need to tell me that."

"Julia Rafael—she's the big one, right? Five-eleven or six feet, bodybuilder's shoulders? Standoffish?"

"She's shy. She came up the hard way, and she's not comfortable with people outside her own sphere yet."

"I wasn't putting her down. That's how I acted when I first enrolled at Stanford. Down there on the Farm with all the rich kids, a scholarship student whose father was a grocery-store keeper in Duluth, and Jewish to boot. The one time I met your Ms. Rafael, she interested me. Any chance she might've done what Aguilar alleges?"

"I can't imagine her coming on to him. Or stealing his credit card in retaliation. But sometimes she does display a curious pattern of behavior."

"How so?"

"First, there's the shyness, which, as you say, comes off as standoffishness. On the other hand, in a professional situation she can be cool and assertive. But if someone says or does something—no matter how innocent—that she interprets as an ethnic, class, or gender slur, she'll lash out. I've had to warn her about that several times."

"Passive-aggressive," Glenn said.

"With a wide swath of middle ground."

"Quite interesting."

"As a case study, maybe, but not when my agency and career are threatened. If Aguilar goes to the Department of Consumer Affairs and lodges a complaint against us, it'll be expensive at best, disastrous at worst."

"DCA licenses you. And Julia."

"Only me. She's a trainee, hasn't put in the requisite number of hours to take the test."

"So you're the liable party."

"If they can prove I had knowledge of what she did."

"Which you didn't."

"No, but . . . Jesus, Glenn, you never know which way one of their hearings may go. I've heard horror stories. Their investigators just show up at your office—and not to ask if you're having a good day. They question you extensively and demand to see your files on the particular case, and if you resist turning them over, they return armed with a subpoena and the firm conviction that you must be guilty. Sometimes they even perform a general audit. If BSIS—Bureau of Security and Investigative Services, the people who control the licensing process—then deem the complaint valid, there's a hearing, whose results can range from a dismissal to the temporary or permanent loss of your license. Even if the complaint is dismissed, it's an all-around expensive proposition, involving lawyers' fees and court costs, to say nothing of damage to your reputation."

"Have you ever been involved in such proceedings?"

"No. During my early years in the business, when I was brash and took foolish risks, any number of complaints probably should've been lodged against me. But I was lucky. Now I keep to the straight and narrow, mostly, and insist my operatives do the same."

"Well, we'll worry about DCA later—if Aguilar even bothers to file a complaint. In the meantime, I'd better take myself down to the Hall of Justice."

"You think you can get Julia out of custody?"

"I doubt it. It's unlikely there'll be a duty judge on the weekend. But at least I can hear her side of the story, try to nose out what kind of evidence they have. Where will you be?"

"Here at the pier, I guess. I've got a lot of paperwork to finish up before the weekend."

"I'll see you there later, then."

After I replaced the receiver, I looked at my watch. It was five-fifteen, the time when Julia, a single mother, would normally be heading home to her young son, Tonio, or calling her sister, Sophia Cruz, to ask her to care for him. I should get in touch with Sophia, alert her to the situation.

I called the flat that Sophia and Julia rented together on Shotwell Street in the Mission district. The phone rang four times before Sophia picked up, sounding distraught.

"Sharon! Thank God!" she said. "I've been trying to get through to Jules for hours. All I got was the machine at the office, and her cell's not working."

Julia, like me, had a bad habit of forgetting to turn on her cellular, but why hadn't Ted or someone else picked up? "When did you call the office?"

"Around three-thirty, when the police came with the search warrant."

We'd all been in the meeting then, phones on the machine. "Did you leave a message?"

"No, I was too upset. The warrant, it was for the apartment and our storage bin. I had to let the police in, and they took a bunch of stuff away from the bin, gave me a receipt. All this stuff that I didn't even know was there, and I can't believe—"

Her words were spilling out breathlessly. I said, "Slow down, Sophia. What kind of stuff?"

"Unopened packages from mail-order places. Amazon. Lands' End. Nordstrom. Packages that had been opened, too. Computer stuff. Fancy outfits."

All items that could easily be bought with a stolen credit card.

"What's going on, Sharon?"

"You'd better brace yourself. Julia's been arrested." I told her what I knew of the charges.

Sophia was silent for a moment. Then she said, "She told you she didn't do it?"

"She told me she didn't know why she was being arrested."

More silence. Apparently I wasn't the only one who was having doubts about Julia's honesty. Now I felt the same reproach toward Sophia that Ted had displayed toward me.

"What?" I said. "You think she's guilty?"

"I don't want to think so. And the stealing isn't like Jules. Even when she was a teenager, turning tricks and dealing, she didn't steal. But the sex thing, coming on to the guy . . . For months now, since she and that Johnny broke up, Jules has been kind of down and sticking close to home. Then a few weeks ago she's off to the clubs, hot to trot and find herself another loser."

Julia had perfectly terrible taste in men, and Sophia rejoiced at the departure of each, while dreading the appearance of his replacement.

I said, "So you're suggesting she set her sights on Alex Aguilar?"

"Might've. I know she was excited when he asked her out to dinner. And she did say she might not come home that night, so I should watch out for Tonio. Not that I'm complaining. Jules has her needs."

I pictured Sophia: a plain woman in her early forties whose two children and husband were long gone from her life. She clerked at Safeway, played bingo at her church on Wednesday nights, and cared for Tonio. That was it, as far as I knew. But she was still young. Didn't she have needs, too?

"Well," I said, "I guess Tonio's your responsibility until bail can be arranged. Are you supposed to work tonight?"

"Yeah, but there's an old lady upstairs can take him."

Tonio was a bright, cheerful eight-year-old who did well in school and didn't seem to suffer from being shuffled off to the various caretakers who helped Julia and Sophia juggle their complicated schedules. All of us at the agency were fond of him and encouraged Julia to bring him to the pier when no one else was available to look after him. "If I can help in any way—"

"No, no. I got it under control."

After I replaced the receiver, I looked at my watch. The wheels at the Hall of Justice turned slowly. It might be hours till Glenn returned to tell me what he'd found out. I could read the Aguilar file. I could start plowing through the week's paperwork.

I could visit the mail room.

Because of the size of the pier and the number of tenants, a mail room had been established near the front entrance, to which the post office and parcel service delivery people had keys. Only one person from each firm had access to the room and made pickups. In our case, it was Ted.

I went along the catwalk to his bailiwick and found him seated behind his desk, working on a crossword puzzle. As long as I'd known him—going back to the days when he ruled the front office at All Souls Legal Cooperative—he'd been a crossword enthusiast, and now I wondered how many words he'd fitted into the little squares over the years.

"Why're you still here?" I asked. "It's Friday night."

"I'm waiting for Neal to pick me up for a weekend getaway to Monterey." Neal Osborn was Ted's life partner. "I've also been waiting for you to ask for the key to the mail room."

"Julia's sister said the police seized a lot of merchandise at their building. I have to know if there's more here."

"I understand. I've had a hard time resisting going down there myself." He stabbed his pen—the showoff always did his puzzles in ink—at the newsprint, then dropped it. "Let's see what's what."

The pier was Friday-night quiet. A light glowed in the offices of the architects on the opposite catwalk, but all the others were dark. Ted and I walked silently toward the mail room—actually a chain-link cage to the left of the pier's arching entrance. He worked the lock, opened the door, and flicked on the overhead light.

The room was divided into bins with shelves above them. Most of the bins were empty. Beside ours sat a couple of cases from Viking Office Supply. "Copy paper," Ted said. He leaned over them, reached into our bin, and grunted in surprise as he pulled out a Jiffy bag.

"What?" I asked.

He held out the bag so I could see. The return address was Coach Leatherworks. The recipient was Ms. Julia Rafael, c/o McCone Investigations.

"What should we do?" Ted whispered, in spite of there being no one to hear us.

"Put it back. That's all we can do. It's evidence. Put it back—and leave it there."

*   *   *

In the three hours before Glenn Solomon arrived at the pier, I read through the Aguilar file and completed my paperwork for the week, but my concentration wasn't all it should have been, and my thoughts kept turning to Julia.

Last year she'd responded to an ad I'd placed in the *Chronicle* for an investigative trainee, no experience necessary—the idea being that I could mold said individual to my own standards while paying a modest starting salary. The application she presented me was the most off-putting I'd ever seen, listing two incarcerations by the California Youth Authority for drug-related offenses and two firings from subsequent jobs, one by a close relative. On the plus side, she'd gotten her GED during her second stint with the Youth Authority and had a solid recommendation from the former director of a federally funded neighborhood outreach program where she'd worked for four years until the government pulled the plug on it.

In California, juvenile records are sealed in order to give the offender a fresh start, and it seemed strange that Julia would choose to reveal hers. When I questioned her about that, she said she feared her history might come out somewhere down the line, and thought it was best to be honest. During the rest of the interview I'd found her honesty to be brutal in the extreme, so brutal that I suspected she was working the angles. But jail time, even in a juvenile facility, teaches you a certain slyness, and it was an ability that would stand her in good stead as an investigator. In the end, mainly because none of my other applicants had standout qualifications, I hired her; she'd proved a fast learner and was also picking up on the interpersonal skills that would make her an asset to the agency. During the time she'd been a member of our little family—as we often referred to ourselves—she'd opened up, begun to trust in her growing friendships with us, become more confident. Now—

Glenn knocked on the door frame and came in. As he sat on one of the clients' chairs—which creaked under his weight—the set of his mouth was grim.

"It's bad?" I asked.

"It's bad."

Normally Glenn cut an imposing figure: tall and heavyset, with a lion's mane of silver-gray hair, he was always impeccably and expensively tailored, even in his most casual clothes. Although generous and kind to those close to him, he was capable of unleashing scathing sarcasm upon his opponents, and had a cobra's sense of when and how hard to strike. A man you would want as a friend, never as an enemy, and during the years he'd been throwing business my way, I'd learned to walk a fine line with him. Tonight, however, he was tired and looked nothing like the aggressive defense attorney whose thundering voice could quail prosecutors and their witnesses.

He slouched in the chair and ran his hand over his reddened eyes, then over the stubble on his chin. "God, I'd forgotten how much that jail depresses me," he said. "Normally I send one of my associates to handle the preliminaries."

"But you went for Julia."

"As I said on the phone, she interests me. Or maybe she reminds me that I come from humble roots, which is not a bad thing. And, of course, I'm concerned for you, my friend."

His words touched me. "Thank you."

"No need for thanks. Anyway, your Ms. Rafael: They're housing her in Jail Two, on the seventh floor of the Hall. High security, no bail until arraignment, and no visitors allowed except me, as her attorney."

"Why high security?"

"Because it's a high-profile case—involving a city supe—and because of 'behavioral problems.' Meaning she resisted arrest and is considered a flight risk."

"You speak with her?"

"Briefly. She claims that the arrest came as a total surprise. Says Aguilar took her to dinner at the conclusion of the investigation, and they parted on amicable terms. Denies making any sort of pass at him, or taking his credit card."

"You believe her?"

"I do. I've got a damned good internal shit detector. She strikes me as a very straightforward young woman."

"Maybe not as straightforward as she appears." I told him about the search and seizure at Sophia Cruz's apartment, and the package in our mail room.

He frowned. "Something's not right. I've never known my shit detector to go on the fritz. She claims she and her sister haven't gone into their storage bin at the apartment building in at least three months. I believe her. But by all indications the D.A.'s got a strong case. I'll know a little more tomorrow, after she's processed and I can take a look at the paperwork, but you'd better be prepared: a source close to the investigation, whom I happened to encounter in the men's room, tells me they have plenty of evidence—and that it leads straight back to your firm."

"Jesus. Because the packages they seized at her apartment house were sent here?"

"That's what I'd guess. Who brings them up from the mail room?"

"Ted."

"He still here?"

"No. He and his partner, Neal Osborn—"

"I know Neal. I've bought books from him." Neal was a secondhand bookseller, dealing on the Internet; Glenn was in the process of amassing a collection of out-of-print volumes dealing with criminal law.

"Well, by now they're on their way to Monterey for the weekend. I don't know where they're staying, and neither of them has a cellular. They won't be back till Monday morning."

"Too bad. I wonder if Ted's noticed an unusual number of packages arriving for Julia."

"He said the one we found in our bin tonight was the first he's seen, and I'm sure that's correct. What about Aguilar's credit card? Did it turn up?"

"Not yet."

"So what happens now?"

"I go over the paperwork when it's available tomorrow, and then we wait till she's arraigned."

"When will that be?"

"Tuesday morning."

"Tuesday!"

"It could be worse. Because she was arrested before four o'clock this afternoon, the case has to go to the D.A. by four p.m. on Monday. If he decides to go ahead with it, it's a Tuesday arraignment. If they'd come for her after four, the arraignment wouldn't've been until Wednesday."

"Poor Jules. So I can't visit her over the weekend?"

"No."

"That's outrageous!"

He shrugged. "Sheriff's department runs the jail and makes the rules. Frankly, they're more generous than most; as you may recall, the sheriff used to be a prisoners' rights attorney. But Julia made a bad mistake when she resisted the arresting officer—even though it wasn't much resistance."

This was going to be a very long weekend—for all concerned.

Half an hour later, when I arrived at my house in the Glen Park district, I left my car in the driveway, illegally blocking the sidewalk, as everyone else did on this congested tail-end segment of Church Street. Parking control understood that we residents settled our disputes privately and politely, and seldom ticketed anyone.

As I hurried up the front steps, I heard the patter of paws behind me and then a yowl. Alice, my calico cat. She nosed frantically at the front door while I unlocked it: *Food! I need food!*

"Hold on, will you?" She streaked down the hallway. I dealt with the alarm system, hung my jacket on the wall rack, and dumped my briefcase and purse on the chair in the sitting room. When I went into the kitchen, Allie was pacing impatiently in front of her food bowl.

"Where's your brother?" I asked her.

For the past few months, Ralph, my orange tabby, had done poorly—weight loss coupled with a huge appetite for both food and water, listlessness, back legs so shaky that he had difficulty climbing up onto the couch. He and his robustly healthy littermate were getting on up there in years, and this sudden decline worried me. We had an appointment at the vet's tomorrow morning.

Hearing his name, Ralph crept tentatively from under the table. This was the cat who once could top the back fence in a single leap, who would run to greet me, tail wagging like a little dog's. Now his tail drooped to the floor. My spirits drooped in a similar fashion, but I patted both cats and babbled with false cheer as I filled their bowls.

In the sitting room I checked the answering machine. A couple of routine calls—I was three weeks overdue picking up my dry cleaning, and even more overdue for my MG's servicing. Nothing from Hy.

My longtime love's silence was another reminder of a troublesome issue, and one I didn't want to dwell on just now. I went back to the kitchen, stuck a frozen lasagna in the microwave, and when it was ready, took it and a glass of Chianti to the table, where I ate as I read my mail. A postcard from my mother and stepfather, mailed at the end of an Alaskan cruise from which they'd now returned. A note and sample menu from my sister Patsy, who, in partnership with her husband, Evans Newhouse, had just opened their third restaurant in the Sonoma Valley. A weird, scribbled card from my half brother, Darcy Blackhawk, in Boise, Idaho. Catalogs and other junk mail that I took to the recycle bin. On the way back, I detoured to my briefcase and extracted the file on the Aguilar case. Went over it again while I finished eating.

As before, I noted nothing unusual. The investigation had proceeded in a straightforward manner. Computers and other equipment had disappeared from the Mission district job-training center Alex Aguilar and a partner had founded. Julia went undercover there, posing as a new client. She studied the dynamics of the other clients for a week, identified a pair of brothers as the probable thieves. Maintained a surveillance at night and photographed them exiting the premises with stolen goods. Followed them and photographed them turning the goods over to a third brother. Called the SFPD Burglary detail, who had arrested the brothers and seized the goods. The trial was scheduled for August, barring a complete breakdown in our overcrowded legal system. End of case.

Until today.

Saturday

•

JULY 12

After dropping off Ralph at the veterinary hospital on Ocean Avenue, where he would undergo a series of tests, I called Craig Morland. His time, I knew, would be somewhat free this weekend, as his significant other, Homicide Inspector Adah Joslyn, was in Las Vegas attending a forensics seminar and undoubtedly indulging her fondness for blackjack. Given the current situation, Craig was the employee whose expertise I most needed to tap into.

But Craig had plans. "I was about to go for my run and then stop by the Friends of the Library bookshop at Fort Mason," he told me.

"Can we meet later, at the office?"

"The office? I don't know, Shar. It's such a beautiful day, I hate to waste it sitting around inside."

It *was* beautiful: clear blue sky, a light breeze, the warm sun making the city shine clean, as if all its buildings were freshly painted. The sort of day we residents hunger for during the fogbound summer months.

"Tell you what," I said, "why don't I meet you at Fort Mason? I'll pick up deli sandwiches, and we can picnic and talk on one of the piers."

"Throw in a few bottles of Sierra Nevada, and you're on."

After a quick stop at the Marina Safeway, I drove past the boats moored at the eastern end of the yacht harbor and through the gates of Fort Mason. The former military base, from which troops and supplies were deployed by ship during World War II, seemed strangely deserted today, and I had no difficulty finding a parking space. That was a surprise, because the facility, now a part of the Golden Gate National Recreation Area, houses forty-some nonprofit organizations, four museums, a nationally renowned vegetarian restaurant, and five theaters, and plays host to thousands of special events yearly. So where was everyone? Out enjoying the beaches and parks, presumably.

I locked the MG and walked over to one of four long beige stucco buildings with red-tiled roofs—former storage depots—where the Friends of the San Francisco Public Library had their bargain bookshop. Craig was seated at a picnic bench in front of it, leafing through an illustrated copy of *Grimms' Fairy Tales*.

"Trying to scare yourself?" I asked.

He looked up and smiled, lines crinkling around his mouth and eyes. "Adah's taken to collecting kids' books. I don't know much about them, but this struck me as a pretty one—although there are an alarming number of hairy, fanged beasts in the pictures."

"The Brothers Grimm were well named."

Craig stood, stuffing the volume into a tote bag that contained several other books, and said, "Let's eat. Not much going on here today, so we should be able to find a good place."

We turned toward the three piers that extended into the bay, passing spaces belonging to such eclectic organizations as the Children's Art Center, the African American Historical and Cultural Society, and Friends of the River. At the middle pier, housing Herbst Pavilion and the Cowell Theater, Craig motioned to the right, then to the left, eyebrows raised questioningly. I pointed to the left, the sunny side at this time of day.

We walked along past rust red stanchions, some still draped in the huge chains that had tethered the military transport ships. A trio of old fishermen leaned on the railing halfway out, and they nodded cordially as we went by. After they could no longer hear us, Craig said, "I don't think I'd want to eat anything they'd catch there."

I glanced at the murky, brownish water and shrugged. "They've probably been fishing here for decades, and they're still above ground."

At the far end of the pier we chose a spot in the sun and sat cross-legged on the warm concrete. I paused to take in the view from the Golden Gate to Alcatraz, watched a sailboat that resembled a Chinese junk glide by. Craig immediately burrowed into the bag of food I'd brought.

"Hungry, are we?" I asked.

"Starved. I'm not much of a cook, and when Adah's gone, I don't eat very well."

Craig was slender, with longish brown hair and a thick mustache. Today he wore shorts, running shoes, and an FBI Academy sweatshirt that was one wash short of the ragbag. A far cry from the buttoned-down, tightly wound agent who had descended upon San Francisco several years ago, determined to nail a lunatic who seemed intent on blowing up every individual in the country who held diplomatic immunity. That case—which I'd eventually solved—had changed Craig, made him doubt much of what he'd previously believed about the Bureau, and in the course of it he'd also met Adah, who had been temporarily assigned to the FBI detail. A year or so later, he resigned and moved west to be with her, and I brought him on board at the agency. A good man, a good operative.

"Sierra Nevada. Yes!" He uncapped two beers, unwrapped our sandwiches and garlic dills, opened the potato salad container. Clinked his bottle against mine and said, "To beautiful Saturdays." As he sipped, however, his expression sobered. "Not that Jules is having much of one."

"You've heard, then."

"It was on the front page this morning. Poor kid. You been able to visit her?"

I shook my head, swallowing pickle. "They've got her in the high-security lockup. No visitors but Glenn Solomon. She told him she didn't steal Aguilar's credit card, but . . ."

Craig paused, sandwich halfway to his mouth. "Come on, Shar. You know Jules. She wouldn't do anything like that."

"I'm not so sure."

"You can't think she's guilty."

"There's a lot of evidence. Packages from mail-order houses in her apartment's storage bin. And one still in our mail room."

"There's got to be a reasonable explanation. . . ."

"I spent a sleepless night trying to think of one."

Craig hesitated. "Look, Shar, you've always stood squarely behind your employees. One hundred percent, you've been there, even when somebody screwed up and did something really stupid. How many times have I heard you say it? 'If we can't trust each other, who can we trust?' And don't give me any bullshit about Jules's juvenile record, or that maybe she's been conning us. She *is* a con woman, but she puts it to positive use—as in closing out her case files."

Craig was as cynical as they come, having blown off the FBI after years of dedicated and meritorious service. His faith in Julia both made me ashamed of my suspicions and gave me reason to hope.

"Okay," I said, "maybe you're right. Maybe she is telling the truth. But if she is, we've got to find out what really went on. That's where you can help."

"I'm with you. How?"

"You're politically informed. Tell me everything you know about Alex Aguilar."

Alex Aguilar, Craig said, had come up from Southern California in the early nineties. "Through volunteer work within the Hispanic community down there, he connected with a very bright USC grad—Scott Wagner—who had a talent for grant writing. When Wagner decided to relocate to San Francisco, he persuaded Aguilar to come along, and together they tapped into federal, state, and private money to establish their job-training program."

"Trabajo por Todos."

"Right. Things went well from the first. Wagner was a natural at administration, and Aguilar is good with people."

"Why the past tense with Wagner?"

Craig took a pull at his beer. "He died last month—a

hiking accident up in Marin County. Anyway, seven years ago Aguilar ran for the board of supes, was elected by an overwhelming majority of people in the Mission. He's in his second term now."

"They say he's got mayoral aspirations."

"Sure, but he's looking years off and positioning himself slowly."

"You know anything about his personal life?"

"It's austere. He's unmarried. Lives in the same Mission-district apartment he always has, drives an old Datsun, takes pride in wearing thrift-shop clothes, like his clients at the center."

"I noticed a certain shabbiness when he came to the agency. It made me wonder if he could afford us, but he didn't flinch at the retainer and paid off promptly. Is he still involved with the center now that he's on the board?"

"Not as much as before. He's hired a good hands-on man, Gene Santamaria, to interface with the clients and the public. I guess Santamaria's an able fund-raiser, too. Aguilar's smart enough to know he can't juggle too many balls without one of them getting out of control."

"Too many balls? What else is he into?"

"Has a business on the side—import-export, goods from Mexico and Central America. Clothing, mainly, that he sells to tourists out of a shop in Ghirardelli Square. He kicks back half of the profits to the job-training center. And, of course, he sits on the boards of any number of Hispanic organizations, including the Mexican Museum, over there in the Landmark Buildings."

"Anything else?"

"That's about it. Have I helped?"

"Some. Now, I have an assignment for you: find out everything else you can about this guy. I want to know exactly where he came from, who his parents are, every detail of his life, from birth onward."

"Shar, my caseload—"

"Shift it to someone else."

"That would logically be Jules."

". . . Right. And everybody else is swamped. Tell you what, call Tamara Corbin, my friend Wolf's partner. See if they can't take on some of it. Otherwise, give it to me."

"Like you don't have other things on your plate."

I took off my sunglasses, looked him in the eyes. "Craig, we're talking about Julia's future. And we may also be talking about the survival of our agency. We'll service our current clients in whatever way we have to. But this cannot wait."

He nodded. "I'll get on it right away."

After Craig left, I tossed the leavings from our lunch in a trash bin, reserving the bottles to recycle at home, and looked at my watch. After one, and the vet had said I shouldn't pick up Ralph till four. Nothing to do at the office; I'd finished my paperwork last night. Nothing to do at home; I'd recently hired an every-other-week cleaning service, and the house was spotless. In the end I wandered around Fort Mason, and on one of my passes along the Landmark Buildings, as the former supply depots were called, I spotted the Mexican Museum. Craig had said Alex Aguilar was on its board.

On impulse I climbed the steps to what used to be a loading dock, pushed through the glass door, and went inside.

A wide central lobby. To my left was a gift shop with a Closed sign in its window. To my right was the museum proper, also closed, but the door stood slightly ajar. I stepped inside, found an unstaffed reception desk, heard a thump from somewhere within. A woman's voice cursed in Spanish. Having been raised in San Diego, close to the Mexican border, I knew what *cagada* meant; most of the Spanish words or phrases I understood were obscene. I went over to an archway next to the desk and peered through it.

A short, slender woman whose black hair was caught up in a ponytail stood amid several crates and a quartet of two-foot-tall ceramic figures, sucking on her left thumb. A hammer dangled from her right hand. When she saw me, she took the thumb from her mouth, wiped blood on her faded jeans, and said, "Sorry, we're closed today."

I stepped into the room. The figures looked to be religious ones: a father offering up an infant to a solemn priest while the mother looked on. The expressions of joy on the trio's faces were surprisingly lifelike.

I said, "Actually, I'm not here to look at the exhibits. I was hoping to get some information about one of your board members."

The woman turned to a crate and began attacking it viciously with the claw end of the hammer. "Well, you're talking to the wrong person. I don't work here. I'm up from Santa Barbara for a temporary show." Her voice had the gentle cadence of one equally fluent in Spanish and English.

"Is anybody else here?"

"Only me. The volunteers who were assigned to help all called in sick. Sick, my *culo*. They couldn't be bothered while the sun's shining." She loosened a nail on the crate, then stuck her finger with a splinter and dropped the hammer to the floor, mouth twisting in pain.

"Let me help you with that." I picked up the hammer

and began working at the nails. As the owner of an old home, I'd become adept at such basic tasks.

"Thanks." The woman sank onto the platform where the ceramic figures stood. She leaned foward, elbows on knees, massaging her shoulder muscles.

"Used to be," she said, "I could set up an exhibit in no time, but I'm out of practice. Normally my curator and his assistants handle it, but I wanted to come up here for a visit, so I decided to take it on by myself. Over-ambitious, I guess. But what's happened to my manners? I'm Elena Oliverez, director of the Museum of Mexican Arts in Santa Barbara."

"Sharon McCone, owner of McCone Investigations here in the city."

"And you're investigating one of the board members?"

"Just verifying facts. Alex Aguilar has been the victim of credit-card fraud, and I'm looking into it."

A frown drew down Oliverez's thick eyebrows. "Aguilar? He's the one on your board of supervisors?"

"Right. Do you know him?"

"No. I suppose he'll be at the private reception for the exhibit tomorrow night—if I ever get these damned figures uncrated and set up."

"What are they, anyway?"

"They're called the Sanchez Sacraments. Executed by a famous Mexican sculptor, Adolfo Sanchez, who lived in the pottery-making center, Metepec. He willed them to my museum. The original collection represented five of the seven sacraments of the Catholic Church, one of which, sadly, was damaged beyond repair." Oliverez suddenly looked melancholy.

I studied the figures she'd already uncrated. The priest

was long-haired but clean-shaven; his eyes were wise and kind. The parents looked young and beamed at their off-spring. "These would be baptism."

"Right. You're Catholic?"

"Lapsed, I'm afraid. But I remember some of my cat-echism. You?"

"Also lapsed, but since I had my little girl, I've felt a small stirring of faith." Oliverez stared pensively at the statues. "This investigation—does Alex Aguilar know you're looking into the fraud?"

"No."

"I see. Well, then I have a proposition for you: I'll gather whatever information I can from him and the peo-ple here at the museum, in exchange for you helping me uncrate the rest of the figures."

I glanced at my watch. Two-fifteen. "I can spare an hour and forty-five minutes. Will that do?"

"Given your skill with a hammer, yes."

"Ralph has diabetes."

"Diabetes!"

Joyce Otani, DVM, nodded solemnly, cradling the cat's frail body against her white lab coat.

"I didn't know cats could get that," I said.

"Diabetes is as much on the rise in household pets as it is in the human population."

"Is it . . . fatal in cats?"

"Oh, no, it's easily treatable, if diagnosed in time. I'm assuming you *will* want to treat it, rather than have him put down?"

Ralph's yellow eyes were fixed trustingly on me: *You've come to take me home.*

"Of course."

"Good." Joyce nodded approvingly. "I'll show you how to give him his insulin shots." She set him on the stainless steel examining table. "Hold him, please."

Insulin? Shots?

"He's already eaten," Joyce said, pulling on rubber gloves. "Unlike people, cats need food *before* they receive their dosage. Will you have difficulty getting him to eat on schedule?"

"No." Like the fifties TV character he was named after, Ralph had never passed up a meal.

The cat was shedding—his typical nervous reaction. Hair stuck to my hands. I patted him reassuringly.

Joyce held up a small bottle. "Insulin. I'll fax a prescription to your usual pharmacy." Then she began a series of instructions involving cotton swabs and hydrogen peroxide. When she pulled the guard from the end of the syringe, I closed my eyes.

Needles. Gaaah!

I opened one eye and saw her seize the nape of Ralph's neck. The tiny needle glinted evilly as she slipped it under his skin.

He didn't even flinch.

"See how simple?" she said, disposing of the syringe in a receptacle by the sink and snapping off her gloves. "You should have no trouble at all."

No trouble at all. Yeah, right.

Forty-five minutes later I left Safeway's parking lot in possession of an insulin prescription from their pharmacy made out to "Ralph McCone Cat," a box of syringes, and a creature that, should his cries be translated into English, would have been heard to wail, "I *hate* this fuckin' cage!"

Even though he'd already eaten at the veterinary

clinic, once home he headed straight for his food bowl. In recognition of his ordeal, I spooned out some of the disgusting, gluey stuff that passes for a catly feast, then put a bit more in Allie's dish. Naturally, he started in on hers.

I put the insulin in the fridge as the pharmacist had told me to and set the box of syringes on the counter. Contemplated them, then stuck them in the cabinet below. In case somebody came over, they might spot the box and think I was shooting myself up. They sure as hell would never believe I was shooting up the cat.

The phone rang. Glenn. "Sorry for taking so long to call," he said. "The paperwork on Julia took an unusually long time to process, and then I had an appointment that I couldn't break."

"What did you find out?"

"I saw the field arrest report. Nothing we didn't already know. They ran her prints; no history in San Francisco, but, as we know, juvenile records are sealed. At least we can rest assured that she's stayed out of trouble as an adult. I spoke with an inspector on Fraud who's helped me out before. He said Alex Aguilar was alerted by the fraud department of his credit-card company to a large number of charges on a card he seldom used; what triggered their attention was an attempt to purchase a first-class airline ticket that was turned down because it was over his limit. An analysis of the charges showed that all purchases went to a third party: Julia, at your business address."

"Damn! Glenn, let me ask you this: do you feel comfortable representing Julia?"

". . . Yes, I do. Remember what I said about my internal shit detector?"

"Uh-huh."

"Well, I met with her after I reviewed the paperwork. And later, in the dentist's chair—which was the appointment I couldn't break—I gave long and serious thought to what my detector was telling me. Even knowing about the packages the police recovered, and the one in your mail room, I feel the same. She's not lying, my friend."

First Craig, now Glenn. Maybe it was time for me to start believing in my formerly trusted employee.

Monday

·

JULY 14

Monday morning I was in my office early, going over the résumés of the final candidates whom Mick had selected for the position of computer forensics specialist. The work of our new department consisted of retrieving messages and files that had been deleted by employees of our clients, often for unethical or dishonest reasons, and was highly complex—at least to me. All the résumés looked impressive.

I realigned the papers, thinking back to my long, unproductive, and depressing Sunday. At nine A.M. both cats were happily eating from their food bowls. I arranged a syringe, a cotton ball, and a bottle of hydrogen peroxide on the kitchen counter, took the vial of insulin from the refrigerator, and rolled it between my palms to warm and mix the solution. Swabbed its top. Yanked the protective guard from the syringe's plunger. Pulled the guard from the needle.

And stabbed myself in the forefinger.

"Damn it!"

Ralph glanced at me, then went on eating. His more high-strung sister streaked for the back door. I set the syringe down, let her out, then returned and examined the contaminated needle. Would it infect the cat? No way to tell.

I took out a second syringe and filled it, but as I was checking for air bubbles, my finger slipped and depressed the plunger. Insulin spurted all over the countertop.

My confidence withered. It took me two more tries before the syringe was properly prepared. Then I couldn't find the cat. He turned up behind the couch in the sitting room, and I had to drag him out. When I grabbed the nape of his neck, he wriggled so hard that I was afraid I'd yank off his fur suit.

I held him down with my elbow and started to insert the needle. He jerked, squeaked, and got away from me. I followed in hot pursuit, brandishing the syringe like a sinister character in a horror film. He led me on a merry chase down the hallway to the front door, where I trapped him and lowered him into a crouch.

Then I stuck the needle clear through a fold of his skin so the insulin shot out the other side.

"Oh, Jesus, Ralphie, I'm sorry!"

He wasn't accepting any apologies. As soon as I removed the needle, he streaked away and hid under the guest room bed.

It was clearly time to call in a reinforcement.

"Nothing to it," Michelle Curley said. "I take care of a diabetic cat for this family over on Chenery Street all the time. Come on, I'll show you." The spiky-haired teenaged neighbor, who took care of my house and cats when I was away, led me to the kitchen and confidently set about loading a new syringe.

"The deal," she told me, "is not to panic."

"I didn't panic," I lied.

"Attitude's everything." She led me to the guest room, got down on her stomach, and slid under the bed. "Hey, Ralphie, dude. What did your mama do to you? Yeah, I know, but 'Chelle's here, and everything's gonna be cool now. There ya go. Not so bad, huh?"

She slid back out, Ralph in her arms. "I don't know why you had so much trouble. He's a pussycat in more ways than one."

"He must still be upset because I took him to the vet yesterday. That's why he fought me."

"He doesn't seem upset." She handed him to me.

Ralph was purring.

"Well, I don't know. He just wouldn't cooperate." I glanced at the syringe in her hand, then looked away.

Michelle frowned, studying me. Then she grinned. "I don't believe it."

"Believe what?"

"Tough private investigator. Crack shot with a three fifty-seven Magnum. Airplane pilot. And you're scared of a little needle."

"I'm not—"

"Ralph picked up on your fear, and you scared him, too."

"I didn't—"

"Listen, Shar, I'm into animal psychology. People psychology, too. If you're that afraid of needles, this is never gonna be a comfortable deal."

"Thanks for the vote of confidence."

"How often d'you have to give him the shots?"

"Twice a day."

"A problem if you go out of town or come home late. And you go out of town and come home late a lot."

I'd thought of that before.

Michelle added, "I can help you out here."

And here comes the sales pitch.

"For, say . . ." She screwed up her brightly lipsticked mouth, rolled her eyes thoughtfully. "For twenty bucks a month, I'll be glad to shoot up Ralph for you."

Michelle already earned a substantial monthly stipend from me. Not that I begrudged her a penny: she was conscientious in the extreme and frequently provided nice personal touches, such as the fresh flowers I'd found in the living room when I'd returned from San Diego after my father died. Still, I sometimes wondered about a kid whose avowed goal in life was to amass large amounts of cash in order to become a real estate mogul. . . .

"Of course," she added, "if you'd rather do it yourself, I'd be happy to work with you for a few months—at only ten bucks per—till you're ready to go it alone."

Yes, she's certainly into people psychology.

I said, "Twenty bucks a month seems fair to me."

After Michelle left, I went to the phone, picked up the receiver, then hesitated and replaced it in its cradle. If Hy was determined to maintain silence, so would I.

Since the events of September 11, 2001, Hy's duties as an international security specialist and hostage negotiator had demanded a great deal of his time, but now he had taken a well-deserved vacation. This week he was at his ranch in the high desert country near Tufa Lake. If the weather was good there, he'd ride this morning, checking the sheep graze that was willed to him years ago by his stepfather. If the weather was bad, he'd be in the comfortable living room by the fireplace, browsing through his collection of western fiction and nonfiction, sampling volume after volume until something caught his interest. But no matter what he was doing, I knew he was thinking of me.

Hy and I had always shared an odd psychic connection, and now I could feel his mood as if he were beside me. Today he was contemplative and patient. Biding his time without feeling particularly anxious. Giving me the chance to decide what direction I wanted our future to take. No pressure, and thus no call.

So why did I feel pressured? And why couldn't I bring myself to call him? Normally, given what had happened during the past two days, I'd've been on the phone to him, seeking his input and reassurance. But now . . .

I glared at the phone.

Why did people want to change things that were functioning perfectly well to begin with? Why did they want more, when less was enough—?

The office phone buzzed, bringing me back to the present. I picked up.

Ted. "There's a Mr. Todd Baylis here to see you. He's with the Investigations Bureau of the Department of Consumer Affairs." His tone was ominous—and with good reason.

The other shoe had dropped.

"Ms. McCone?" Ted asked formally when I didn't respond.

"I'm here. Tell Mr. Baylis I'm finishing up with something, wait five minutes, and show him in."

I used those minutes to calm myself so I could project a professional appearance.

Todd Baylis was a stocky man with thick blond hair,

a cleft chin, and a bone-breaking handshake. As he sat on one of the clients' chairs, his gray eyes assessed me through a pair of chromium-rimmed glasses. I thought I caught a hint of meanness in the set of his mouth, but supposed that could just be my reaction to the threat his presence implied.

I sat behind my desk, anchored his business card under my stapler, and said, "What can I do for you, Mr. Baylis?"

He set his briefcase on the desk, opened it, and took out a file. "Last month your agency contracted with a client named Alex Aguilar."

"That's correct. He hired us to investigate several incidents of theft at his job-training center in the Mission district."

"Shouldn't that have been a police matter?"

"Of course, but . . . I assume you live in the Sacramento area, Mr. Baylis?"

He nodded.

"Are you familiar with San Francisco?"

"Not intimately, no."

"Well, there are problems here. I love the city, but I'd be the first to admit to them. Our police department has been in what I'll politely call a state of disarray since last fall, as well as being chronically understaffed and overburdened. Agencies such as mine take up the slack."

"Who was assigned to the Aguilar investigation, Ms. McCone?"

He knew that; it would have been detailed in Aguilar's complaint. So why was he asking?

If I weren't cynical, I'd say it's to verify the facts. But I am cynical, so I'll say it's because he thinks taking an aggressive stance will give him power over me.

I said, "Julia Rafael handled it. My only Spanish-speaking operative. I assume you're here in response to a complaint from Supervisor Aguilar. And I assume you're aware that Ms. Rafael has been arrested."

Now the hint of meanness around Baylis's mouth grew more pronounced. He curled his lip, revealing unnaturally white and even teeth.

"That's true, Ms. McCone," he said. "Mr. Aguilar has lodged a complaint with my department—against you, as Ms. Rafael's employer."

A chill settled on my shoulders. I folded my hands on the desk and said as coolly as I could manage, "Ms. Rafael has denied Mr. Aguilar's allegations. Because of the timing of her arrest, we won't know if the district attorney intends to go forward with the case until this afternoon."

"Has she been released on bail?"

"No."

"And why not?"

"You'll have to consult with her attorney on that. Glenn Solomon, of Solomon and Associates." I handed him one of Glenn's cards, which I kept in a wooden box on the desk.

Baylis's eyebrows raised a fraction; obviously he knew Glenn by reputation. "Perhaps after she's arraigned we could meet so I could hear her side of the story?"

"Of course. I'm as anxious as you must be to clear up this false allegation."

"And perhaps you could provide me with a copy of her case file and report?"

I nodded and buzzed Ted, asked him to print them. When I stood to show Baylis out, he said, "That's all right, Ms. McCone. I know the way."

* * *

"I'm sorry, my friend," Glenn said. "This complaint to the DCA worsens the situation."

"I gather it isn't the type of problem you care to handle. Any suggestions as to someone who might represent me?"

"The person I think you want is Marguerite Hayley—Maggie, for short. Extremely sharp woman, specializes in this area. Degrees from Berkeley and Yale, taught for a while at Boalt Hall. She doesn't work cheap, but she gets the job done."

"She's here in the city?"

"Tiburon. Why don't I put in a call to her, get the ball rolling."

After considering my options for a few minutes, I buzzed Ted and asked him to set up another agency meeting for that afternoon. "Check everyone's schedule, and try to find a time when they can all attend. And until then, don't mention Todd Baylis's visit to anyone." My employees deserved to know what was going on, but it was better presented to the whole group at the same time, in a straightforward manner, rather than having them hear it by word of mouth.

"Will do." Ted's tone was curt.

"What's wrong?"

"How long have we worked together in one capacity or another, Shar?"

"Eons."

"And when was the last time you knew me to gossip about sensitive material?"

"Never."

"Then why do you feel compelled to warn me against it now?"

". . . I don't know."

"Could it be that your distrust of Julia has spread to the rest of us?"

"Ted, no. But this is a really bad time; I'm trying to handle a type of situation I've never encountered before. Never thought I *would* encounter. I guess I'm doing it badly. If I implied—"

"That's okay, so long as you don't imply anything like that to the others."

"I would never—"

"Look, Shar, you're talking to the grand poobah here." The title he'd created when I'd promoted him and upped his salary last year. "One of the items on the job description I've concocted for myself is to help you keep things in perspective. Be the in-house psychologist to the often stressed-out boss. Truth is, when one trusted person lets you down, you may have a tendency to expect the worst of others. I'm cautioning you, is all. So say thank you, and let me get on with setting up this meeting."

"Thank you and please get on with it."

No wonder I loved and valued Ted.

After I replaced the receiver, I got up and paced— from the desk to the window and back to the desk. I'd been spending too damn much time in the office lately, mired in reports and fiscal matters and personnel issues. But those things weren't what had drawn me to the business; field work and the chase had. I needed to get out of here, take action. But what?

The phone buzzed. Ted said, "An Elena Oliverez on line two."

Who . . . ? Oh, yes, the woman whom I'd helped uncrate the ceramic figures at the Mexican Museum on Saturday.

"How did your opening go?" I asked her after we'd exchanged greetings.

"Very well. I met your Mr. Aguilar. He's quite attractive, in a scruffy way. Charismatic, too."

"Were you able to learn anything about the fraud case?"

"It wasn't the time to bring it up. I did mention it to a couple of the museum employees, though, and they knew nothing more than what appeared in the newspaper. However, I did hear some interesting information. Mr. Aguilar has been out of sorts for about a month: extremely nervous and short-tempered. One of the other directors mentioned an outburst at a board meeting."

"Over . . . ?"

"Nothing in particular, just a sharp exchange of words with one of the members. I'm well acquainted with such incidents, from sitting on my own museum's board."

"When was this?"

"A month ago. Could his short temper be related to the fraud case?"

"I doubt it. A month ago he didn't even know his credit card was out of his possession."

"Well, he didn't seem stressed last night, and he left this morning on a trip to Mexico and Central America. A buying trip for a business he owns."

The import shop in Ghirardelli Square. "Anything else?"

"That's all I could find out."

"I really appreciate this, Elena. And, as thanks, I'd like to take you to lunch before you leave town."

"I'd like that, too, but I'll have to take a rain check until I return next month to dismantle the exhibit. I'm flying home to Santa Barbara this afternoon. Our daughter is driving my husband crazy. It's not that Arturo's an inept father; Gaby's a real handful. Exactly as my sister and I were, only my mother—Gabriela, my daughter's named after her—had to cope all alone. Anyway, I'll call you before I come back up. I'd like to talk with you about your work; I've had . . . some experience with crime myself."

And, having imparted that tantalizing bit of information, Oliverez ended the call.

Another bit of interesting information: Alex Aguilar was out of town. Meaning that if I visited Trabajo por Todos, I wouldn't run the risk of encountering him.

As I drove along Mission Street toward the job-training center, my eyes were assaulted by a riot of color. Red, white, and green Mexican flags fluttered in the wind outside a bakery. Pink, saffron, and turquoise mobiles twirled lazily in front of an Asian market. Artichokes, oranges, avocados, grapefruits, and limes were heaped in the outdoor bins. A black lowrider was painted with brilliant flames. A woman strolled along wearing a purple and green sari. Several walls were painted with intricate multihued ethnic murals. Sound blasted my ears: salsa and rap music, honking horns, shouts, and the shrieking brakes of a Muni bus. The air was thick with the smell of frying tortillas, exotic spices, sesame oil, curry, and good old American grease. When I stopped for the light at Seventeenth Street, I saw a red, yellow, and blue cloth parrot fall from above, its wings fluttering. It bounced off a parking meter and landed on the sidewalk. When I looked up, I spotted the laughing brown face of a little girl at a third-story window.

In the late 1800s the Mission became a way station for

the waves of immigrants inundating the city. Newly arrived Irish, Germans, and Italians settled there, creating a solid working-class neighborhood. Then, in the 1930s, came the Latin Americans—a flood tide that reached its peak in the '50s—and for decades the district was predominately Hispanic. Now yet another ethnic transition is taking place as Asians, blacks, and caucasians move in. The result is a melting pot in the truest sense of the word. The area has its problems—gentrification that threatens to displace longtime residents, drugs, crime, homelessness, and lack of funding for critical services—but it's also a place where ground for community gardens is broken, where colorful street fairs celebrate diversity, where clubs and restaurants and boutiques take hold and siphon off money from more advantaged parts of the Bay Area. Many years ago I lived near the heart of the Mission, and I'm not all that far from it now; it was an interesting place back then, but today it is positively vibrant.

Of course, you still can't find a parking space. . . .

I circled the block where the center was located, cruised along Capp Street. No spaces, but a chain-link fence opened onto a small parking lot, and I saw a sign for Trabajo por Todos posted on a rear entrance. I pulled in and wedged my MG into a narrow space between two monster SUVs.

Concrete stairs led up to the entrance, which was unlocked. Inside I heard the chatter of female voices. I walked along an industrial-carpeted hallway, glanced through a door from which the voices came. Women—at least fifty of them—sat at long tables, their sewing machines' clacking and whirring competing with their conversation. A garment-manufacturing company, but not a sweatshop; years before, I'd investigated abuses in one of the latter, and I could tell the difference. These workers looked happy and productive, and were probably unionized and well compensated.

A sign beside the elevator indicated that the job-training center was located on the second floor. I opted for the stairs. I hadn't been able to swim at my health club as often as I would've liked recently, so I took my exercise when and where I could.

A series of arrows painted on the pale green walls directed me through labyrinthine hallways, past closed doors where no light shone behind the pebbled glass windows. No surprise: much of the office space in the city was vacant these days, especially in areas considered marginal. Finally, at the end of the last hallway, a set of double doors opened into the center's headquarters.

The kid at the desk in the small reception area had lime green hair and multiple facial piercings. So much for bringing the occupationally disadvantaged into the mainstream. I was reminded of my half brother, Darcy Blackhawk, who had had purple hair and piercings when I met him, but had recently removed the hardware and dyed his hair back to its original black in an attempt to reconnect with his Shoshone roots. Personally, I doubted that Darcy, a former substance abuser, would ever reconnect with much of anything; he lived in a world of his own manufacture—a safe haven from the demons that plagued him in this one.

"Help you?" the receptionist said.

"I hope so. I'm a freelance writer, and I'm interested in doing an article on your organization. Is there someone I could talk with?"

"That would be my dad, Gene Santamaria. I'll see if he's available." He picked up the phone, spoke into the receiver, set it down. "He'll be out in a few minutes. Please have a seat."

So much for first impressions. Santamaria's son was cordial and efficient enough to impress even Ted.

I sat on a metal folding chair and studied the notices posted on the bulletin board across from me. They were mostly in Spanish, advertising—as much as my rusty language skills would permit me to make out—everything from a fiesta of food and dance to a battered-women's shelter. The door behind the reception desk stood open, and from inside came the sound of laughter, a baby crying, and a strident voice that could only be an aerobics instructor's.

It was five minutes before a big bald man with a swooping mustache that reminded me of Hy's stepped through the door. He glanced at the receptionist, who nodded toward me, then came forward, extending his hand. "Gene Santamaria, program coordinator. And you are?"

I rose and took his hand, coming up with my half sister's name because I'd been thinking of Darcy. "Robin Blackhawk, struggling freelance writer." Actually, Robin Blackhawk was a law student who planned to transfer from the University of Idaho to Berkeley in September.

Santamaria let go of my hand and stepped back, appraising me and raising his bushy eyebrows. "Struggling? I didn't think struggling writers dressed with such style."

I'd worn my Donna Karan suit today because I had an appointment with an important client that afternoon. It was a two-year-old outfit that still seemed like an extravagance, but one which, Ted assured me, presented the proper image for the owner of a successful and growing agency.

God, sometimes I longed for the days when all I wore were jeans!

I said to Gene Santamaria, "Don't let my style fool you—this suit is left over from when I was a dot-commer."

"Ah, yet another casualty of this hideous economy."

"Yes, but it's enabled me to get back to the things I really care about. Writing, and publicizing those who deserve it. Such as your job-training program."

"And in what publication will the article appear?"

"I'm writing it on spec, but I hope to place it in the *Chronicle*'s Sunday magazine. Other newspaper magazines as well."

He considered that, then nodded. "I happen to have a half hour free. Let me show you around, and later we'll talk in my office."

Santamaria led me through the door at the rear of the reception area. From the right came the strident voice I'd noted earlier, interspersed with thumps and groans. "Aerobics class?" I asked.

"Yes. The purpose of our center is to produce applicants who are fully employable in every sense of the term—and that means being attractive and physically fit. Now, over here"—he motioned to the left—"is our language lab. Clients study English using workbooks and tapes—supplemented, of course, by classwork."

A child wailed in the next room. "Our day care center."

I peered through the open door, saw a roomful of toddlers playing with colorful toys. Cribs were lined up along the far wall. A woman was squatting on the floor, comforting the crying child, who was gesturing wildly at a little girl who possessively clutched a Tonka truck.

Santamaria shrugged, smiling. "I'm a father myself, but I don't know how our volunteers manage. Now, over here to our right is the computer room. An invaluable skill today. Apple and Hewlett-Packard donated the machines."

I started to look inside, but my guide pressed onward. "Classrooms. The courses being conducted at the moment are 'Getting Along'—basic business etiquette— and bookkeeping. In addition to regular classroom work, we've made arrangements with a large auto repair shop, an electrical contractor, and a major insurance company to take on clients as apprentices. And here is the cafeteria; clients interested in the food service industry work with volunteers to provide free breakfasts and lunches five days a week. We'll go to my office now."

He led me down a narrow hallway to a series of modular cubicles. "These cubicles were donated by a dot-com firm that closed its San Francisco branch last year. No high administrative overhead here; we take what's offered to us, and eighty-two percent of every cash donation goes directly to servicing our clients."

Santamaria's cubicle was small and spartan: desk, computer workstation, file cabinets, one chair. He motioned me into the chair, picked up the phone and said to hold all his calls, then sat behind the desk, hands folded. "What else can I tell you about the center, Ms. Blackhawk?"

I took out my voice-activated tape recorder. "Do you mind?"

"Feel free."

"Thank you. First, I'd like to get some background on Trabajo por Todos. I understand it was founded by

Supervisor Alex Aguilar and a grant writer named Scott Wagner."

"That's correct. Supervisor Aguilar was a social worker in Southern California. When he moved north, he contacted Mr. Wagner on the advice of one of his colleagues. It was an effective and productive association."

"And Mr. Wagner is now deceased?"

"Yes, unfortunately. Two months ago he died in a hiking accident up in Marin County."

"And then Supervisor Aguilar hired you?"

"Yes. I oversee fiscal matters and fund-raising, as well as the day-to-day operations of the center."

"A large responsibility."

"I have good support staff, both paid and volunteer."

"I understand Alex Aguilar is not so active in the organization."

"Also correct. Alex has his duties on the board of supervisors, as well as an importing business that brings revenues our way."

"Is it possible I could talk with him?"

"Sorry, no. Alex is out of town. Perhaps when he returns."

"What about your clients? I'd like to use a few personal success stories in the article."

"Ah, I can certainly provide you with that." He opened his desk drawer and extracted a file folder. "Testimonials to our success."

I glanced through it. Computer-generated text, along with smiling photographs. "Would it be possible for me to talk personally with some of these people?"

"Of course, Ms. Blackhawk. Read through the file, then call me. I'll be glad to put you in touch with whoever you wish."

I reached for my tape recorder and stood, but didn't turn it off. "By the way, Mr. Santamaria, I noticed an article in the paper last weekend about Mr. Aguilar. Apparently he's been the victim of credit-card fraud?"

"Yes, that's correct. However, it doesn't apply to our organization. Why do you ask?"

I shrugged. "Just curious. I myself was once a victim of identity theft."

Gene Santamaria rose from his chair. "That must have been a nightmare, Ms. Blackhawk. I know that Alex has been very troubled by the situation."

I started to speak, but he looked at his watch. "Did I say I had half an hour? I've enjoyed our conversation so much that I've run fifteen minutes over."

Santamaria hadn't once glanced at the time since we'd begun talking, but now that I'd mentioned the fraud case, our interview was ended.

From the car I called Ted to ask what time he'd been able to set for the agency meeting. Owing to everybody's conflicting schedules, he told me, it would have to run over the noon hour.

"Fine," I said. "Why don't you order in food—"

"I've got it covered. The consensus was pizza."

"Coffee and—"

"The carafes're full of freshly brewed caf and decaf. Sodas're in the cooler."

It was five after eleven, time for one more stop. I took the Aguilar file from my briefcase and looked up the supervisor's home address. It was on San Jose Street between Twenty-fourth and Twenty-fifth, not much of a detour.

The apartment building was one of those bland types

constructed in the sixties: three stories of dirty white stucco with rectangular picture windows facing the street; the windows were framed above and below by decorative panels that probably once had been turquoise but now were a peculiar shade of blue. Rust stains had accumulated at their corners. The curtains on all the windows were closed against the decidedly unscenic view of a utility pole and a hideous orange house across the pavement, but one of the three garage doors on the ground level was open, and a talk radio show was playing. I left my car blocking the driveway, went over, and stuck my head inside.

A red-haired man in dirty jeans and a grease-streaked T-shirt stood with his hands on his hips, staring angrily into the engine compartment of a battered old Ford Falcon. "Piece of shit," he muttered.

"Excuse me," I called.

He started. "Excuse *me,* lady. Didn't know anybody was there. But this thing *is* a piece of shit, you know?" He wrinkled his freckled nose.

"I know." I motioned outside at the MG.

"That one looks like a real classic car. Mine . . . Well, that's what I get for trusting my cousin Joey. He works for Xavier Motors, used-car joint over on South Van Ness. This thing comes in—God knows how they drove it onto the lot. Joey gets it cheap, sells it to me at cost. He's gonna help me fix it up, my great mechanic cousin. Sure, he is. I ain't seen him since. Let me ask you this: why're all guys called Joey fuckups?"

With a flash of sadness, I thought of my brother Joey, who had committed suicide with an overdose of drugs and alcohol. Yes, he'd been a fuckup. A lovable one, but a fuckup nonetheless. . . .

"Ah, hell," the man said, tossing the filthy rag he held

into the Falcon's engine compartment, "you don't wanna hear about it; *I* don't wanna hear about it. What can I do for you?"

"I'm looking for information on your fellow tenant Alex Aguilar."

The man scowled. "Aguilar? What's the bastard done now?"

"What did he do to make you call him a bastard?"

He took a step back, held up his hands. "Whoa, lady. I don't even know who you are."

No need to conceal my identity; this guy wouldn't tell Aguilar about my visit. I gave him one of my cards.

He studied it, looked up with a gleam in his eye. "He in trouble?"

"Could be."

"Good. I'm Patrick Neilan, by the way. Live downstairs from Aguilar. What d'you wanna know?"

"Start with my original question: Why's Aguilar a bastard?"

"He's lived here for eight, nine years, right? So he thinks he owns the place. Polices everybody. Don't put your recycle bins there; don't put out your garbage till the morning of pickup; don't leave your junk mail in the lobby. You have a party, make a little noise, he doesn't warn you; instead he calls the cops. He's got an in, see, on account of being a supervisor, so you can't complain to them. I tried complaining to the landlord once, but a lot of good it did me."

"What about consulting an attorney? The guy's violating your rights."

"Lady, I could barely afford this car. How can I afford a lawyer? Nah, it's just easier to tone down the noise at the parties."

"Does Aguilar have parties?"

"Shit, no. He's too busy saving the world."

"What about women friends?"

"Some, but they don't last."

"Last month, did you see him with a tall Hispanic woman? Strong looking, multiple ear-piercings, cropped hair?"

He thought, shook his head.

"Maybe if I brought a picture around . . . ?"

"Maybe."

"The other tenants—how many apartments are there?"

"Six, but only four're occupied."

"How do the others feel about Aguilar?"

"About the same as I do. Angela Batista, woman who lives across from him, says if he had a vicious dog—like the one attacked and killed that woman in Pacific Heights a couple years ago—she'd take her chances with the dog."

A very different portrait of the supervisor than what had appeared in the press and his campaign literature. I told Patrick Neilan that I'd be back that evening to talk with his fellow tenants.

Mick glanced covetously at my untouched slice of pepperoni pizza. I motioned for him to take it. I'd just finished explaining the current situation to my staff, and had no appetite whatsoever.

"So that's how it stands at present," I concluded. "We'll know late this afternoon whether the D.A. is planning to go forward with the case against Julia. If he does, we'll also know what evidence they have against her.

But, regardless of what he decides, BSIS may still pursue the complaint against me."

Craig asked, "What's the likelihood they'd do that?"

"I don't have a clue. As we all know, state budgets for the various administrative departments have been drastically slashed. That could work in our favor. Why pursue a specious complaint when there's no funding for pursuing the serious ones? On the other hand, we're a high-profile agency and the complainant is also high-profile. BSIS was created to enforce the standards set for our industry, and if Alex Aguilar decides to make a commotion, they've really no choice but to pursue and resolve it. Private investigators have taken some bad hits in the press lately, and you can't blame BSIS for taking aggressive action. Tomorrow I'm seeing an attorney who specializes in this area—someone Glenn Solomon recommended. Maybe then I'll have a better feel for what might happen."

"So as for now, Shar?" Ted asked.

"We ought to be prepared for the worst, on all fronts. Friday, it looked as if we'd be expanding. Today we're in a holding pattern. Your paragon of the paper clips will have to wait." I turned to Mick. "I've gone over the résumés you gave me, and I like all three of the candidates, but I think we should hold off on offering employment to any of them."

"Shar, these people are the cream of the crop, and they're going cheap because of the rotten economy. If we wait, we'll lose them. One in particular, Derek Ford—"

"We'll talk later, in my office. Charlotte, I'm afraid I'm going to have to ask you to hold off on your assistants as well."

The petite brunette's mouth pulled down with disappointment, but she only nodded.

"And," I added, "we'll have to tighten our belts all around. Take good care of our current clients, but in a way that doesn't strain the budget."

"Well," Ted said, "we can all chip in for the next batch of pizzas."

"I don't think it's that dire yet"—I flashed Mick a mock glare—"provided this one goes on a diet."

Mick grinned sheepishly. He was tall, but lately—because cooking and dining out were hobbies of Charlotte's and his—he'd entered love-handles territory.

"Okay," I said, "we're out of here. Craig, I want to see you in my office right away. Mick, I'll buzz you later."

"Alex Aguilar," Craig said, opening his file. "Born, Long Beach, thirty-six years old. Father, Hector, worked the docks at Terminal Island, is retired now. Mother, Celia, held various service industry jobs and is also retired. Alex is the youngest of four children. A sister, Teresa, is a housewife in Crescent City; another, Maria, has a beauty salon in Modesto. The brother, Jim, manages a Denny's in Grass Valley."

"Average middle-class family, then."

"Middle class, yes. But not so average."

"How so?"

"The Aguilars have a tradition of activism within the Hispanic community. Now that they're retired, the parents work with various nonprofit organizations in the L.A. area. One sister currently volunteers with a literacy program, the other with a battered-women's shelter. The brother is on his county's board of supervisors."

"And now Alex has built on his own record of community service to a potential mayoral bid."

"Right. Aguilar graduated high school in Long Beach, enrolled at San Diego State the next fall, majoring in political science. Dropped out after three semesters— money was short—but remained in the area, working as a waiter. Rematriculated a year and a half later, received his B.A. after another six semesters. Took a job as a social worker for L.A. County immediately upon graduation."

"Don't most social workers have at least a master's degree?"

"Apparently Aguilar did volunteer work during college that qualified him. And L.A. County wasn't paying enough then to hire fully credentialed people. Aguilar quit and came up here eleven years ago."

"Okay, that's bare-bones background. What about the personal stuff? Who is this man, aside from what his campaign literature and press releases claim? Was it political ambition that prompted him to give up a secure job as a social worker and come up here to start a job-training center? What romantic relationships has he had? What do his old friends say about him? His enemies? His barber? His bank teller?"

Craig frowned. "Shar, forgive me for saying so, but it sounds as if you're launching a vendetta against the guy."

"Well, Aguilar's already launched a vendetta against this agency. Having Julia arrested was one thing, but he didn't have to file a complaint with DCA. He could just as easily have come to me and asked if I had knowledge of her actions. He could have taken a respectful and professional approach, but he chose not to."

"Now that you mention it, his reaction was somewhat extreme."

"And that's not all. I've found out Supervisor Aguilar's private persona does not mesh with the public image." I related what Patrick Neilan, Aguilar's cotenant, had told me. "I'll find out more this evening when I talk with the other tenants of the building. And in the meantime, I want you to keep digging."

"Right. But what about this belt-tightening you were talking about? I'll have to fly down south, or co-opt people at other agencies there. I've already farmed out two clients to Tamara Corbin—"

"Do what you have to."

"Shar, this is Derek Ford."

Derek Ford was tall, lean, bespectacled, and clad in a black leather cap and a long black leather coat. His smooth facial features looked Eurasian. A tattoo of linked scorpions showed above the vee neckline of his black silk shirt. My first take on him was of affluence and confidence. From his résumé, I already knew that he was highly intelligent.

And he wasn't supposed to be here. I'd told Mick to hold off on hiring anyone for his department.

I contained my displeasure with my nephew and said, "Mr. Ford, I'm glad to meet you, and I'm very impressed with your résumé. But Mick should have explained our situation. We've had to impose a hiring freeze—"

"Call me Derek," he said, taking my offered hand. "Mick's explained everything, and it doesn't matter to me. I really want this job, and I'm here to offer my services, free of charge."

". . . Free of charge?"

"Yes."

"That's a first. Please, sit down, Derek. You too,

Mick." When we were settled, I added, "I'm not used to people volunteering to work for me. Will you explain why you are?"

"Because, until your problems are resolved, I can afford to. I made a fair amount of money in the dot-com boom, and unlike many of my colleagues, I didn't spend it on ten-buck martinis, fast cars, and cocaine. I grew up in a home where frugality was considered a virtue; both of my parents are college professors, but there were five of us kids, and they were determined we'd all get at least an undergraduate education, so everyone pulled his own weight. You flip burgers after school or bus dishes on weekends, you learn the value of a dollar pretty quick."

I liked what he said, liked the way he looked me in the eye as he spoke. "And exactly why do you want the job so badly?"

He grinned, glanced at Mick. "Because I can learn a lot from this guy."

"Your résumé says you have a degree from Cal Poly. You didn't learn enough there?"

"I'm well educated, yes. And like I said, I profited from my early job experience, even though the company I was with crashed and burned. But I've got enough sense to realize I'm only competent in my field. Mick is a genius at what he does. Some of the advanced concepts he's working on . . . well, I want to help him develop them."

I glanced at Mick.

He smiled smugly: *See? I've always told you I was a genius. Now you're hearing it from a total stranger.*

"What kind of concepts?" I asked my nephew.

"If I could explain them to you, they wouldn't be advanced."

Mick had come a long way since the sorry day when

his parents shipped him north to me, as penance for such sins as hacking into the Pacific Palisades Board of Education's mainframe and selling the confidential information he gleaned to his fellow students. Now he had concepts. Concepts that could only benefit my agency . . .

Now he also had a talented assistant.

"Okay, Derek," I said, "here's the deal I can offer you: you come to work for the genius and me; I don't pay you a salary until the agency's current problem is resolved; I do, however, enroll you in our health care plan, which is a pretty good one; your 401(k) plan will kick in if and when you begin receiving a salary. Should we be unable to offer you a permanent position because our situation worsens, you'll retain your health care benefits for a period of three months after we terminate you. If you do achieve permanent status, your pay will be retroactive from the date you started."

He blinked, and the corners of his mouth quirked up. "That's very generous, Ms. McCone."

"Everybody here calls me Sharon or Shar. So is it a yes?"

"It's a yes."

"Welcome aboard. When would you like to start?"

"Now?"

"Fine. Go help this man"—I motioned at Mick—"work on those concepts I can't possibly understand."

After Mick and his new assistant left my office, I made a note on my scratch pad to purchase for my nephew a baseball cap I'd recently seen in a catalog. One of the things you could have embroidered on it was "Genius."

*   *   *

"The D.A.'s going forward," Glenn's voice said on the phone. "Arraignment's at ten tomorrow morning."

"But that's when I'm meeting with Marguerite Hayley over in Marin."

"No reason for you to be present."

"But I want to be there for Julia's sake. . . . And what about her bail?"

"She says she can't afford it, insists she'll just stay in jail."

"No way. She's been there long enough. The agency will pay—"

"I'll handle it. I'm convinced she's not a flight risk, and I'd like to invest in her future."

"That's very good of you, to go out on the limb for someone you barely know."

"I know Julia well enough. And, as I told you before, she interests me. Things I've been hearing via the grapevine interest me, too."

"Oh? What?"

"We'll talk tomorrow. I'll take Julia directly from the Hall to my office. You meet us there as soon as you're done with Maggie."

"That guy, I see him in the paper, always smiling. Smiling when he's sucking up to the voters here in the neighborhood, too. But at home, he's like an ugly dog with sharp teeth."

Angela Batista was the only tenant of Alex Aguilar's building who had been home when I began ringing doorbells that evening. We were seated on the sofa in the small living room of her cluttered top-floor apartment across the hall from the supervisor's; the curtains were drawn, and only a dim floor lamp illuminated her broad features and high-piled black hair.

"You listen to me," she went on. "I am part owner of the Mission's newest, hottest tapas restaurant. Café Gastrónomo. Everybody who is anybody eats there. I am connected to the establishment in this city, and let me tell you this: that guy has got them fooled."

I picked up the coffee cup Angela Batista had placed on the table beside me, sipped, and tried not to gag. The concoction, she had informed me, was her personal variation on one of the popular International Coffees line. To me, it tasted like instant to which she'd added an inappropriate herb, such as oregano. I hoped to God she wasn't offering it at her hot new restaurant.

"That guy," she went on, "I see him on television, at one of the Giants games, with the mayor. Smiling. I see him at the opening of our new low-income housing development, with one of the governor's people. Smiling. I see him in the newspaper, at the hospital with that little boy who was hit by a Muni bus on Mission Street. Smiling. But here I see him like he really is."

"Not smiling."

"Not smiling. He scowls. He snarls. He tells everybody what to do. The garbage, it can't go out till he says so. He polices the laundry room. Leave your clothes in the dryer overnight, and he puts them in the trash. This apartment doesn't come with garage space, but if I park my car one inch over the curb by *his* garage, he calls the cops and I get a ticket. Those apartments in this building that're empty? The people left because of him. The others? They probably won't talk to you because they're afraid of him. Now, me, I am not afraid of him. He is scum. And the people who come to see him?" She threw up her hands in disgust.

"What kind of people?"

"Cheap women, the kind I chase off the sidewalk in front of my restaurant. Men that would sooner cut you than look at you. This one—R.D.—he lived there for weeks last month. He was an ex-con—I could tell; my brother-in-law's one. But my brother-in-law's just a stupid pachuco doesn't know enough to stay outta trouble. This R.D., he was plain evil. I tell you, he must've had something on that Aguilar, for him to let him stay. They'd fight, in there. Loud voices, and one time I heard things breaking."

"What's R.D.'s full name?"

"I don't know."

"What does he look like?"

"I don't know. What do any of those scum look like? Scars, tattoos. Evil."

"And you say he left last month?"

"Yeah, right around the time you were asking about, when Aguilar says that woman ripped off his credit card."

"You sure you don't remember the woman?"

"I never saw her. But you listen to me: if she did rip off Aguilar, the more power to her. That guy deserves every bad thing happens to him."

I was silent, my hand hovering over the coffee cup. Angela Batista's hostility toward Alex Aguilar was understandable, but why did the well-connected owner of a hot new restaurant continue to live in such an unpleasant situation?

"Ms. Batista," I said, "why don't you simply move, or consult your attorney?"

Her gaze slid away from mine.

"Ms. Batista?"

After a moment she said, "Moving is expensive; attorneys' fees even more. My restaurant has only been open seven months. It's hot, yes, but it's yet to make a profit. My life savings are sunk into it, and I have no extra money."

"Perhaps if you talked to one of the influential people who frequent the restaurant . . . ?"

Her mouth pulled down ironically. "Oh, yes, that would bring me much goodwill from my customers. Aguilar is one of them; he eats there often, both with friends and in the company of his influential colleagues."

"You must have some recourse——"

"No, no, I don't." Batista stood. "You must excuse me now, Ms. McCone," she said. "I have to be at the restaurant by nine o'clock."

As I was leaving the apartment, I shook Angela Batista's hand, looked into her eyes. And what I saw there surprised me: for all her angry rhetoric, Batista was afraid.

Light shone from under the door of one of the lower-floor apartments. According to Patrick Neilan, this one belonged to Vanessa Lu, a teacher at the nearby Happy Days Preschool. When I knocked and explained who I was and what I was after, Lu—trim and athletic in pale blue sweats—looked wary. When I mentioned Neilan, her reserve melted and she invited me inside. The apartment, because it faced the street, was a mirror image of Angela Batista's, but uncluttered and simply furnished with items like those I'd seen in Cost Plus ads. Lu asked me to be seated at a teak dining table and, mercifully, offered mineral water with lemon slices rather than a noxious coffee concoction.

"Alex Aguilar," she said in answer to my question, "is

a classic case of someone who's out of his depth in public and compensating with petty tyrannies at home. I suppose Patrick's told you about all the rules and regulations?"

"Angela Batista's gone into them as well."

"I don't know her, except to say hello to, but I'm sure she's had her run-ins with Alex. We all have."

"What exactly do you mean, 'out of his depth'?"

"I don't think Alex was ready to be thrust into the limelight as a supervisor. The rumor is that he was pushed into campaigning by the district's Hispanic community, and didn't really expect to win. So far, he's holding his head above water, but he's beginning to show the strain of treading too hard. And strain always shows first at home."

"What kinds of run-ins have you had with him?"

"Well, he dumped my trash all over the sidewalk once, because I put it out too early. And he yelled at me for spilling detergent in the laundry room. Since then I've kept my distance. I've learned to avoid emotional storms that are about to break. Now I put out my garbage when he says to, do my laundry at Tidee Clean, and generally keep a low profile."

"Doesn't it bother you, to have to go out of your way to avoid upsetting a fellow tenant?"

She smiled, running her hand through her short, rumpled hair. "Sure, it bothers me, but the apartment is relatively inexpensive for this city. My place of work is within walking distance, so I don't need a car, and I can put money aside to buy a house someday. I'm not about to throw all that over for the sake of going up against an inadequate personality who will probably be history in a few years."

"History? I thought Aguilar was setting his sights on the mayor's office."

"He—or his people—may be setting their sights, but I suspect that one way or another Alex will self-destruct."

"Interesting. Did you ever encounter a recent houseguest of his, a man called R.D.?"

"Hispanic man? Tall, with a scarred face?"

"Yes. Angela Batista mentioned him. She said he might be an ex-con."

"That wouldn't surprise me. Those scars, and the tattoos . . . He was here for two weeks, maybe three, then left. We passed each other in the entryway, but never exchanged a word, or even a nod. You know, I've taken self-defense classes, and I'm not a timid person, but that man frightened me. If he'd been the one making the rules here, rather than Alex, I might've given serious thought to finding another apartment."

It was full dark when I left Alex Aguilar's building. While the street itself was quiet, in the distance I could hear sirens overriding a cacophony of other sounds: music blaring, cars honking, dogs barking, a man shouting, another voice wailing. As I walked the two blocks to where I'd left my MG, a bottle shattered on the sidewalk behind me. I whirled, saw a figure dart between two buildings.

It's not personal, McCone, and this is not a bad neighborhood. Hell, you used to live only a couple of blocks away, near an intersection whose four corners are now occupied by trendy establishments.

Footsteps rushed up behind me. A hand tugged on the strap of my slingbag. I tightened my grasp, yanked it away. Before I could turn, the person gave a high-pitched giggle and ran off.

A kid playing a stupid prank, that's all. The real predators come out much later than this, in the dangerous hours.

My MG was parked at a barely acceptable angle at the next corner. I took the keys from my pocket, hurried toward it. Stopped.

"Damn it!"

The convertible top had been slashed, a big gash extending its entire width. I looked through the window, saw that my briefcase was gone. It contained files, my tape recorder and Palm Pilot, an expensive pen the staff had presented me on my last birthday, a sterling silver business card case . . . No sense in even reporting the theft; such items were never recovered. My mistake, anyway. Stupid to leave it in plain sight.

I inspected the damage to the top, saw it was not repairable. They probably didn't make tops for this model anymore; I would need a costly custom job—and at a time when I could least afford it. Jesus, how could everything in my life turn to shit in such a short time?

Once I got home, after a warm shower and a cool glass of wine I abandoned my resolve and, with some nervousness, dialed Hy's ranch.

A month ago he'd asked me to marry him. I'd told him I'd think about it, but had gotten no further than trying to figure out why the concept of marriage filled me with an emotion bordering on dread. Two weeks ago he'd told me he was flying up to his ranch and would remain there, waiting to hear my decision. So far I had made none, and hadn't felt right about calling him. But after the events of the past four days, I needed to hear his voice, to ask for his input.

He didn't answer, and for some reason the machine wouldn't pick up.

Monday. Fucking Monday.

Tuesday

·

JULY 15

"First of all, I recommend that you cooperate fully with the DCA's investigator"—Marguerite Hayley consulted the notes she'd taken while I explained the situation—"Mr. Baylis. He may have an unsympathetic or even antagonistic attitude, but, as you yourself admit, he's simply doing his job. You should provide him with whatever records he requests, assuming they contain nothing confidential, and agree to attend all meetings with him. For my part, I will immediately let BSIS know that I've been retained to represent you, and that you are committed to cooperating."

I nodded, envisioning cash flowing out of the agency's coffers. Everything about Hayley's office in her home high in the hills above Tiburon spoke of exorbitant fees: the dark blue Chinese rug, the worktable and clients' chairs that were either original Chippendales or good imitations, the softly lighted oil paintings that reminded me of the Dutch masters. Hayley herself, a petite white-haired woman in her mid-sixties, was dressed in a tan suit that probably cost more than my entire wardrobe; gold and diamonds winked at her earlobes and on her ring fingers.

My expression must have reflected my thoughts, because she smiled gently and said, "Don't feel that this office reflects my fees, Ms. McCone. They're well within the normal range. It just so happens my late husband left me well off, and I like to work at home."

"With that view, I'd want to spend as much time here as possible." Behind her a glass wall opened onto a balcony; I could see the Golden Gate and the entire sweep of the bay. Fog was pouring through the Gate, obscuring the bridge's midspan, but on either side the sun shone—an eerie-looking phenomenon that told me the city would be socked in by early afternoon.

"It *is* lovely," Hayley said absently, consulting her notes. "Now, from what you've told me, I know you're well aware of the seriousness of the charges and what the possible penalty could be. I should add that if this goes to a hearing and you lose, you also will be assessed the cost of the investigation and prosecution. My goal in contacting BSIS is to prevent them from taking it that far. Are you at all interested in trying to settle early, accepting some level of probation?"

"Absolutely not! I haven't done anything."

She nodded approvingly. "All right, then, we'll wait it out, see how the investigation progresses. I'll talk with BSIS, meet with their people, and review the file. I'll speak with the investigator as well. I'll work my contacts and put you in the best possible light. You have an excellent reputation and a clean record, so there's a good chance I can get the case dropped. If there's already a deputy attorney general involved, I'll get in touch for a little lawyerly jostling. Should be fun." Her blue eyes twinkled.

"What about the case against Julia Rafael? If it's not proven, won't BSIS drop the case against me?"

"Possibly, but they could still go forward. In an administrative proceeding, the burden of proof is different from that of the courts. Just because the district attorney can't prove the charges against Ms. Rafael beyond a reasonable doubt doesn't mean that BSIS can't prove those against you by the lower clear-and-convincing-evidence standard. But don't fret about that now. I'll be in close contact with Glenn Solomon about Ms. Rafael's case. We'll share evidence, facts, and tactics. The best all-around solution would be if we could prove the theft and credit-card fraud never happened, but that's unlikely. Now, this brings us to a subject that I sense you're not going to like, because you strike me as a person with a great deal of loyalty to your employees."

"That's true."

"And commendable. However, you should be prepared for the possibility that you may have to let Ms. Rafael go. In effect, distance yourself from her in order to save your license."

As I started to protest, Hayley held up her hand. "The law assumes that you know what your employee has done. Ultimately, it may be a matter of disproving that assumption. But let's not get ahead of ourselves just yet."

"All right. What's your opinion of the case we have?"

She folded her hands on top of the pad on which she'd been taking notes. "So far, we don't have a case, Ms. McCone. We have Ms. Rafael's claim of innocence, and by now Glenn has received details of the evidence against her. We have some facts and, frankly, a great deal of conjecture. We need more facts and a framework to place them in. Normally at this point, I'd bring in my own investigator, and he'd set about developing that."

"But . . . ?"

"But there's no need for him, now, is there? Who better to build our case than the party with the most to lose?"

As I drove back to the city, I tried to shore up my sagging spirits. I was equal to the task, wasn't I? Look at the cases I'd solved single-handedly. Look at what the agency had collectively taken on. And it didn't matter that this case was deeply personal; I'd solved that type of case before. I'd once foiled a woman who was trying to steal my identity. I'd tracked down the mother who gave me up at birth, and the father who only suspected my existence.

Doesn't get more personal than that.

But I couldn't build any resolve or enthusiasm. Everything seemed to be crashing and burning around me. Hy had suddenly changed from the easygoing man I'd fallen in love with to a man with a mission. My cat had diabetes. I was riding across the bridge—which was now totally socked in—in a car whose top was held together with duct tape.

My *life* felt as if it could use duct tape.

As Glenn ushered her into his office at two that afternoon, Julia—in the denim jacket and jeans she'd been wearing on Friday—looked shabby next to his tailored elegance. Her eyes widened as they took in the leather furnishings, oriental carpets, and dark, polished wood. Fog wrapped around this high floor of Embarcadero Four, making it seem that we were trapped in some remote but luxurious alternate universe. Certainly a universe as remote as one could get from Julia's everyday world. I wondered if the expression on her face was similar to what Marguerite Hayley had seen on mine as I sat in her office contemplating fee scales that morning.

Glenn steered Julia toward one of the armchairs facing the desk. I said hello and smiled at her from the other. She nodded and tried to return the smile, her lips trembling.

Glenn sat behind the desk, clasped his hands on the vest that stretched over his well-rounded stomach. Several weeks ago he'd confided to me that at the urging of his wife, interior designer Bette Silver, he'd taken to working out on "one of those contraptions that threatens to seize and strangle me if I anger it." So far, his new regimen had produced no visible results.

"Have you been waiting long?" he asked me.

"An hour or so. But I've kept busy." I motioned at the copy of the California Penal Code that I'd set aside when they arrived.

"Ah, some light reading." To Julia, he added, "Sharon is the only person I know who actually enjoys law books. She delights in bringing obscure statutes to my attention. Did you know that in California it's illegal to trap birds in public cemeteries, but not in private ones?"

Julia shook her head.

"Neither did I, and what she expects I'll do with the information is beyond my understanding." Glenn leaned foward then, removed a file from the briefcase he'd set on the desk, suddenly all business. I'd seen him make such abrupt switches of mood in court, much to the confusion of his opposing counsel.

"Bail," he said, "wasn't as bad as it might've been. Twenty-five thousand. The judge accepted my argument that she's a long-term resident of the community, single mother, gainfully employed, has family and friends to lend support."

Julia said softly, "You shouldn't've paid it."

"Of course he should have," I told her. "It's bad enough you were in jail for three days."

"I've been in jail before. And you know I don't like to owe what I can't afford to pay back."

"Then don't flee the country, and eventually you'll owe me nothing," Glenn told her.

The corners of her mouth twitched in a faint smile.

"Now," he went on, "as to the evidence: Julia tells me she concluded her investigation for Alex Aguilar on June thirteenth. He asked her if she'd like to go to dinner to celebrate a satisfactory wrap-up to the case. Friday the thirteenth. Wouldn't you know it? Why don't you take it from here, Julia, tell it to Sharon as you told it to me?"

She shifted toward me in the big chair. Her eyes were deeply shadowed and troubled. "Okay, he asked me to dinner, and I said yes. I justified it by telling myself it was a business meal, no big deal, but I admit I was attracted to him. And it'd been a long time since I had a real date. Anyway, we went to this tapas place in the Mission that's owned by a neighbor of his."

"Café Gastrónomo?" I asked.

"Yeah. Lots of important people go there; they kept stopping by our table. People I never thought *I'd* meet. Afterwards he suggested we go back to his place, have some more wine. And I did. Stupid, huh?"

"I've done stupider things. Go on."

"I was there about an hour. We drank; he played some music, had a couple of phone calls that he took in the bedroom. Then he started to put the moves on me, but I could tell he wasn't really into it. I mean, it felt like he was . . . following a manual, or something." She glanced at Glenn, flushed.

Glenn spread his hands. "Consider me as you would your parish priest. Nothing anyone says can shock me."

"Great, and me not even Catholic anymore. To say nothing of you being Jewish."

Her response startled me. I'd expected her to be as intimidated by Glenn as she was by his office, but apparently in the short time they'd spent together, they'd built a rapport.

"Anyway," she went on, "a guy acting like I'm some kind of machine he's trying to program is a total turnoff to me. I said I had to go home and relieve the babysitter, got the hell out of there. Wouldn't even let him drive me. And that was the end of it."

I asked, "You didn't hear from him again?"

"No."

Aguilar couldn't have been too upset at Julia's rejection; the next Monday he'd complimented her work to me. I turned to Glenn. "What evidence does the D.A. have?"

He opened his folder, paged through it. "The packages they seized from Julia's storage bin. No credit card; since it hasn't turned up anywhere incriminating by now, I doubt it will. Aguilar's complaint alleges that he last used his MasterCard at Café Gastrónomo on the night of June thirteenth. However, on July seventh he received a call from Citibank's fraud division, asking about unusually frequent and high purchases beginning on June fourteenth. All the charges were placed by computer and were to be sent to a second party—Julia Rafael—at McCone

Investigations. That's where it leads back to your agency."

"Wait a minute," I said. "The orders must show the e-mail address they originated from."

"Yes, they do. All were placed late at night from the main computer at Trabajo por Todos."

Relief flooded me. "Well, there you have it. Julia didn't have access to their computer after she concluded her investigation. Someone who did must've stolen Aguilar's credit card and placed the orders. I don't know why the D.A. is going forward—"

Glenn shook his head.

"What?" I said.

"There's a matter of a key," he told me. "One to the job-training center that Julia used while she was investigating. Aguilar claims she never returned it."

I looked at her. "But you did."

She shook her head, gestured at Glenn. He was holding up a key on a metal chain.

Julia said, "I forgot to give it back. I don't know how I could've, but I did."

"So what's your gut feeling about this?" Glenn asked. "Is she a truth teller, or have we misjudged her?"

We were alone in his office, Julia having gone home to be with her son. She'd refused Glenn's offer of a cab, saying she preferred to walk over to Market Street and take BART. She hadn't much money with her and didn't want to accept any from either of us.

I said, "Sometimes she's a truth teller. She's also a bit of a con woman—but then, so am I. Nobody who doesn't possess a sneaky, shifty side gets very far in our business. You walk a little to one side of the line, a little to the other, and hope you don't stray too far. But I do know this: Julia's not stupid. And only a fool would have attempted a scam like this. So, yes, in this case at least, she's a truth teller."

Glenn nodded, fingering the key to the job-training center.

I said, "I wonder why the police didn't find that. You said it was mentioned in the search warrants for her home and my offices."

"It was in a cluttered container in her office desk; they must've overlooked it. We stopped by to pick it up on the way here." He hesitated. "I suppose Maggie Hayley mentioned to you that you might want to distance yourself from Julia."

"Yes. I refused."

"How are you feeling about that now?"

I considered before I spoke. "I don't want to give up on her. She's come so far since I hired her. Ms. Hayley's convinced me that our best strategy is to prove the crimes didn't happen the way Aguilar says."

"That would be an excellent solution, my friend. Why don't you get started?"

Fund-raiser dies in fall

by Kristine Winter
Chronicle Staff Writer

Scott Wagner, fund-raiser for the Mission district's Trabajo por Todos, died in a hiking accident at Olompali State Historic Park in northern Marin County on Sunday, June 22. Wagner's body was discovered at the bottom of a steep ravine on

Monday afternoon by a maintenance man who was repairing a drainage pipe. Wagner, 34, was an experienced hiker and frequent visitor to the park, according to Ranger James White, who spoke with him shortly after his arrival that morning.

"This is a tragic loss for Scott's friends, associates, and Trabajo por Todos' clients," said Alex Aguilar, co-founder with Wagner of the center. "His spirit, tenacity, and talents will be very much missed."

A memorial celebration of Wagner's life is to be held at the center's headquarters at 2141 Mission Street at five P.M., Sunday, July 6. Contributions in his honor to the job center will be welcomed in lieu of flowers.

I hit the Print icon and waited while a copy of the *Chronicle*'s June 23 article on Scott Wagner's death slid from the machine. Then I backed up and started another search for Olompali State Historic Park. Their Web page gave a brief description and directions: It was on Highway 101, just above Novato, some thirty miles north of the city. The park hours specified day use only, and it was well after six. Still, I called the phone number listed on the site, hoping to reach Ranger White, but got only a recording. Then I went to my old armchair and rested my feet on the low sill of my office's big, arching window. Stared out at the shifting fog.

When investigating a person's life, look for the unusual—even if the unusual appears to have nothing to do with the matter at hand.

The man who trained me as an investigator, Bob Stern,

had embedded that—and many other valuable concepts—
into my mind, and I, in turn, had frequently recited them to
my operatives.

Look for the unusual.

Damned right. Tomorrow morning I'd head for northern
Marin County.

Wednesday

·

JULY 16

The directions to Olompali State Historic Park instructed northbound drivers to continue past the park on Highway 101 and, at the next opening in the median strip, make a "safe U-turn" south.

Sure, I thought as I waited for traffic to clear. Huge trucks, passenger cars, and SUVs rumbled past, some in a gaggle, others spread out, all going too fast. I'd be lucky if I got to the park by sundown.

But then, miraculously, a break appeared, and I shot across into the far lane. Headed south to where a wood-and-stone sign marked the park entrance.

I drove along a winding access road across a sun-browned meadow toward the western hills—sun-browned, too, and thickly forested with darker vegetation. A jackrabbit bounded across the pavement, and I braked hard to avoid hitting it; it ran along the side, as if it were racing the MG, then veered off into the underbrush.

The road ended in a parking lot where several vehicles, including a horse trailer, sat. A rider astride a roan was starting up a dirt trail, the horse picking its way carefully. I got out of the car, took off my light jacket, and threw it into the back. It was warm and clear here, unlike in the fogbound city. Maybe in the high eighties, with a cloudless sky. I stood still for a moment, savoring the heat and the scents that filled the air—dry grass, eucalyptus, and bay laurel. Then I went to pay the park fee and started toward a paved pathway that led to a distant cluster of buildings.

There weren't many people in this part of the park, just a couple sunning themselves on a blanket spread next to a huge iron pot that looked as if it should contain witches' brew. I nodded to the sunbathers and walked toward the buildings. The closest was a curious hybrid, the back part a two-story adobe in poor repair, the front a characterless shingled box with aluminum-framed windows. Brick steps led up to the box; I climbed them and peered through the dusty windows into a dark room where building materials and assorted junk lay about.

A quick inspection of the adobe and a nearby yellow frame house turned up no one, but sounds came from across the path, where wide, moss-covered steps led down into an area that was laid out like a formal garden. Eucalyptus, oak, walnut, and some of the tallest, most spindly palms I'd seen outside Southern California shaded the area, and a man in work clothes was tossing a fallen limb into a wheelbarrow near a huge cairn of stones at the garden's center. I went down the steps and saw that the stones—artfully piled some twenty-five f high and another twenty-five feet in circumference—were actually a fountain surrounded by an empty pool. In between the stones at various levels from top to bottom were large, cavelike spaces where ferns, agapanthus, and calla lilies grew. Two small children were running around in the pool and ducking in and out of the lower caverns in a game of hide-and-seek.

The man tossed another tree limb into the wheelbarrow and straightened. "Okay, you two, I'm not gonna tell you again," he called to the kids in a deep, Spanish-accented voice. "Climb on outta there."

The kids scaled the pool's wall and ran across the garden toward the steps, squealing when they narrowly avoided crashing into me. The man took off his Giants cap and wiped his sweaty face with his forearm, then nodded to me and shrugged. "The parents should watch them, but they don't. Me, I'm not paid to babysit, but they could get hurt in there."

"Yeah, they could. Do you know where I can find Ranger James White?"

"Sorry, ma'am, he doesn't work here anymore. Can I help you?"

"If you have a few minutes to answer some questions."

He jammed the cap back over his longish black hair, sat down on the edge of the fountain, patted the concrete beside him. "I don't take a break soon, I'll get a heatstroke. Days like this, they make me wonder why I don't get a job in a nice, air-conditioned office building. This thing was filled"—he jerked his thumb at the fountain—"I'd jump right in."

I sat beside him, gave him one of my cards, introduced myself.

The man studied the card, then said, "I'm Ray Rios, park maintenance. So, Ms. McCone, how come you drove all the way up here?"

"A client has asked me to look into a fatal hiking accident that happened last month."

"You must mean Scott Wagner. Only fatality we've had all the years I've worked here. I was the one found his body. An accidental fall. Why would somebody hire you to look into it?"

"My client's a relative, wants closure. You know how that is."

Rios nodded. "Well, it was a Monday afternoon, June twenty-third. I'll never forget. I'm pulling a broken drainage pipe up past the Miwok village. Springtime, there's a lot of runoff from up above. Pipes collect it, dump it in the stream, stop erosion. I'm going back to my Jeep for one of my tools when I see something blue in the ravine, so I climb down, and it's a dead body, face in the water. I turn him over and it's Scott. His head is all bashed in. Face was pretty bad, too."

"You knew Scott Wagner, then."

"Most of us did. He hiked here once, twice a month."

"It's a long way to come from the city for a hike."

"Scott told me he grew up in Novato, had been hiking here since he was a kid. Guess he felt connected to the land. He was a good guy, raised funds for some nonprofit. Offered to help us get a grant to keep the restoration going, but he died before we could do anything."

"That house looks like it could use a lot of restoration." I motioned at the adobe with the shingled addition.

Rios nodded. "The old Camillo Initia adobe. Later the Burdell family home. This place has some history. Spanish land grant, site of a battle during the Bear Flag Rebellion in the eighteen-forties. Initia sold out to a rich Marin family—the Blacks—in the eighteen-fifties, and Olompali was passed along ten years later to the daughter, Mary, when she married Galen Burdell, the San Francisco dentist who invented tooth powder. She was the one planted this garden. Loved plants, old Mary did. Went as far as Japan for some of them, actually got them to grow here."

He shook his head, smiling wryly. "Crazy family, though. Mary's stepmother died from blood loss or something while Doc Burdell was doing surgery on her teeth. After that, old man Black disinherited Mary and took to drinking, used to come up here and ride around on horseback, so drunk they practically had to tie him to the saddle. He died, and when they read his will, Mary got so pissed off at being disinherited that she tore his signature off the will and ate it. Was arrested, caused a big scandal."

This was all very interesting, and normally I'd be fascinated by the crazy family—possessing one of my own—but Rios's storytelling wasn't furthering my purpose in coming here. "Could you show me around?" I asked. "Take me to the place where you found Scott Wagner's body?"

"Sure." Rios stood. "My Jeep's over there, beyond the stone bridge."

As we walked toward the steps that led up toward the adobe, he said, "Bet you can't believe that was once a twenty-six-room mansion, real fancy country estate. Remained in the Burdell family till World War Two, when they sold it. After that a lot of different people lived here. Jesuits used it as a retreat. Was a hippie commune in the late sixties, and they nearly burned the house down during a naked wedding. The Grateful Dead leased it for a time—a wild time." He paused, thoughtful. "Speaking of the old days, here's something you might be interested in."

We'd reached a Jeep that sat around a curve in the path. I slid into the passenger's seat and asked, "What?"

"For a long time there was a guy hanging around here, Dan Jeffers. A leftover from the hippie years who went away in the seventies, came back in the mid-nineties. Guess he spent the best days of his life here, felt the place was home. Strange guy; you could tell he'd done—was still doing—way too many drugs. Not a bad guy, though, and I felt sorry for him. He had a permanent place to crash—Novato, or maybe up in Los Alegres—and he'd disappear for months at a time. But every once in a while he'd show up here, asking if he could trade grunt labor for staying in one of the cold rooms off the old dairy barn, and I'd let him. Shouldn't've—insurance—but the boss didn't need to know, and Dan never caused any trouble. The thing I'm getting to is that Dan was staying in the cold room the week before Scott Wagner died, but as soon as I found the body, he disappeared, and I haven't seen him since. Makes you wonder."

"About what?"

"Well, maybe he saw something that scared him off."

"Are you saying you don't think Wagner's death was an accident?"

Rios's lips tightened, and he gunned the Jeep up the dirt trail. "I'm not *sayin'* anything. Just wonderin', is all."

He drove swiftly, past an old wooden horse barn topped by a cupola and a grouping of small white buildings—once a blacksmith's shed and housing for ranch workers, he explained—that clustered around a declivity dominated by one of the largest bay laurel trees I'd ever seen. "Down that road to the right," he added, "is today's staff housing."

I looked the way he pointed, saw a collection of mobile homes about a quarter mile down a second dirt track that led toward the freeway. Beyond it Rios slowed, moving off into the high grass to avoid a dip in the trail and motioning at a dilapidated corrugated-iron structure to our left. "The old dairy barn where I let Dan Jeffers stay."

The trail narrowed, became rutted, and began rising, oak and bay laurel and madrone crowding in. We crossed a bridge over a stream, rounded a curve, and came to a large clearing where several rustic bark-and-reed huts stood.

"Miwok village," Rios said. "Tribal members are building it, preserving the old ways, trying to show how their people lived. Miwoks've been on this land since six thousand BC. The name Olompali means 'kitchen rock,' from the boulders they used for fixing their food. But the village project is stalled now. Old story for the Indians— no money. But you ought to know all about that. At least, you look Indian."

"I am—Shoshone." It still seemed strange to lay claim to my heritage; until I'd learned I was adopted, and located my birth parents, I'd thought I was Scotch-Irish with one-eighth Shoshone blood—my appearance the result of a recessive gene inherited from my great-grandmother. And Rios was right: "no money" was an old story for all the native people; my birth father, artist Elwood Farmer, donated his own time and funds to teaching in and providing supplies for the underfunded reservation schools of western Montana.

The trail became narrower, deeply rutted now. Rios downshifted, steered around the worst dips.

I said, "This Dan Jeffers, what d'you know about him? Where did he come from? What did he do for a living?"

"I think he came from someplace north. Mendocino County, maybe. One time, while he was helping me prune what's left of old man Burdell's orange trees, he mentioned his hometown was where the Citrus Fair is held. As to what he did for a living, I doubt it was much. He might've picked up other odd jobs. Sometimes he collected recyclables from our trash barrels, redeemed them for cash. Maybe he got government disability money—a lot of those burned-out druggies do. He had a car, at least, even if it was a clunker."

"What kind of car?"

"Old VW van. Real leftover hippie vehicle. Wonder it ran at all."

"What color?"

"Some tan, mostly rust."

"You recall the license plate number?"

"With my memory, I'm lucky I recall Dan." He pulled off to the side of the trail under another giant bay laurel, whose twisted trunk must have been six feet in diameter.

"You know," he said, "there might still be some of Dan's stuff in the cold room off the dairy barn. After I show you the place where I found Scott Wagner's body, we'll go there."

Rios led me through thick underbrush, along a deer track that angled away from the trail for some fifty yards until it came to the edge of a ravine. The drop wasn't too steep on this side—some five gradually sloping feet— but on the other, sheer rock rose sharply toward the treetops.

"Stream's dried up now," he said, "but last month it was still running pretty good. The cops said if Scott hadn't died from the injuries caused by his fall, he might've drowned before he regained consciousness."

I let my gaze travel to the tangled vegetation at the top of the rocks. "What's up there?"

"Grassland. There's an old stone wall at the top. Wagner probably left the trail at the bridge below the Miwok village, climbed up to the wall to take in the view. At this point you can see north to Mount Saint Helena, south to Mount Tamalpais."

"But why did he come here to cross the stream? He must've known it wasn't possible."

Rios shrugged. "Probably he was looking down at the water, lost his balance. Soil at the top was disturbed, like he'd loosened some rocks and slipped. You seen enough?"

"Yes."

We went back to the Jeep, and Rios made a U-turn. I gripped the sides of the seat, trying to cushion myself against the roughness of the ride. At the old dairy barn, he brought the vehicle to a stop.

The barn was open on one side, its interior dark, with small shafts of light penetrating where the iron roof had rusted through. When we approached, noises came from the far reaches as mice or rats scurried for cover, and a gecko ran across our path. Rios raised a flashlight he'd brought from the Jeep and shone it around inside. An old tractor, oil drums, tools, buckets, stacked lumber, cabinets, and doors.

"It's a hold-all for equipment and other stuff that nobody wants," he said. "You got someplace this big, you can shove junk in here and forget about it. Back this way are the cold rooms where Dan used to sleep."

A thick-walled concrete building with high, boarded

windows and missing doors stood toward the rear of the barn. Rios led me there and motioned me inside. The first room felt cool and damp and smelled musty, and contained nothing but mouse droppings. I crossed the cracked concrete floor and peered through a second door, saw sheets of warped plywood leaning against the wall, a rusted metal desk beside them. A rolled sleeping bag and a backpack were propped in one corner, and a scattering of Budweiser cans and cigarette butts lay on the floor.

I went over and examined the sleeping bag. It was worn but of fairly good quality, and nothing was rolled inside it. The backpack was equally worn and held a couple of changes of clothing. In a side pocket was an empty prescription drug vial. I took it out, held it up to the light. The label was made out to Dan Jeffers, for the painkiller Vicodin, and had been filled at a pharmacy in Los Alegres, the next town north on the Highway 101 corridor. There was one refill left.

"Okay if I take this?" I asked Rios.

He shrugged. "Don't see why not."

"Thanks." I stood, slipping it into my purse. We left through a second door that led from the rear room and down a short flight of steps. Minutes later Rios had me back at my car. As he drove off, I waved and called out my thanks for the tour.

Back in my car, I paused to contemplate the possibility that I might be going off on a tangent, making more of Scott Wagner's death than the circumstances warranted. Still, Ray Rios's thinly veiled suspicions and the leftover hippie who had gone missing as soon as Rios discovered Wagner's body intrigued me. And I was very close to Los Alegres.

Before I started north, I called the office. "Did Craig go to Southern California?" I asked Ted.

"Yes, last night. He called in this morning, said he probably wouldn't be back till tomorrow. You can reach him on his cell."

"Anything else?"

"Mother One called." After some confusion over phone messages, Ted had taken to differentiating between my adoptive and birth mothers as One and Two. "She asked me why you didn't reply to the message she left on your home machine last night."

"And you're supposed to have the answer to that?"

"Maybe she suspects I'm omniscient. Why *didn't* you reply?"

"I worked late, and by the time I got home I was in no mood to— Why am I telling you this, if you're so all-knowing?"

Ted laughed. "Getting people to tell me things is how I acquire my vast stores of knowledge. Anyway, she wanted to remind you not to forget your brother John's birthday on Thursday."

"What's wrong with her? I never forget his birthday."

Ted didn't respond. Both he and I knew exactly what her problem was: ever since my other brother, Joey, committed suicide last year, grief had made Ma cling tightly to her surviving children. I said, "If she calls again, tell her I haven't forgotten and I'll get back to her tonight. Is that it?"

"Jules came in. She's sitting at her desk, staring at her monitor, but I can tell nothing's happening there. She won't talk to any of us except for little grunts and mumbles."

"At least she came in. We'll just have to give her some space for a while. Will you buzz Mick for me, please?"

"Computer Forensics Department, Ford speaking," a smooth voice said.

"Derek?"

"Yes. How may I help you?"

"It's Sharon. You sound . . . very formal."

A silence. "Let me turn you over to Mick."

"Yo, Shar."

"What's going on? Derek sounds like an SBC online technician."

"And how does one of them sound?"

"Robotic and insincere."

Mick repeated the phrase, and in the background I heard Derek laugh. "Okay, I agree it's too much," my nephew said. "But we're kind of trying to define our persona."

"Your . . . persona?"

"The face we want to present to the public."

"Why does it have to be different from the one you've been presenting all along?"

"Well, the clients that this department's aiming at are somewhat different from the agency's as a whole."

"Oh? How?"

"For one thing, they're more corporate. Upscale. We need an image that will give them confidence in us."

An image. God help me!

I said, "I don't have time for this discussion, Mick." *Although you can be sure there* will *be a discussion—soon.* I added, "Right now I need you to pull up some information for me."

"Sure. What?" He was all business now—the "image" I liked agency employees to project.

"The Citrus Fair. Where is it held?"

"I can tell you off the top of my head. Last year Sweet Charlotte and I did the festival circuit—Gilroy for garlic, Sebastopol for apples. You know."

I knew. California has more gala celebrations involving food than anywhere else on earth, and sometimes I worry about a population that so worships what it puts into its collective mouth. The absolutely worst example of such events is the now-defunct Slug Fest in the Russian River town of Guerneville, during which chefs vied to create the best dishes containing the huge, slimy banana slug. "So the Citrus Fair is held at . . . ?"

"Cloverdale. Northern Sonoma County. Every February since the late 1800s. But get this: there hasn't been enough citrus grown in that area to create the fair's displays in decades. So where d'you think they get it?"

"Southern California?"

"Nope. Florida!"

Yes, the world had gone quite insane.

I asked Mick to begin a search for people in Cloverdale with the surname Jeffers and get back to me with the information. Then I ended the call and set off for Los Alegres.

I'd learned to fly at the small airport on the eastern side of the old-fashioned river town, so I knew the central district and had no difficulty locating ABC Drugs, next to the municipal parking structure two blocks off Main Street. I left my car in the structure and went into a store that was a cross between this century's drugstore and last century's five-and-dime. Aisles of utilitarian merchandise—over-the-counter medicines, personal care items, household cleaning products, school supplies, greeting cards, and wrapping paper—alternated with what my half-Jewish, half-black friend Adah Joslyn calls "tchotchkes": ornate figurines, potpourri, American flag doormats, whimsical windchimes, T-shirts imprinted with cutesy sayings ("Ex-lovers Make Great Speedbumps!"), Beanie Babies and teddy bears, scented candles, a bank shaped like a toilet that made flushing noises when coins were deposited. Looking at the assortment, I wondered not so much why anyone would buy it as why it had been manufactured in the first place.

Finally, at the rear of the store, I found the pharmacy. A basket full of fuzzy toys called "Mr. Love Weasel" sat next to a rack of literature on rheumatoid arthritis. I picked one up, saw a heart-shaped patch on its underside that read "Squeeze Me," and fulfilled its wish. The thing giggled and writhed in my hand as if we were engaged in foreplay. I dropped it, looked around to see if anyone was watching me.

Not the pudgy young man who lounged behind the counter. He was moving his lips as he read an issue of *Playboy.* When I said, "Excuse me," he took his time before setting the magazine down and coming over to wait on me. Not too bright or ambitious, and just as well. Such an individual wouldn't be inclined to question the scenario I'd constructed on the way up here.

I took the prescription vial from my purse and laid it on the counter. "My friend Dan asked me to bring this in to be refilled. You deliver, don't you?" I'd seen a van with the drugstore's name parked outside.

"Uh, yeah, but there's a charge."

"That's okay. Dan's in too much pain to come in for it,

and I can't wait till it's filled. He doesn't remember if he's picked up any prescriptions since he moved, so he asked me to check to see if you have the right address."

The clerk sighed and reached under the counter, bringing out a looseleaf binder. He squinted at the name on the vial, flipped pages, ran his index finger down one. "Dan Jeffers, one-oh-three Rose Court. That it?"

"Yes. When can he expect delivery?"

He sighed again. "I guess we can have it to him by five this afternoon."

The young man obviously had a wonderful future in the workforce.

I located Rose Court on a city map I bought at the drugstore. It was a short block off Fifth Street, only a few blocks away. Most of the small frame houses were well cared for, their postage-stamp yards neatly groomed, but number 103 was an unpainted wreck with a sagging porch and cardboard taped over broken windows. A pair of rusted patio chairs, their webwork trailing, stood beside a deflated kiddie pool in the weedy front yard.

I went up on the porch, where an old sofa was piled with mildewed cardboard cartons, and rang the bell. After a second ring, a sallow, gaunt woman in a bathrobe answered. She clutched the robe tightly at her throat, her other arm folded over her midriff, as if she was in pain.

"Danny?" she said when I asked for Jeffers. "I haven't seen him in a month or more, but I've been in the hospital, so that doesn't mean anything. Did you try out back?"

"No, I didn't."

"The studio, that's his. This place belongs to his mother. I rent it from her; she's in a rest home now, and Danny has the use of the studio."

"You pay your rent to him?"

"No." Her mouth twitched, and her knuckles whitened as she twisted the robe's fabric. "Management company handles the house. Danny, he's . . . well, you must know. Look, I've got to lie down now. I'm *always* lying down, goddamn it. Studio's at the end of the path to the right of the house. If Danny's there, tell him to stop in some time."

The cracked concrete path led to the back of the deep lot. There, under a gnarled pepper tree whose heavy limbs rested on its roof, stood a small brown-shingled structure with a Dutch door; the upper half of the door was slightly ajar. I called out for Jeffers twice before nudging it open.

The interior was one tiny room whose only light came from narrow windows to either side; a door at the rear opened onto an even tinier bathroom. A makeshift loft— plywood, supported by metal braces and thick wire— hung from the rafters, blankets and sheets drooping over its edges. The space below was in chaos: clothing heaped on the floor; take-out cartons and beer cans littering a low table; magazines and newspapers strewn on a rumpled futon-style couch. The walls were decorated with curling and torn Grateful Dead posters; the floor was covered in a dirty grass-cloth mat; a lava lamp on the table was cracked, liquid pooled beside it.

I turned the knob on the lower half of the door and stepped inside. The air was stale, the heat intense. I moved around the room, examining its contents; on the couch, beneath a June 17 issue of the *Chronicle,* I found an ashtray full of cigarette butts and marijuana roaches. I pawed through the rest of the newspapers, but they all predated that edition.

The bathroom was in the same state of disarray as the

main room, towels crumpled on the floor, the fixtures filthy. In the medicine chest, prescription vials were jumbled together. I read their labels: various painkillers, sleep aids, a sample kit of Zoloft—an antidepressant that I'd seen advertised on TV. An empty fifth of an off-brand bourbon stood atop the toilet tank.

As I searched, I grew cold in spite of the trapped heat. Then my vision blurred, and I felt a curious dissociation from my surroundings. I grasped the door frame, cradled my forehead in the crook of my elbow.

Jesus, it's just like Joey's wretched trailer in Anchor Bay. The last place he lived before he moved to Humboldt County and killed himself. . . .

After a moment the feeling passed, and I went back to the main room. I warned myself I shouldn't draw parallels between my brother and Dan Jeffers, but there was a sense of déjà vu about the situation: I'd gone to Joey's trailer, found out how bad his life was, and then heard that he'd ended it. Now I'd gone to Dan Jeffers's last known address, found out how bad *his* life was, and . . .

Doesn't follow, McCone. You're just overreacting to a similar set of bad circumstances.

My phone buzzed. Mick.

"Turns out Jeffers isn't all that common a name, at least in Cloverdale," he said. "I found only two. You want the addresses and phone numbers?"

"Please." I'd come this far. Why not?

Cloverdale is the northernmost town of any size along the Highway 101 corridor in Sonoma County, nestled in a valley on the banks of the Russian River, where the wine country blends into the redwoods. Years ago, the highway narrowed and became the town's main street, bringing a fair amount of business to local merchants, but then a bypass was constructed, and Cloverdale was largely forgotten by motorists pressing on to points north and south. Next the lumber industry that formed the economic base for the community became severely depressed. The town was well on its way to ruin when it was discovered by people looking to escape the high housing costs of the greater Bay Area, and as I exited the freeway, I saw a number of new shopping centers and housing developments that had been constructed in response to the migration.

It was well after two, and I hadn't eaten anything since my breakfast of coffee and V8 juice. At the south end of town I spotted the Owl Cafe, an establishment I'd noted many times while driving through and always planned to visit. No time like the present, and the number of big rigs in its parking lot hinted at good food. I pulled in but remained in the MG as I called the local numbers Mick had given me. A machine at the first told me I'd reached the residence of Susan and John Jeffers. I didn't leave a message. The woman who answered my second call sounded wary when I asked if she knew Dan Jeffers. Yes, she told me, she was his sister-in-law, Patty. Could I stop by later to talk about Dan? I asked. She hesitated, then agreed to see me.

Inside the café I ordered a cheeseburger and, while waiting for it, considered various strategies. Overcoming resistance on the part of a relative who is probably inclined to be protective toward the person you're investigating can be tricky. On the other hand, if the person is in trouble or missing, the relative may be likely to open up in the hope of learning something or gaining reassurance. Initially I'd have to feel my way with Dan Jeffers's sister-in-law.

The Owl Cafe was busy, even this far past the noon hour. Waitresses delivered steaming plates of food to the booths and tables. I watched people come and go, many stopping to chat, as if it were a social club. And as I watched, the owls watched me.

It seemed there were hundreds of them: stuffed owls, wicker owls, glass owls, ceramic owls, salt-and-pepper-shaker owls. Owls on the place mats, owls on the napkins. Yellow eyes staring from every nook and cranny. No one else in the café seemed to find them unusual or be paying them any mind.

It made me reflect upon the human capability for normalizing situations. These people probably ate meals here several times a week under the scrutiny of the big-eyed birds and had long ago ceased to notice them. Just as I'd long ago ceased to notice the noise from the traffic on the Bay Bridge above our offices at the pier. Just as, until recently, I'd considered a certain other aspect of my life well within the bounds of normalcy . . .

It isn't normal to live this way, McCone.

What's wrong with the way we live?

It's scattered. Not rooted. We need stability. Commitment.

Oh, Jesus, Ripinsky, not the "C" word!

What's wrong with the "C" word?

It's . . . unnecessary. I mean, it's implied in everything we do and say.

Sometimes implied isn't enough. Sometimes things need to be spelled out, written down. . . .

My food arrived. I banished the troublesome memory, dove into the burger.

Food, the great tranquilizer.

*   *   *

Dan Jeffers's sister-in-law, Patty, lived in a mobile home park near the south end of town. Rosebushes bloomed in profusion next to a walkway that led to a covered deck at the side of her doublewide, and a trio of evil-looking garden gnomes leered out at me from beneath their branches. At my approach a small, wiry woman with blond hair and a dark, leathery tan came to the top of the stairway.

"Ms. McCone? I'm Patty Jeffers. Come on up, have a seat. I'm just waiting for my husband to get here."

The deck was crowded with wrought-iron furniture and flowering plants. In one corner a fan rotated on a table, stirring the plants' branches but doing little to alleviate the heat, which must now be in the mid-nineties. My T-shirt was stuck to my back, and I pulled it free before sitting down.

Patty Jeffers stood in front of me, clasping and unclasping her hands. "Lemonade," she said. "I've got some made up fresh. Would you . . . ?"

"Yes, thank you."

She hurried inside, returning less than a minute later with a pitcher and three glasses. "My husband," she said as she poured. "I called him at work because, frankly, after I spoke with you I wasn't sure I should. Meet with you, I mean. And after all, Dan's his blood relative, not mine. Lou—my husband—said it was all right, but he wants to be here, and—" She paused, cocking her head. "His car. That's him now."

Lou Jeffers was a tall, balding man in mechanic's coveralls with the name of a Ford dealership embroidered on them. He greeted me, squeezed his wife's shoulder reassuringly, and took the glass of lemonade she offered.

When he sat down and stretched out his long legs, they bisected the floor space.

"So," he said, studying the business card I handed him, "you're interested in Danny. Why?"

"I believe he witnessed an accident I'm investigating."

Jeffers exchanged a knowing look with his wife. "What accident?"

"A fall that a hiker took at Olompali Regional Park in June."

Patty Jeffers said, "I told you—"

Her husband silenced her with a frown. "Why?" he asked me.

"Why . . . ?"

"Why are you investigating it?"

"A family member wants details. For closure."

He nodded, staring down at his glass of lemonade. After a moment he raised it, took a swallow, and turned to his wife. "What the hell, Pats. We don't know where Danny is. Don't even know what really happened. Maybe if we talk with this lady, she might help us find him."

"If you think we should, okay."

Jeffers said to me, "If we tell you what we know about this . . . accident, and some time down the road you find Danny, will you let us know where he is? We haven't seen or heard from him since the end of June."

"Of course I will."

"Okay, then. You go first, Pats."

She leaned forward, rolling her sweat-beaded glass between her hands. "A Monday. June twenty-second or -third. Around two in the afternoon. Danny showed up here, asking for money. Now, that wasn't anything new; he does it all the time, and when we can, we're happy to oblige. Danny, he hasn't been right for a long time—"

Lou Jeffers cleared his throat, and Patty glanced nervously at him. "Anyway," she went on, "this time it was different. Usually when Danny asks for money he acts real charming. But that day he was . . . kind of desperate and demanding. To tell the truth, he scared me. So I told him he'd have to ask Lou. And Danny went off to see him at work." She looked at her husband.

Lou said, "Pats is right; he *was* desperate. I took a break; we went to a bar in one of the shopping centers. He was knocking back Scotches, telling me this crazy story. He said he'd seen this guy he knew killed, beaten unconscious and pushed off a ledge into a ravine at that park down in Marin where he hangs out."

I leaned forward. "When did it happen?"

"The day before, Sunday afternoon. Danny freaked, hid in this room where he stays down there, got stoned, took some pills. That's what he always does when the going gets rough." He grimaced. "He got so wasted, he decided the whole thing never happened; but the next day somebody discovered the guy's body, and then he *really* freaked. Came here, asking for money so he could leave the area."

"You give it to him?"

"Only what I had on me. It wasn't much. I told him he should just go to the cops, tell them what he saw, but he said if he did that he'd be a dead man."

"Why?"

"Because of the guy who did the killing. According to Danny, he was one bad dude."

"Dan *knew* the killer?"

"Yeah, he did. He said it was really a weird coincidence, because he hadn't seen the guy for over ten, fifteen years. And then there he was, killing somebody right before Danny's eyes."

Armed with what personal history his relatives could provide about Dan Jeffers, I headed back to the city. Traffic between Cloverdale and Santa Rosa was light, but once I reached the Sonoma County seat, it came to a dead stop due to multiple feed-ins. I used the drive to consider Jeffers's claim that he'd seen Scott Wagner murdered.

On the one hand, the story could have been nothing more than the hallucination of a substance abuser. Jeffers might have seen Wagner fall and manufactured the rest. On the other hand, his family had described him as genuinely frightened, and the man hadn't been seen since. It made sense to treat seriously the possibility that Scott Wagner might have been murdered, and by someone Jeffers knew.

A background check on Wagner was in order. I'd need to know if he had enemies or was substantially different from the clean, altruistic image projected in a profile the *Chronicle* had run on him last fall. When a person is murdered in a manner that isn't random, there's usually some shameful secret or connection just waiting to come out.

As for locating Dan Jeffers, I wondered if I had enough information to proceed with a search. He'd dropped out of Cloverdale High School in the mid-sixties, which would make him in his fifties now, and had gravitated toward San Francisco's Haight-Ashbury district. Lou, who was two years younger, hitched down to visit him once and found him living in a dilapidated Victorian on the Panhandle of Golden Gate Park with eleven cats, five dogs, and thirteen other people, two of whom, Lou later learned, were loosely affiliated with the

Manson Family. After that, Dan only communicated with his family by postcard or an occasional collect phone call; Lou recalled mailings from Taos, Mexico, Belize, Costa Rica, Peru, and finally from various U.S. locations where Dan was apparently following the Grateful Dead from concert to concert.

"Deadheads, they called themselves," Lou told me. "Dead *in* the head, if you ask me."

Dan's Deadhead phase had ended around 1988, when he called from San Diego asking for a loan. A buddy and he were going into business, buying a juice bar. Lou invested two thousand of his savings in the enterprise and didn't hear from Dan for a year, when he called to hit him up for another loan.

"He said the juice bar failed. I thought, that's Southern California; how can you fail with a juice bar? But then, fool that I am, I gave him more money to start a surfboarding business. He blew that, too. About the time he hit me up for the next loan, I'd figured out he was spending my money on drugs, so I cut him off."

Dan finally turned up at Lou and Patty's place on a rainy winter night in 1997. He was emaciated and frail and explained that he'd recently been released from a state-mandated stay in a drug rehab center. Lou and Patty took him in and later arranged for him to have the use of the studio at his mother's Los Alegres property.

"I helped him fix up an old van, and Pats tried to teach him about budgeting his money. We made sure he visited the doctor and filled the prescriptions for his meds. But then we realized he was getting hold of other drugs that the doc hadn't prescribed. And he was spending a lot of time down at that park, smoking grass and pining away for the good old days. Tell the truth, I was sick and tired of trying to deal with him. And I guess that's why I wasn't very sympathetic when he came to me with the story about the murder down there. Like I said, I told him to go to the cops, but when he wouldn't, I gave him what money I could and hoped he'd go away for good. And he did. I feel awful about it, but you know what? I don't miss him. I don't miss him at all."

Abruptly the Santa Rosa traffic jam eased, and the vehicles in front of me began to move. I ran up the RPMs and shifted into a higher gear.

Is that how I feel about Joey? That I don't miss him?

Yes and no. Certainly he wasn't a burden like Dan Jeffers. He never asked any of us for a thing. But we worried about him, all the time. And I don't miss the worry.

No, I don't miss the worry at all.

But I do miss Joey.

It was after six when I got back to the pier. None of my employees' cars were parked in their spaces on the floor below our catwalk, but a faint glow came from the office Julia shared with Craig. I looked in and saw her slumped at her workstation. The computer's screen saver displayed a school of colorful fish.

When she realized I was there, Julia swiveled to face me. She was a mess, her clothing dirty and wrinkled, her hair greasy. Why had she come to the office in such a state? We stared wordlessly at each other, and then she attempted a smile, but it turned into a defensive smirk.

For a moment I flashed back to my conversation with Marguerite Hayley: *You may have to let her go. In effect, distance yourself from her in order to save your license.*

How easy it would be. Cut her loose, contribute to the costs of her criminal trial, but set the wheels in motion for

BSIS to drop the case against me. And get on with business as usual.

Except that I'd always know that I hadn't given her a fair chance.

Or had I? The evidence against her was overwhelming, her explanations flimsy at best. Was I blinded by my fondness for her? Or had I perhaps not been asking the right questions? It was best to find out now, while my options were still open.

"My office," I said. "Five minutes."

Julia entered the office tentatively and waited till I asked her to be seated. She'd used the five-minute interval to visit the restroom and wash her face. It was only a slight improvement, but I took it as a good sign.

She said, "I want to thank you for asking Glenn to represent me. And for standing by me."

"The agency is behind you one hundred percent. Craig's in Southern California, investigating Alex Aguilar's background, and I've been pursuing leads of my own."

"Wish I felt it would help, but it just seems like more of the same."

"How so?"

"Well, look at my work history since I got out of CYA. First I get fired from my maid's job at the motel because a guy groped me and I smacked him. My fault—I shouldn't've lost it. But then there was my boyfriend stealing from my uncle's convenience store where I was working. Did my uncle believe that I didn't know the guy was lifting stuff? No—he canned me, too. And then when I thought I was set with the neighborhood outreach program, the feds pulled the funding. Story of my life."

She sounded as if she was on the verge of a full-blown pity fest, so I said, "Well, history's not going to repeat itself this time. We're going to get to the bottom of this. Do you remember what I taught you about looking at the facts of a case?"

She nodded. "Look at the surface facts first, then look at what lies beneath them. Look for a motive."

"Right. Eventually everything goes to motive. I've analyzed what surface facts we have, and I think the charges against you—and the agency—are the result of a carefully orchestrated plan on the part of Aguilar. We need to know the reason behind it."

"Because I wouldn't sleep with him?"

"No, that's not enough for a plan of this scale. Now, I'm going to ask you some questions, based on things I've found out over the past couple of days, and I want you to think carefully before you answer them."

"Okay."

"Scott Wagner—as I recall, he was your main contact at the job-training center. What was he like?"

"Nice guy, very helpful, gave me free run of the place. We got along fine."

"You heard he died?"

"I saw the story in the paper after I wrapped up the case."

"You hear anything else about his death?"

Julia frowned. "From who?"

"In the neighborhood, maybe from somebody you met at the job-training center."

"No. I thought about going to his memorial service, but there wasn't much point. I mean, I didn't know him all that well."

"Okay—Aguilar. Had you ever met him before I assigned you to the case?"

"No. I'd've remembered."

"What about his administrator at the job-training center, Gene Santamaria?"

"I never even saw him. I don't think he'd been hired yet."

"Is it possible you might've met Santamaria somewhere else at some point, and not remembered the name?"

". . . I suppose I could've."

I made a note of that. "What about the clients at the center? You know any of them from before?"

"There's a woman who was in the CYA same time I was, but we weren't close, and I hadn't seen her for maybe five years until I ran into her at the center. We just said hello—didn't talk or anything. That's usually the way it is when you come across somebody you've been inside with, if you've got your life together."

"Anybody else?"

She thought. "A guy named Rocco something. I see him around my neighborhood, but we've never even said hello."

"Okay, here's another name for you: Dan Jeffers."

"Jeffers . . . Nope."

"What about someone who goes by the initials R.D.?"

"Just R.D.?"

"Yes."

She shook her head. "Doesn't mean anything to me."

"Ask her if she knows a drug pusher named Johnny Duarte."

Craig stood in the doorway, laptop in hand, travel bag

slung over his shoulder. "You know him, Jules?" he added. "Do you?"

Julia paled and pressed a hand to her lips. In the silence that followed, the traffic on the Bay Bridge sounded louder than normal.

I said, "Well, Julia?"

She swallowed, cleared her throat. "Johnny . . . He's, you know, the guy I was dating last winter."

I hadn't met him, but I'd heard plenty. For a while they'd been quite an item. On Valentine's Day he'd sent her a dozen roses and a box of Godiva chocolates. Then, a few weeks later, the romance was over. "You were dating a *drug pusher*?"

My tone made her shrink into her chair. "I didn't know he was one; I swear it. I met him at this club on Eighteenth Street in January. He told me he worked for a marketing company whose accounts were in the telecommunications field. I didn't have any reason not to believe him. He dressed well, not flashy or anything, had a nice car, a nice condo, always had money to spend."

"Didn't it occur to you to check him out? You have the resources."

Julia's eyes flashed. "Yeah? Is that what you would've done? I've heard those stories about Hy keeping his past a secret from you."

Her reaction was one she'd displayed before—a quick, defensive segue from fear to anger—and it brought out anger in me, too. What she'd said displayed little understanding of my relationship with Hy, past or present.

I said, "We're not talking about me here. When did you find out Johnny Duarte was a drug trafficker?"

Julia's eyes moved from side to side, like a cornered

animal's. For a moment I thought she might bolt from the office. Finally she slumped forward, covering her face with her hands.

"When, Julia?"

"Last week in February. There's this narc I know— Tom Leary. Johnny and I ran into him on the street one day. He busted me once back when, but since I've gotten my act together, he kind of treats me like a little sister. That night, though, he was *cold*. And the next morning he called me, told me I was dating a major drug distributor, made me come down to the Hall and look at the file they've got on Johnny. I freaked, called Johnny, told him it was all over."

"You tell him why?"

"No, no way I was gonna let him know I was onto him. I said an old boyfriend was back in my life, and I'd had to choose between them. Johnny was cool about it."

I nodded, drumming my fingertips on the desk. My next question was one she wouldn't like, but I had to ask it.

"Why didn't you tell me about this?"

"Wasn't any of your business!"

"When you came to work for me, what did I tell you about your private life?"

She thought, running the tip of her tongue over her upper lip. " 'Your private life is your own, except when it reflects badly upon the agency. Then we need to talk.' "

"Didn't you think the subject of your relationship with Johnny Duarte was one we needed to discuss?"

Julia looked down at her hands.

Craig, who was leaning against the doorjamb, shifted. I sensed he was about to say something in her defense, so I held up a staying hand.

"Julia?"

". . . I was embarrassed. I mean, I should've known what he was. Hell, I used to *work* for guys like Johnny."

She'd had a rough five days and was close to the breaking point. I backed off some. "We all want to believe we have good judgment about the men we're involved with. You overlooked the little signs that would've told you Duarte wasn't what he seemed. But after you found out about him, you should have come to me."

"I know." She looked up, more resigned than upset. "I guess this means you're firing me."

I shook my head. "No, but I am sending you home to do some thinking."

Her lips twisted wryly. "Sort of like I send Tonio to his time-out corner?"

"Something like that. I want you to take tomorrow off. Review everything that's gone on in your life since you came to work here, to see if there's anything else you should have told me."

"Shar, I swear—"

"It could be something insignificant, that didn't seem important at the time. For one reason or another, you've become a target, and we have to figure out why."

After Julia left the office, Craig moved to the chair she'd occupied. "I think," he said, "that Alex Aguilar found out Julia had dated Johnny Duarte. He was probably afraid she'd discovered the connection between them and might use it against him after he put the moves on her. So he decided to frame her, maybe trade dropping the charges against her for her silence."

"And what is that connection?"

"Let me tell you about my trip down south." He set his laptop on the desk and booted it up. "Most of the people I spoke with in the L.A. area confirmed the public details of Aguilar's life. But in San Diego I began running into resistance. The owners of one of the restaurants where he worked during the time he dropped out of college wouldn't talk about him. In fact, they seemed disturbed that I had come around asking questions. Naturally, that intrigued me, so I kept digging. A former roommate who still lives in the area threatened to call his lawyer if I persisted. A woman who did volunteer work with Aguilar refused to see me. Finally I came up with the name of an old friend of his who lives in Banning—that's Riverside County—and he agreed to talk with me, on the condition of anonymity."

"A lot of closemouthed people down there."

"More like a lot of frightened people. But the guy in Banning is tough—ex-con gone straight, owns a motorcycle dealership. He wasn't about to let Aguilar's pals shut him up."

"Aguilar's 'pals'?"

"His term. He claims that shortly after an article on Aguilar appeared in the national press, touting him as San Francisco's best future prospect for a Hispanic mayor, some of Aguilar's people paid him a visit, warned him that a certain area of the supervisor's past was not to be discussed. They offered him money, and when the guy refused it, they threatened him. He ran them off, started sleeping with a baseball bat next to the bed."

"Who are these people?"

Craig shrugged. "From the description the guy in Banning gave me, I'd say your garden-variety Mission-district thugs."

"So you think they paid visits to all of the people you tried to contact?"

"Uh-huh."

"And what is this area that's off limits to discussion?"

Craig smiled thinly. "Aguilar's drug dealing."

"Ah." I nodded.

"During the time that Aguilar dropped out of college—and after he rematriculated—he worked as the UCSD liaison for Johnny Duarte. Naturally, this is information that won't enhance his present position or future mayoral bid."

I nodded, thinking of what I'd learned that day. San Diego, my old hometown, appeared to be pivotal to the case. Alex Aguilar had sold drugs for Julia's ex-boyfriend there. Dan Jeffers had lived there around that time, scamming money from his brother that he probably used for drug buys. Dan had seen "a bad dude" he used to know kill Scott Wagner at Olompali. Johnny Duarte? Possibly. But why?

"Shar?"

"Sorry. I found out something today that adds another puzzling angle to the investigation." I told him about Dan Jeffers's claim that he'd seen Scott Wagner killed.

Craig frowned. "Wasn't Wagner a squeaky-clean guy? I remember reading a profile of him someplace: fundraiser, on the board of the Sierra Club and other environmental organizations, all-around do-gooder. That type doesn't make a good candidate for premeditated murder."

"No. I want you to run an in-depth background check on him, see if you can come up with something that would prove him otherwise. And while you're at it, run one on Gene Santamaria, Wagner's replacement at the center. I'll also need you to try to locate Dan Jeffers."

"Will do. So what are your thoughts about Duarte?"

"Well, Julia obviously doesn't know about his connection to Aguilar, or she would've mentioned it. And it seems extreme for Aguilar to have worked out this elaborate a frame on the basis of what she *might* know."

"Right. Unless he and Duarte have an ongoing profitable relationship."

"You mean drug trafficking. It's possible. That shop in Ghirardelli Square interests me; they could be bringing in drugs in shipments of merchandise from Central America. I'll have it checked out."

"Well," Craig said, "my other assignment is obvious—find out everything there is to know about Johnny Duarte."

"No, I need you to follow up on Scott Wagner, Gene Santamaria, and Dan Jeffers for now. I'll tackle Duarte."

Johnny Duarte's favorite hangout, Julia told me when I called her later, was a club on Twenty-fourth Street called Holidaze. I got a detailed description of him from her.

I asked, "As far as you know, Duarte's never seen me, right?"

"He never came to the office. In fact, he didn't seem all that interested in what I did for a living. Mostly we just talked about him—and then it turned out what he said was lies."

After I ended the call, I went to the armoire that served as my coat closet, and contemplated the outfits I kept there for occasions that required something other than business attire or sweaters and jeans. The little black cocktail dress was too formal for the Mission; the baglady ensemble was appropriate in some quarters, but not for the clubs; the prim-and-proper corduroy jumper from L.L. Bean—even a member of the bridge-and-tunnel crowd wouldn't wear it for a night out in the city. But the slim leather pants and short matching jacket would work, if I mated it with the red silk T-shirt.

I carried the outfit and a bag of miscellaneous makeup and costume jewelry to the restroom. Washed my face and pulled my hair into a ponytail. Then I proceeded to tart myself up with heavy eyeshadow, mascara, blusher, and bright red lipstick. When I was dressed and surveyed myself in the full-length mirror on the back of the door, I had to admit I looked like a woman any self-respecting drug trafficker would be eager to meet. The long, red enamel earrings that matched the silk tee were a particularly nice touch. Before I left the office, I took my .357 Magnum from the safe and slipped it into my bag. I didn't like to carry the gun under normal circumstances, but tonight I'd feel better with it close at hand.

Eight-thirty, and Twenty-fourth between Mission and South Van Ness was humming. People entered and exited the BART station; couples gathered on the sidewalk, talking about where to go for dinner or clubbing; others strode along, eager to reach their destinations. They were dressed in casual and business attire, expensive urban chic, or the latest in hipster style—thift-shop acquisitions such as baggy pants, oversize formal jackets, and garish sneakers, or floral-print shirtwaist dresses from the sixties paired with hiking boots. Intermixed with them were the old and the poor, the shifty-eyed and the wild-eyed; and, as always, the homeless sprawled like so many bundles of rags in doorways. I joined the throng of those in a hurry and, moments later, entered Holidaze.

The club had a travel motif—posters on the wall, models of airplanes hanging from the ceiling. Although there was a bandstand and small dance floor toward the rear, both were dark and vacant. Music played over a sound system—at the moment, the old song about seeing the pyramids across the Nile. The bar was relatively uncrowded, and I had my choice of seats on its short leg by the front windows, from which I could see the entire room.

Tables, most of them occupied, dotted the floor, and booths lined the far wall. From Julia's description, I spotted my man in the center one. He was heavyset, with more muscle than fat, and wore a black patch over his right eye—an old injury, Julia had told me, that he wouldn't talk about. His hair was thick, well styled, and faintly streaked with gray; his blue silk shirt looked expensive. I put his age at mid- to late thirties. A glass full of pale amber liquid sat before him, but he ignored it as he leaned forward, talking intensely with a small, shabby-looking man in a faded denim jacket. After a moment he grasped the man's forearm and spoke more emphatically. The man—

"What'll it be, miss?"

The bartender. "Uh, wine. Chardonnay."

"We have Kendall Jackson, Deer Hill—"

"The house will be fine," I said, ever conscious of the agency's tightened budget.

When I looked back at the booth, the little man was gone, and Duarte was making a call on his cellular.

For the next half hour Johnny Duarte sat alone, sipping his drink and making call after call. I nursed the wine—which was quite dreadful—and tried to think of a way to approach him. Finally he turned off his phone, signaled for another drink, and looked around the room. His eyes lit on me, and he smiled; the eye patch made him look like a rakish pirate.

I smiled back, and Duarte motioned for me to join him.

Why wasn't it this easy when I used to haunt the clubs, looking for guys?

The first thing I noticed as I slid into the booth opposite Duarte was his aftershave—too much of it and too pungent. The second, as he introduced himself and we shook hands, was his immaculate manicure. I once again gave my name as Robin Blackhawk, with mental apologies to my half sister. Robin's area of study was civil rights law; she would have hated someone like Duarte, who gave his people a bad name.

"So, Robin Blackhawk," Duarte said, "tell me about yourself."

"There's really not much to tell. I'm from Idaho, came out here for a change of scene after my divorce. I'm currently staying with friends and looking for a job."

"Doing what?"

"Anything where I can make a lot of money and not do much work."

Duarte's good eye regarded me thoughtfully. "That's a tall order. Do you have any particular skills?"

"I'm good with people. I can sell anything. And I believe in situational ethics."

"Meaning?"

"If it benefits me, it's ethical."

He laughed and signaled to the cocktail waitress, motioned at my wineglass. "I like the way you think."

I said, "Now it's your turn to tell me about yourself."

"I am a businessman—in marketing for the telecom-

munications industry. Currently unmarried like yourself.
I like fine dining, auto racing—as a spectator only—and
traveling to exotic locales. I own a condominium on
Upper Market with a large deck and a panoramic view of
the city, but I'm not particularly domestic. I have no
houseplants, no pets, and have yet to figure out how to
use the convection oven. When I throw dinner parties,
they are catered. And I am enamored of women with high
cheekbones and black hair in ponytails." He leaned forward, taking my hand.

"Although," he added, "the red lipstick and earrings
have to go."

So he's into control.

"You think so?" I asked.

"Most definitely."

I picked up my cocktail napkin and rubbed at the lipstick. Pulled the earrings off and dropped them on the
table.

Duarte nodded his approval. "Now we will go to La
Vida Loca. It's much livelier than this place, and the
owner is a friend who will give us a good table."

At 2:15 the cab I'd taken from the club dropped me at
my car. At 2:27 I was home, fuzzy from the wine Duarte
had plied me with—although, surprisingly, he'd acted
quite the gentleman—and tired from a long day and too
much frenetic dancing. The evening had paid off, though;
I was now equipped with much more information about
Johnny Duarte than he was aware he'd imparted to me.
When under the influence of a considerable quantity of
single-malt Scotch, even the most streetwise drug dealer
is no match for this private investigator—wine or no
wine.

The cats were asleep on the couch in the sitting room, Ralph butted up against Allie. He didn't move as I passed by, but her eyes followed me anxiously. As kittens they used to sleep curled up together, but later they decided they hated each other, and the snuggling ceased. I didn't know whether to take this newfound affection as a good or a bad sign, but was too preoccupied to contemplate it. Instead I patted them both, and went to check the answering machine. Only one message, from Marguerite Hayley, saying she would be meeting with Todd Baylis and an official with BSIS in Sacramento on Friday. "That will buy us some time," she added. "I trust your investigation into this matter is going well?"

I made a mental note to call Hayley in the morning, before I again donned my Robin Blackhawk persona for three appointments Ted had set up for me with former clients of Trabajo por Todos. Then I went back to the bedroom, dropped my clothes on the floor, and crawled between the sheets without turning on the light.

Thursday

•

JULY 17

I set the typed transcripts of that morning's interviews with former clients of Trabajo por Todos on the desk and began going through them, refreshing my memory and highlighting the important parts.

Pete Infante, data-entry clerk, Bank of America: "Hey, this is great. Back when I was unemployed, I'd sit around my mom's house watching daytime TV and see these commercials. Some guy smiling and saying he went to this or that college and now he's making good money in such and such a field. But those colleges, they're expensive, and what're you gonna do if you don't have a job and are living over your mom's garage? Then a friend of mine, he told me about the center, that it's free. I went in; they gave me tests, pointed me at the computer lab—and here I am. . . . Yeah, that was two years ago, a little more. . . . Right, Alex Aguilar and Scott Wagner were the head honchos then. I didn't see much of Scott; he was busy raising money. Alex, he was around a lot. . . . What do I think of him? He's okay. Pushy, though. One of those guys who wants things his way, and right now. And he took advantage of the clients—made us turn out for his political rallies, stuff like that. Not that I minded much. I'd've probably turned out, anyway."

Marina Reyna, nurse's aide, San Francisco General Hospital: "I go to Trabajo por Todos after I come up from Ciudad Juarez to live with my *tio* and his *familia*. My *inglés*, it was not very good, and I don't know the right way of things here—how to behave and dress so somebody will give me a job. They teach me all that and send me here to Ms. Evans, who is a friend of Mr. Wagner and hires people from the center. . . . Yes, I know—I knew— Mr. Wagner. A nice man. *Muy bueno*. It is terrible, what happen to him. . . . Mr. Aguilar? He is . . . You will put this in the paper? No? Okay, then. He is . . . I don't know the word. Someone who makes people do what he wants. . . . Manipulates, yes, that is the word! He and Mr. Wagner sometimes argue about that. Mr. Wagner say it is not right to use *los clientes* that way. . . . Oh, yes, Mr. Aguilar gets very angry when they argue. And those of us who hear them become afraid for Mr. Wagner."

Juan Salcido, mechanic, Len's AutoWorks: "It's a great job-training program. My parole officer steered me to it, and I really owe him. It's not easy for an ex-con to get any job except for real shit work, but the center's connected with these firms all over the city who don't discriminate because you've made a mistake and done your time. I like my job; I like the people I work with. They give me respect, man, and what more can you ask? . . . Wagner and Aguilar? Now, that was a weird combo. Oil and water. . . . Who was oil and who was water? Aguilar's oily as they come. Wagner was pure water. You couldn't find a better man. The day I interviewed for this job? My truck was broke down. Something, huh? Auto mechanic with a busted truck. But Wagner hears about it and loans me his car. A class act, huh? Aguilar wouldn't've loaned me the sweat off his balls—oops, excuse me, ma'am. . . . Did they argue? No, I didn't see any of that. But Wagner was really worried about something the week before he died. . . . I don't know how I knew; I just could tell. I asked him about it, and he said the situation would work itself out and the center would go on, with or without him. . . . Yeah, that's what he said: *with or without*."

I pushed back from my desk, swiveled around, and stared out the big, arching window at the bay. A sailboat glided by, carrying a quartet of people, probably on their way to dinner at one of the restaurants up the channel. Maybe the Islais Creek Resort—where I had had a near-fatal encounter a while back. It had recently reopened, under the direction of a celebrity chef, and I'd been meaning to try it and banish the bad memories.

Not tonight, though. It was almost six, and in two hours I was due at Johnny Duarte's condominium for one of his catered dinners and "a talk that may result in our mutual benefit."

A talk that might give me more insight into his present relationship with Alex Aguilar. I wouldn't go to Duarte's alone, however; I'd have Craig waiting outside as backup. And I'd go armed. No need to take foolish risks when you're dealing with a potentially dangerous individual.

And Duarte *was* dangerous, as I'd discovered from the things he'd let slip the evening before.

During the time we spent together, Johnny waxed philosophical: "Like you, I very much believe in the concept of situational ethics. That is the basis I operate on. Not everyone can or should do so. There are the masses, and for them there must be standards and laws. But those of us who, by virtue of superior intelligence, rise above the masses must be free to set our own standards and enact our own laws."

He'd also bragged of his friends in high places: "You would be very surprised at the powerful people I know, and at what they are willing to do for me. Last year, for example, I wanted to evict the tenants of an income property I own here in the Mission. One call to city hall, and it was accomplished. And my contacts in the police department provide protection for a business I run on the side."

I knew what that business was, and it didn't surprise me that the SFPD employed cops who would look the other way. As for the evictions, earlier this afternoon I'd researched the history of several properties owned by Duarte, and found that the removal of six tenants from a multiflat building on South Van Ness had been facilitated by an attorney who was a major contributor to Alex Aguilar's campaign fund.

After another drink, Duarte lapsed again into philosophy, skating dangerously close to the nature of his second business: "When people make foolish choices, they deserve the consequences. Drugs, for example: addicts are weak and stupid; they take drugs, and then they die. We are supposed to feel this is a bad thing, but it is not. Drugs are nothing more than the tool by which these people are removed from the gene pool."

As the evening wore on and Duarte drank more, he began to drop increasingly blatant and unwise hints about his dark side, in an obvious effort to impress me.

"I walk through dangerous territory, but I am very sure-footed."

"People, even powerful people, can be made to do anything. If money won't sway them, coercion will."

"It takes a brave man to kill. I am a brave man. And proud of it."

I wasn't impressed, especially by the latter statement. I had killed, more than once, and hadn't felt either brave or proud. On bad nights, dreams of those acts—justifiable though they had been—still returned to disturb my sleep. Hy, during his years as a pilot for a corrupt charter service in Southeast Asia, had also taken lives—with far less justification than I—but afterward was overwhelmed by remorse and guilt, which it had taken him years to come to terms with.

But the Johnny Duartes of the world felt nothing after they committed their crimes. Instead they went on and on, perpetrating greater and greater horrors, convinced that their "superior" intelligence, wealth, and connections were justification enough. That was what separated them from Hy and me, however flawed we might be: their lack of humanity.

"I don't like this," Craig said. "The guy is not your typical street pusher. I'd feel better if you met him in a public place."

"I can't do that. He won't discuss what he wants to in public. I'm armed, and you'll be right outside the building if I need you."

"I don't like you taking a weapon in there. If he picks up your purse and feels how heavy it is—"

"Craig, you've been in a relationship too long. You

forget that a man does not handle a woman's purse on the first date."

"How do you know what this asshole might do? He's a loose cannon."

I smiled and patted my bag. "Then it's good that I have *my* 'cannon' along, isn't it?"

"I'm glad *you* think this is a joking matter."

"I don't. But, for God's sake, lighten up."

I moved away from where our cars were parked around the bend from Johnny Duarte's building on Upper Market. A chest-high barrier blocked the precipitous drop from the sidewalk to the rooftops of the buildings below. The day had cleared while I'd been away from the city, but now the sun had fallen behind the western hills; purple shadow wrapped the far-flung vista. I closed my eyes and took a deep breath as my hair streamed back on a sudden breeze; I caught the odor of someone's barbecue. A fine summer evening in the city—and a rarity, since July was normally a cold, fogbound month.

Craig came up beside me. I said, "I'll be all right. Really."

"I must be cursed."

"Why?"

"Because all my life I've been surrounded by women who're tougher than I am. First my mother and my grandmother, later my younger sister. My classmates in college and at the Academy, my colleagues at the Bureau. Then Adah. Now you."

"Count yourself lucky, Morland. In a crisis, there'll always be some broad around to defend you."

I received an immediate answering buzz at the door of Duarte's building. The lobby beyond it was spacious, with a rock wall and exotic plantings; a stairway led to the floors above. I climbed all the way to the top, found the door to his condo open, and called out his name as I stepped inside.

A woman greeted me. She was tall and slender, in slim-fitting jeans and a ribbed tee; her thick blond hair was permed and spilled to her shoulders. "Ms. Blackhawk," she said, "I'm Harriet Leonard. Come in, please. I have a note for you from Mr. Duarte." Her accent sounded Australian.

I followed her down a hallway to a living room that opened onto the spacious deck Duarte had mentioned the night before. The view was spectacular, the furnishings expensive, but the space felt unlived in. Harriet Leonard went to a secretary desk on one wall, picked up a square vellum envelope, and extended it to me.

I slipped my finger under the flap and took out a card printed with Duarte's name.

Robin—
I very much regret that I will be unable to keep
our appointment tonight. Urgent business takes
me out of town. Perhaps when I return, we can
meet to discuss our matter of mutual interest.
                                   —J

When I looked up, Harriet was studying me. She said, "Would you like a drink before you go? I know I'd like one. It's the least Johnny can do for us, after he stood you up and made me wait around to give you his note."

"Why not?" In spite of her gracious manner, I sensed an edginess in the woman, perhaps a need to talk.

"Red wine all right?" she asked.

"Fine, thanks."

She went to a small bar cart and returned with two balloon glasses, handed one to me, raised hers, and said, "Cheers." After taking a sip, she sank onto the leather sofa, and I took a chair across from her.

I said, "You're a friend of Johnny's?"

"Business associate. Oh, hell, you must know. I deal for him. He recruited me eight months ago. Let me guess about you. You recently met him at one of the clubs. He told you he was a marketing exec with business interests on the side. Then he wined and dined you, threw out a lot of pop psychology about superior intellect and the survival of the fittest, and offered to discuss a business proposition. Am I right so far?"

"Except for the dining part. All *we* did was drink."

"Cheap date, you are. Tonight must be when he intended to reveal the true nature of his business and dazzle you with the unheard-of profits you'll make if you'll 'step over the line of conventionality.' "

". . . I guess so."

"Oh, don't give me that look of shattered innocence. You aren't young or stupid enough to have believed him. I didn't, and I've been fooled by countless men with countless schemes. But I walked in here knowing exactly what I was signing up for."

I sipped wine. Harriet had chosen a very good vintage. "And did you realize those 'unheard-of profits'?"

"I do all right."

"But not as well as Johnny claimed you would."

"No, but now I can't get out; I'm hooked on the lifestyle. Before, I was a secretary in a brokerage firm— dreadful hours, dreadful pay. I never want to go back." She frowned. "That's why I'm worried."

"About what?"

"Johnny. I snooped at that note you've got there. He said he had to go out of town, but his car's still in the garage. And take a close look at his handwriting—doesn't it seem strange?"

"I wouldn't know. I've never seen his handwriting before." But as I examined the card, I saw what she meant: some of the letters were irregularly formed, as if he'd written them while stressed.

"Well, I have seen his writing, and it looks strange to me. Also, when he called to ask me to come over here and give you the note . . . Well, he sounded . . . not himself. In fact, he sounded scared."

"Scared? That's not a word I'd associate with Johnny—and I hardly know him."

"Exactly. But he *was* scared, and not hiding it at all well. I had the feeling . . . Well, this is absurd, knowing Johnny, but I had the feeling that he was making the call under duress."

"Why?"

Harriet thought, compressing her lips. "Well, I didn't hear any other voice in the background, if that's what you mean. And he didn't use any code phrasing to tip me off, like people do on crime shows on the telly. But there was something . . . *something*. I just can't say what. And Johnny being afraid . . . Well, it makes *me* afraid."

Friday

·

JULY 18

"So that's where we stand, after a week," I said to my staff members. "Any ideas?"

We were assembled in the conference room for our regular Friday afternoon meeting. Craig was making a note on a legal pad. Charlotte stared at the white presentation board where I'd drawn a crude diagram and a timeline in red Marks-A-Lot. Derek leaned over and consulted with Mick, who shook his head in the negative. Ted was frowning and fingering a scratch on the round oak table, which, like my office armchair, was a relic of our days at All Souls Legal Cooperative and had been lovingly refinished by him. And Julia, back from her one-day "time-out," bowed her head, picking at her fingernails.

Charlotte said, "Your timeline doesn't go back far enough."

"Oh?"

"It should start when Alex Aguilar was in San Diego, dealing drugs for Johnny Duarte."

I extended the line up the left-hand side of the board and scribbled, "A.A. dealing, J.D."

"And you should indicate when Dan Jeffers was down there."

"Right." I scribbled again.

Craig asked, "How major a distributor is Duarte, anyway?"

"He's got a lock on the Mission, according to my contact on Narcotics." My contact being my former lover and good friend, Captain Greg Marcus, who headed up the detail.

"And how major was he in San Diego?"

"Middling. He handled the university and environs."

"Any idea who he worked for?"

"No, but my contact's looking into it." I turned to Julia. "You haven't remembered anything about any of the other names on the board, have you?"

She shook her head, looking somewhat hurt. That morning she'd told me she hadn't been able to recall anything else about her personal life that could conceivably discredit the agency, and I believed her, but I knew memories had a way of cropping up unexpectedly. If Julia had remembered something personally damaging in the interim, she might have been tempted to withhold it unless I probed.

"Okay," I said. "We have Alex Aguilar, who, according to one of his fellow board members at the Mexican Museum, has been touchy and out of sorts lately. He lodges the complaint against Julia, then leaves for a buying trip in Central America."

Derek consulted with Mick again. Mick said, "Go ahead, speak out. Shar even listens to me occasionally."

"Derek?" I said.

He cleared his throat—nervous because as a new hire he was unsure how he fit into our tightly knit operation. "That import-export business of Aguilar's—I think somebody should look into it. Central America, the drug angle . . ."

"And that's just what I was about to ask you to do."

He looked both pleased and relieved. "I'll see what I can find out online, but somebody else should check it out in person; I've got no experience as a field investigator."

"I'll handle that, after you get me the information. Next we have Scott Wagner, who, if you can believe the account of a drugged-out witness, was beaten to death and pushed into a ravine up in Marin County. What did your background check on Wagner turn up, Craig?"

"Apparently his private persona was identical to the public. No arrest record, exemplary on-the-job and academic histories. Everyone I talked with spoke highly of him. A very ethical, stand-up guy."

Which didn't fit with being beaten to death and pushed into a ravine. "What about Gene Santamaria?"

"Much the same. Impeccable credentials, long record of work with nonprofits in the Pacific Northwest, which is where he's from."

"Any connection with Aguilar or the other people we're looking at before he came to work at the center?"

"Negative."

"Okay, next we've got the witness, Dan Jeffers, who recognized the killer and took off shortly afterward. Any luck in locating him, Craig?"

"No trace of him since he visited his brother in June, but I'm still on it."

"Okay, you may as well also try to find out what kind

of business took Johnny Duarte out of town, and where. The woman I talked with, Harriet Leonard, described him as sounding frightened, but he doesn't strike me as a man who's easily intimidated. She also told me Duarte's job with Heritage Marketing is legitimate—a front to cover for his drug distributing—so start with them."

He nodded. "What about this R.D.? The one who was staying with Aguilar for a while?"

"Pretty difficult to trace someone when you only have a description and initials," Charlotte said.

Mick frowned at her. "I don't know about that."

"Come on, Mick."

"I'll bet you."

"Bet me what?"

"Dinner at Piperade."

"Done."

The two of them were always wagering for food; before I'd given Mick an incentive package along with the go-ahead to establish our computer forensics department, he'd performed unusually difficult chores or overtime work in exchange for restaurant meals.

Ted spoke up. "Shar, those files you had me copy after your briefcase was stolen—I've been thinking that the theft may not have been random. After all, one was on Aguilar. What if somebody's keeping an eye on you, monitoring what you're doing about the situation?"

That should have occurred to me. "Good point. It *was* taken while I visited Aguilar's building for the second time that day."

Charlotte said, "Maybe Aguilar himself has been watching you. How certain are we that he actually went to Central America?"

"We aren't certain. Craig—"

"I'll look into it."

Julia shifted in her chair, glanced up, troubled.

"Yes, Jules?" I said.

She hesitated, then shrugged. "You know, I'm kind of unimportant."

"What's that supposed to mean?"

She folded her hands on the table, hunched her shoulders. "I'm just a trainee here. Haven't even closed that many cases yet, and nothing major. I've got a juvie record, am a single mom struggling to get by, don't have any power or influence. Nada. So why would anybody go after me? What if this doesn't have to do with me at all? What if the person behind it is really after *you*?"

All heads turned in her direction.

"Go on," I said.

"This morning I reread the Private Investigator Act, especially the part about the owner of the agency being responsible for the employees' actions. If the D.A. proves his case against me, I'll only go to jail. I'm not saying it's no big deal, especially because I'd be separated from my kid, but my family would take care of him, and when I got out I could always get some kind of job. But you, Shar—you stand to lose a profession and an agency you've worked hard for. If I wanted to get revenge on somebody, that's what I'd go after."

Of course.

"Good reasoning, Jules. It's a possibility we need to explore."

She shrugged again and looked down at her hands, but her lips curved in a small smile.

I turned to the presentation board, where an arrow connected Alex Aguilar's name to Julia's. Now I wrote my own name and drew another arrow.

"Okay," I said, "who's willing to work late tonight, and maybe over the weekend?"

To a person, they volunteered.

They worked for food. Ted brought in burgers and salads and fries from Miranda's, our favorite waterfront diner. He supplied soft drinks and mineral water, and brewed pot after pot of coffee. Each operative took a given time frame and went over the agency case files, searching for a disgruntled client with a possible connection to Alex Aguilar, Johnny Duarte, or the shadowy R.D. I shut myself in my office and tried to think back on the cases I'd handled for All Souls Legal Cooperative. Under the buyout agreement for the poverty law firm, all files were supposed to have become the property of the remaining partners, but as I recalled, I'd kept mine. Unfortunately, I couldn't remember what I'd done with them.

Hank Zahn, my best male friend and founder of All Souls, might know, but he and his family were on a two-week vacation in British Columbia.

What about Rae Kelleher? I picked up the phone and called my one-time assistant at the Sea Cliff home she shared with her husband, my former brother-in-law, Ricky Savage.

"Hey," she said, "you'll be at my signing on Sunday, right?"

Oh, God, I'd clean forgotten it. After Rae had married Ricky, a country music superstar, she'd quit the agency to write what she called "shop-and-fuck novels." But instead of sleazy best-selling prose, she'd written what the *New York Times* had recently described as "a gem of a first effort," and would be signing copies at a local bookshop on Sunday afternoon. Rae was terrified at the prospect of the signing and convinced it would be poorly attended. There was no way I, or any of her other friends, could miss it.

"I'll be there," I said with more enthusiasm than I felt. "Now I've got a question: d'you remember the day we moved from All Souls to the pier?"

"Yeah. You— Jesus!"

In the background, young voices had begun to screech, and now Ricky yelled, "Cut it out! Red's on the phone!" Lisa and Molly, the youngest of his six children with my sister Charlene, were visiting for the weekend. There was good reason we called them the Little Savages.

Rae said, "Your nieces are driving us crazy. Why do you ask? About the move, I mean."

"My old files—I kept them, but I don't remember what I did with them."

"No surprise. You and Hank were both pretty ripped that night, celebrating you closing out your last open file."

The morning of the agency's move, I'd been going over the old files in a fit of nostalgia when I'd come upon the only unsolved one—the first investigation I'd undertaken for the co-op. As I read the inconclusive report, I realized the case's obvious solution, and by evening I'd closed it. Then Hank and I had indulged in too many celebratory glasses of cheap wine.

Rae added, "I'll never forget that night. I was still living at the Victorian, and came home around ten. You and Hank were drunk as skunks and trying to load that awful armchair you still have in your office onto the rental truck. Between the three of us, we got it aboard, and then you rushed back inside for your file boxes. Hank told you they weren't yours to take, but you said, 'Fuck it! As of today, I've closed every single one of them. That makes them mine.' And he laughed and stuck them on the truck."

"I remember that much, but where are they now?"

"In the crawl space above your home office. Hank and I put them up there while you were in the bathroom, throwing up."

"Not one of my finer hours."

In the background, Ricky's voice was now competing with my nieces'.

Rae sighed. "Got to go play wicked stepmother, before my husband goes into serious meltdown. You want help getting those file boxes down, give us a call. We'll bring Lisa and Molly over, lock them in the crawl space for the weekend."

Ted was hanging up the phone when I stopped at his office to ask him to tell the others that we'd meet at nine tomorrow morning, to go over our individual findings.

"Damn! That call was for you," he said. "I buzzed your office, but you didn't pick up."

"Who was it?"

"Marguerite Hayley. She said to tell you that the meeting with BSIS was productive, and that Todd Baylis will contact you on Monday about obtaining additional documents and setting up a meeting with you and Julia. You're to cooperate in any way you can."

"Something to look forward to." I told him to take money from petty cash to buy pastries for the morning, then headed home to review the All Souls files.

*   *   *

On my front steps I ran into Michelle Curley, who had just finished giving Ralph his shot. She'd been browsing the Internet for information on feline diabetes, and while she helped me drag down the dust-covered boxes, she chattered knowledgeably about such things as blood glucose levels, creatinine values, and Somogyi rebound. As I was descending with the last carton, she got so wrapped up in trying to persuade me to buy a measuring device called a Glucometer Elite that she let go of the ladder and I almost fell on top of her. I thanked her for her efforts on Ralph's behalf, said she should price the meter, and got her out of there as quickly as possible.

There were seven cartons on the floor of my home office. They contained only the reports I'd delivered to whichever All Souls attorney had assigned me to investigate a given case—not depositions or briefs or actual court documents—but that should be enough to refresh my memory. All in all, it was pretty ordinary stuff: employee background checks, interviews with witnesses in civil cases, skiptraces. Most of the time I hadn't even met the client.

Of course, there was the Albritton case, which had resulted in a murder conviction, but the killer had long ago been paroled and eventually moved out of state. The perpetrator of the 1956 "Two Penny Murder," whom I'd helped bring to justice decades later, had died of a heart attack in prison. I'd sent con artists and embezzlers to jail, returned children to the custodial parent, unmasked insurance fraud, recovered stolen property, and, in a few cases, allowed people whose misdeeds had really harmed no one to retreat into obscurity. In the end, I had to conclude that none of the cases I'd worked during my tenure at All Souls could have provoked serious retaliation. The majority of them were simply not important enough and had happened too long ago.

Their very ordinariness depressed me. At the time, the co-op's attorneys and I had thought we were on the cutting edge, out to change the world. But what had we really accomplished? We'd settled petty matters for semi-indigent clients, most of whom had then turned around and complained about having to pay for our services, even though our fees were based on a sliding scale, according to their income levels. And what was I accomplishing now? The clients were better off and tended not to complain as much, but . . .

Okay, McCone, so you're not performing brain surgery or forging world peace, but don't forget that what you do makes it easier for the clients to get through in this world. It's a legitimate service, and a damned important one.

Somewhat reassured of my position in the grand scheme of things, I left the files strewn on the floor, went to the kitchen, and poured myself a glass of wine. Fog misted the window over the sink, and the temperature in the house was edging downward. Instead of turning up the furnace, I went to the sitting room and lit a fire, then curled on the sofa, contemplating my major cases since I'd established the agency.

The most personal had involved the attempted theft of my identity. But the woman responsible was still in a mental institution, and in the unlikely event she was released, the state would be required to notify me; thus far I'd heard nothing. Ted and his partner, Neal, had been the targets of a series of antigay harassments that the entire agency had worked to bring to a halt, but the homophobe who had perpetrated them was firmly ensconced in prison. A man who had killed his wife in order to inherit her fortune was on death row, and it struck me as unlikely that he had the outside connections to set in motion such a scheme. Maybe someone at the agency would come up with something less obvious, but I had my doubts—

The phone rang. I started, looked at my watch. Close to midnight. One of my operatives? Hy, tired of my silence and demanding a response to his proposal? I snatched up the receiver.

Silence, but the kind that tells you someone's on the line.

"Hello?"

More silence.

"Hello!"

A click.

All right, first you invaded my car; now you've invaded my home. Next it's my turn.

Watch out, you bastard.

Saturday

·

JULY 19

"And now in local news . . ."

I'd gotten into the habit of watching the morning TV news during the war in Iraq, and hadn't yet been able to break myself of it. Today, I decided as I advanced on the little set in the kitchen, would be a good time to change my ways. The news was too depressing—who needs the forecast of a record federal deficit, a movement to recall the state governor, slaughter abroad, and duplicity at all levels of government first thing in the morning? Such reportage would set a bad tone for what already promised to be a difficult day. Better to find out what was going on from tomorrow's *Chronicle,* when the events' sharp edges would be blunted by the passage of time and lack of live film footage.

I had my finger on the Off button when I caught the words ". . . body of a man found Friday evening on the rocks below Devil's Slide has been identified as that of John H. Duarte, thirty-seven, of San Francisco."

A grainy photograph of Johnny Duarte appeared on the screen. I turned up the volume.

". . . Mr. Duarte, who is thought to have fallen while walking on the treacherous cliffs along Highway One, was spotted by a hiker shortly after six last night. Emergency service workers recovered his body an hour later." An aerial film showed the cliffs and the recovery operation. "According to a friend, Harriet Leonard, Mr. Duarte, a marketing executive, had been absent from his Upper Market home since Thursday evening, although his car was parked in the garage. Anyone with information concerning his fall is asked to contact the San Mateo County Sheriff's Department. In other news—"

I punched the TV off.

Fell, while walking along the cliffs?

I don't think so.

I went to the sitting room, located the receiver of the cordless phone in the wood basket—what was it doing there?—and called the Marina district apartment that Craig shared with Adah Joslyn. He answered, told me she was working today; I could catch her at SFPD.

"What's happened, Shar?" Craig asked. "You sound upset."

"I'll brief everyone on it at our meeting. I'm running a little late, though. Will you tell them I'll be there as soon as possible?"

"Will do."

"Thanks." I broke the connection and dialed Adah's number at the Hall of Justice.

"Why do I think you want something?" she asked.

"Because I never call you at work otherwise."

"Not true. You called three weeks ago to cancel our swim date."

Adah, like Craig, was big on physical fitness and had nagged me into joining her athletic club. I love to swim, but in a year I'd used the pool fewer than two dozen times, and was considering canceling the membership.

"Okay," she added, "what is it now?"

I could picture her: sitting at her desk, trim and elegantly dressed even on a Saturday, a pencil stuck into her closely cropped curls, frown lines marring what was otherwise a flawless honey-tan countenance. Adah liked to refer to herself as the department's "poster child for affirmative action," but that alone didn't account for her rapid rise through the ranks. She was a damn good investigator, and in the past year she'd also proved herself a good diplomat, having tactfully distanced herself from a rash of scandals that threatened to cripple the already troubled department.

I said, "A Mission district drug distributor, Johnny Duarte, took a tumble off of Devil's Slide yesterday. Has San Mateo County contacted you about it?"

"Hmmm. Sounds familiar. Yeah, here it is. They copied your pal Greg Marcus on it, too. Circumstances don't point to an accident. Duarte was dressed casually, but not like you would for hiking; Gucci loafers don't provide much traction. Also, there was no vehicle belonging to him in the vicinity."

"How'd they identify him?"

"His wallet was in his pants pocket."

"And no autopsy results yet?"

"McCone." She clicked her tongue. "You should know better than to ask. Pathologists are even more backlogged than I am. Does this have to do with the problems at the agency that Craig's been telling me about?"

"Yes."

"Anything San Mateo—or I—should know?"

"Yes to that, too, but I'm running late for a meeting."

"Come by the apartment this afternoon for a glass of wine. We'll talk then."

I was on my way out of the house when the phone rang. Ma, I thought. I'd planned to call her the night before and then got sidetracked. If I picked up, she'd want to talk for a long time, and I hated to cut her short. Although she was happy with her new husband, Melvin Hunt, and received frequent visits from my brother John and his two sons, Joey's death had hit her hard, and she seemed to need constant reassurance that the rest of us were there for her. For a moment I debated letting the call go on the machine, then rushed back inside.

"Hey, McCone."

Hy. Now, of all times.

"Hey, yourself. How are you?"

"Good. Feeling like a jaunt in Two-Seven-Tango." The sexy red Cessna 170B we jointly owned, a magnificent tail-dragger capable of speeds up to 120 miles per hour. It was currently tied down at Tufa Tower Airport near Hy's ranch.

He added, "What say I pick you up at North Field, take you on a picnic at that grass strip near the reservoir in Lake County? On the way, we can hit the aerobatics box at Los Alegres, put Tango through her paces; she hasn't had a good workout in weeks."

Take me on a picnic in an isolated place; hold me hostage till I'll talk about our future.

Somehow, the idea didn't alarm me as much as it would have a week ago, and genuine regret crept into my voice as I turned him down. "There's a crisis at the agency," I told him. "Something I could use your input on."

"Okay—change of plans. I'll fly down later today; we can talk about it tonight. I've got to be in the city on Sunday, anyway, to lend moral support at the book signing."

The idea appealed to me. We'd have a nice evening, a productive exchange of ideas about the situation with the agency, and a good time in bed. Now that I could anticipate Hy's arrival, I realized how much my body had been aching for his. And Sunday we'd have brunch at a favorite restaurant, attend the book signing, spend more time in bed.

Maybe I'd even get away without a discussion of marriage.

After I finished briefing my people on Johnny Duarte's "accident," we turned our attention to the cases they'd gone over the previous evening.

Mick led it off. "Last Christmas you conducted that investigation for the mayor's office—about the official they suspected of leaking sensitive information from city hall."

I'd thought of the case myself. "Right. That architect who worked on the other side of the pier, Tony Kennett, was a friend of the official and tried to steal the disk of my final report so his buddy could find out what we had on him. My investigator friend, Wolf, was at the party and helped me apprehend Kennett. Kennett was fired, and the official's no longer working for the city."

"Not directly, but I found out he's now on Aguilar's staff, in a low-profile position. Apparently the folks around city hall have short memories, or else they don't care."

"So maybe the guy persuaded Aguilar to set this thing

up. Question is, does he have that much influence over the supervisor?"

"I'll have to find out," Mick said. "Also there's Kennett. He was unemployed as of June."

"Get on it, Savage."

He saluted me and left the conference room.

Charlotte said, "I've got something promising. Last year you handed me a skiptrace in a child custody case. The father had fled the area with his ten-year-old daughter; I followed the paper trail to Palm Desert. When I located them, the mother wanted the daughter escorted home by Atwater Security—that outfit that specializes in transporting juveniles to the custodial parent or, if they're out of control, to special schools."

"I remember. I wasn't comfortable with Atwater's operatives, so I asked you to go along. Their team—what were their names?"

"Tracy Escobar and Mike Fairchild. They went to the kid's school and, in my presence, flashed badges at the principal and teachers. Acted like they were cops, in flagrant violation of the Private Investigator Act."

"And after I read your report, I gave it to the head of Atwater. He fired them both. So what's the connection to Aguilar?"

"Escobar now runs the language lab at Trabajo por Todos, and was romantically linked to Aguilar last fall, before he met Julia."

"Revenge might be a motive there, but if he's no longer seeing Escobar . . ."

Craig said, "It turns out Aguilar *did* go to Central America. He's in Guatemala City as we speak, and his traveling companion is Tracy Escobar."

"Well, keep working on it," I told Charlotte.

"But wait, there's more!" When she let loose with one of her throaty giggles, I realized she was parodying those TV commercials where sellers entice viewers to phone in and buy merchandise with the promise of additional free goodies.

"It had better not be a Salad Shooter," I warned.

"Nope, it's a deadbeat dad I tracked down last month. He's had his wages garnished to the point where he'll be eating Tuna Helper with cat food till he's of retirement age. His name is Patrick Neilan—"

"And he lives in Aguilar's apartment building." Neilan had bad-mouthed the supervisor to me. Did he genuinely dislike him, or had he recognized the agency's name and tried to throw me off by distancing himself?

Charlotte said, "You want me to talk to him?"

"No, I'll pay a personal visit to Mr. Neilan."

Patrick Neilan's garage door was raised, and his broken-down Ford Falcon still sat with the hood up, in the same state of disrepair as when I'd last seen it. I rang the bell of his apartment and, after half a minute, received an answering buzz.

The apartment was at the front of the second floor, over the garage space: one small room, a bath, and a kitchen. Neilan had fashioned a sleeping alcove in a narrow hallway between the kitchen and the bath; he had to step on the mattress in order to fetch us coffee. The other furnishings had come either with the unit or from a thrift shop; aside from a couple of snapshots of two small children attached to the refrigerator by magnets, there were no pictures, no knickknacks—nothing that spoke of the man who lived there.

He saw me looking around and shrugged, his wide mouth pulling down. "It's a place to sleep, not home."

"Where is home?"

"About half a mile away. My family settled in the Mission after the oh-six quake, never even thought of leaving. My father's a cop, his father before him, all three of my brothers. Even my sisters married cops." He shook his head. "Me, I had bigger ideas, so I went to Golden Gate University, got a business degree, met my wife there. We had two kids right away, I was working a day job at a small accounting firm, and another at night— security. Doesn't give you much time for the things that matter."

I knew about those nights working security; it was how I'd put myself through UC Berkeley—having little social life, even less sleep, but finding time to study during the long midnight hours.

"I've been there," I said.

"Well, you can probably guess the rest of the story, then. I'm gone day and night. The wife is working at an insurance agency. Her boss is single, makes good money, and next thing I know, she's out the door. But she's not really gone, because there's the child support."

Neilan's blue eyes grew dull, and he ran a hand through his already tousled red curls. "I tried to make the support payments on time, but I lost my day job, and the security firm cut way back on my hours. I love my kids, but what can I do? I've gotta live, don't I? After I missed a couple of months, the ex cut me off from seeing the kids. I moved to this dump to save money and forgot to give her the new address. She isn't speaking to anybody in my family, so she hired detectives to track me down. Why she needed them, I don't know; I'm not more than ten blocks from our old apartment. Anyway, she got a judgment against me, and now my wages're garnished down to practically nothing. I can't pay my rent, so next month, streets, here I come."

A familiar saga of the working poor, and my firm was responsible for it.

Neilan appeared to be thinking about what he'd told me. "Ah, hell," he said, "you shouldn't have to listen to this. *I'm* even sick of listening to it."

I liked Neilan, and certainly couldn't see him as a man who would help Alex Aguilar frame Julia. Besides, I felt bad about my agency's role in his financial downfall.

"Patrick," I said, "do you remember the name of the detective firm your wife hired to track you down?"

"Not offhand. Mc-something. Wait a minute! That was you?"

"One of my employees, yes."

"Jesus." He shook his head, frowning. "Stuff like that—how can you sleep at night?"

Good question, but so often I didn't see the end results of the cases I contracted for. "Look," I said, "maybe I can make it up to you."

"Don't see how that's possible."

"Just give me a minute. D'you think you're a good security man?"

He considered, eyes moving thoughtfully. I liked it that he took time before answering.

"I'm not bad," he said. "I can read people, and I'm observant; I'm quick at picking up on little things that don't seem right. I put details together in a way that the other people who work with me don't. Why?"

"That's how I was when I worked in security. My supervisor noticed it and recommended that I be trained as an investigator. How about if I test your aptitude for investigation while you pick up some extra money? I'm not promising anything, but depending on your performance, we might be able to talk about a trainee position with my agency."

Surprise and pleasure transformed his freckled face. "I could go for that. What d'you want me to do?"

"It concerns the building's other tenants, particularly Alex Aguilar."

Ghirardelli Square sits on the lower slope of Russian Hill, a stone's throw from Fisherman's Wharf. The red-brick complex, which used to house a chocolate factory, a woolen mill, and other enterprises, was refurbished in the 1960s as space for specialty boutiques and restaurants, and incorporates large, attractive outdoor areas. Los Colores, Alex Aguilar's shop, was off the main courtyard on the north side of the complex—a pricey location.

I spotted the shop when I reached the top of the stairway from Beach Street, and moved toward it, giving wide berth to a white-faced mime who was entertaining a group of tourists. If the truth be known, I'm terrified of mimes; for some reason they zero in on me, and countless times their antics have humiliated me in front of total strangers. An understandable aversion, perhaps, but I'm also terrified of bagpipers, and not a one has done anything more to me than insult my eardrums. Go figure.

The windows of Aguilar's shop were decorated with a display of colorful weavings that swayed and fluttered in a breeze from the open door. Inside I encountered a four-foot-tall wooden plant with large leaves in various shades of green and with yellow fruit on long stalks; it was a moment before I noticed the snake that rested in an undulant pose amid the foliage, red tongue extended evilly. I touched one of the leaves, and it fell to the floor with a clatter.

Behind the plant, someone laughed. I peered through its branches and saw a young Hispanic woman with up-swept hair and long silver earrings. She said, "That's the fourth time it's happened today. The plant fits together with pegs, and they come loose."

I retrieved the leaf from the floor and took it around to her. "I'm glad I'm not the only clumsy one."

She set it on a glass display case containing jewelry. "No harm done. Look around; let me know if I can help you with anything."

I moved about the space, browsing. The goods were interesting: exotic clothing, carvings, colorful wooden boxes, paintings with an iridescent quality that resembled stained glass. I'd have to tell Ted about the rack of brilliantly dyed handwoven vests; his new fashion statement was tending toward the south-of-the-border look.

On the surface, at least, Los Colores appeared to be a legitimate operation—Derek's assessment when I'd phoned the agency before I drove over here. His Internet search had shown nothing about Aguilar's business that could be construed as illegitimate: after three years, the shop was turning a tidy profit; it had an excellent credit rating and belonged to all the right retailers' associations.

I moved to the glass case, examined the jewelry. A pair of hammered copper earrings caught my eye, and I asked the woman if I could see them. Three hundred fifty dollars. Well, of course. Aguilar would have to charge high prices to make the rent. I was about to hand them back to her when someone came through the door behind me and a familiar voice said, "Maria, do you know where I can reach Alex? It's an emergency."

I turned. Harriet Leonard stepped around the wooden plant. When she saw me, she whirled and headed back outside.

I set the earrings on the counter and followed. Leonard was moving swiftly across the courtyard. She looked back, then speeded up, nearly crashing into an old man with a walker. I started to run as she disappeared down the stairway that led to Beach Street.

The mime whom I'd seen earlier began running along at my right, his movements aping mine.

Jesus Christ, not this again!

"Go away!" I shouted.

He mimicked the motions of my mouth.

"Asshole!"

More mouth motions. People flocked behind us, laughing.

All right for you!

The stairway was a couple of yards away. I feinted to the left, speeding up. Darted to the right, grabbed the handrail, and started down.

Behind me I heard a grunt as the mime smacked into the wall at the top of the stairs.

Next time you'll know better than to mess with me, buddy.

Of course, by the time I reached street level, Leonard was gone, and I felt guilty about the mime. What if he'd been hurt? Lately I'd felt all sorts of urges to retaliate against people who annoyed me—which they seemed to do with increasing frequency—but I'd acted on few of them, and never done bodily harm.

What was *wrong* with me, anyway?

Chalk it up to the times. People dying needlessly both here and overseas; entire countries being laid to waste; a once-robust economy in the tank; tax cuts for the rich, while our educational and health care systems foundered; an overall in-your-face, "I got mine, so fuck you" attitude —it was enough to reduce the most even-tempered individual to sheer rage.

No, my attitude wasn't extreme, only misdirected.

I headed for my car, looked at my watch. Three-thirty. Hy's ETA at Oakland Airport's North Field was five. It would take him forty minutes or so to tie down Two-Seven-Tango and catch a ride with one of the many people he knew at the field, to the place nearby where he garaged his decrepit Morgan. If the car started—and during the past year it hadn't been too reliable in that department—he'd be at my house by six-thirty.

I could try to track down Harriet Leonard, but given my lack of a phone number or address for her, that might be a time-consuming proposition. And I'd earlier promised Adah I'd stop by her place to discuss what I knew about Johnny Duarte. In the interests of staying on my friend's good side, I turned the MG toward the Marina district.

The roses around the fountain in the courtyard of Adah and Craig's Spanish-style apartment building on North Point Street were blooming in profusion this year. I went over and smelled a coral one whose scent was particularly exotic, before I climbed the private stairway to their second-floor unit. When Adah let me inside, her big white cat waddled out from under the coffee table and sank his fangs into my ankle.

"Charley! What the hell? Stop it!" I shook him off and glared at his owner.

Adah, looking relaxed in running shorts and a tee, rolled her eyes and clapped her hands at the cat. He retreated to the bedroom. "Sorry about that," she said. "He's pissed at the world."

"Why?"

"Vet told us he's 'officially obese' for the second year in a row. We've got him on short rations."

"I suppose that's better than having to stick him with a needle twice a day, like Ralph."

"I don't know. When he's in this kind of mood, I think I'd *enjoy* jabbing him." Adah led me to the kitchen, poured us wine, and we took our glasses to the deck that overlooked the communal vegetable garden the tenants had planted in the narrow space between the building's wall and the back fence.

"Johnny Duarte," she said when we were settled. "What d'you know about him?"

I detailed my contact with Duarte, ending with Harriet Leonard's flight from the shop in Ghirardelli Square.

Frown lines appeared between Adah's eyebrows. "This Harriet Leonard's beginning to interest me. San Mateo County picked up her name as a friend of Duarte's from a news broadcast, asked me to question her. She lives a couple of doors down the street from his condo, in a rental property he owned. I went over there after lunch, and although she denied it, I could've sworn she was packing for a trip."

"You find out anything from her?"

"Not much. She told me about him phoning her and asking her to give you the note canceling your date. Didn't say anything about him sounding scared. Friday night she went back to the condo to see if Duarte had returned, and a reporter showed up, so she gave him the interview. I asked about her relationship with Duarte; she said they were good friends. Seemed more nervous than upset about his death, though, and kept looking at her watch."

"So you . . . ?"

"Passed on the information to San Mateo County, asked if they wanted me to order a surveillance. They were less than impressed with the nuances I'd picked up on, and said no. So I called it a day. Not my jurisdiction. I've got enough problems on the job without taking on theirs."

I—and everyone else who kept up with the news— was fully cognizant of those problems. Like any major city's police department, the SFPD had always had its organizational and political difficulties, but the previous November, following an incident now labeled as "Fajitagate," all hell had broken loose. Three off-duty police officers, including the son of the deputy chief, had allegedly accosted two men outside a bar and grill on Union Street, demanding they hand over a take-out bag of steak fajitas. When they refused, a fight broke out, the officers fled, and one of the men called the police.

The incident spawned accusations by the district attorney's office that the department had covered up the off-duty officers' misconduct, and eventually resulted in multiple grand jury indictments of officers all the way up the chain of command—including the chief of police. The chief, who was close to retirement, took medical leave; when most of the indictments were later quashed, the mayor named the deputy chief—father of one of the accused—acting chief. In time, the son was let go for administrative reasons, but the damage had been done, and a recent report on an unrelated incident, alleging that a police captain had ordered a subordinate's name withheld as a potential suspect in a kidnapping, had only worsened the situation. Morale within the department, seldom high in recent years, was now at an all-time low.

I asked Adah, "How are things down at the Hall?"

"They've been better." A loyal cop, she steered the conversation away from the controversial subject. "So Leonard wanted to get hold of Aguilar, and panicked when she saw you. Why, d'you suppose?"

"Why did she panic, or why did she want to get hold of him?"

"Both."

"I think she wanted to get hold of him to warn him about Duarte's death. Her behavior tells me that Aguilar may have been doing business with him out of that shop."

"Drug business."

"Right. Everything my new hire, Derek Ford, has been able to learn about the operation points to it being legitimate, but Aguilar does make frequent buying trips to Central and South America. He could be importing drugs as well as merchandise."

"Well, that would bring the supervisor down, now, wouldn't it? And end Ms. Leonard's 'career.' No wonder she was scared of you. She's probably found out who you are, suspects you're investigating him."

"I was going to try to locate her, but from what you tell me, she's probably long gone by now."

Adah nodded, frowning again. "You know, here's Aguilar, the product of a family dedicated to community service. He makes a slip in college, does some dealing. But finally that's behind him; he's on track again with the job-training center, charitable activities, board of supes, and potential mayoral candidacy. Why would he team up with Duarte again?"

"Pressure. Duarte knew about his past."

"Okay, if Aguilar is doing business with Duarte, why would he call attention to himself with these false accusations against Julia?"

"Don't know."

"Well, that's what you better find out, girl. That is very definitely it."

When I arrived home, I found Hy's long, lanky body sprawled out on a chaise longue on the deck. Ralph lay draped over his feet. The cat had wanted nothing to do with me since the insulin-shot fiasco on Sunday, and his haughty expression when he looked up conveyed-that he had found someone far better to associate with.

Hy said, "There you are. I was beginning to wonder if I'd have to spend my whole evening with this creature. Michelle came over to give him his shot, told me about his diabetes." He shifted his legs, and Ralph slid down and slunk into the house.

I leaned over to give Hy a kiss, then sat on the chaise next to his. "D'you believe it? A cat with diabetes?"

"I'd believe anything these days." He looked and sounded tired; even though his stay at the ranch was supposed to be a vacation, I was sure he'd spent a good deal of it fielding phone calls from RKI's clients and operatives around the globe.

"So what's the crisis at the agency you need to talk about?" he asked.

Suddenly I wanted to insulate the two of us in a warm cocoon where no problems—his or mine—could touch us.

"Talking can wait. I have a better idea." I got up and reached for his hand.

He said, "I like your way of thinking."

We were lying in bed, and I'd just finished outlining the events of the past nine days, when Alice shot through the partly open glass door from the deck, launched herself through the air, and landed on Hy's chest, where she industriously proceeded to groom his thick, dark-blond mustache.

"McCone, this cat is weird."

"She doesn't get it from me."

"Or me. I'm only a potential stepdaddy."

I tensed, and he must have felt it, because he said, "I didn't come down here this weekend to force the issue. I've said my piece, told you what would please me; and in time you'll say your piece, tell me what would please you."

"And if they're not the same?"

"McCone, we love each other. We'll negotiate something."

Relief washed over me; at least he wasn't taking the all-or-nothing stance I'd feared.

"But remember," he added with a wicked grin, "I've negotiated successfully in four different languages with guys carrying semiautomatic weapons, who didn't at all mind dying. Can you top that?"

"No. But right now I'm only interested in negotiating one thing—which one of us gets up and calls out for a pizza?"

Sunday

·

JULY 20

Rae signed another copy of *Blue Lonesome* with a flourish and smiled as she handed it to the customer. A Clean Well-Lighted Place for Books, in the Opera Plaza complex, was mobbed with her friends, Ricky's music industry associates, three of his six children, and, apparently, strangers who had read the glowing review of her novel in that morning's paper. During the time she'd been with Ricky, Rae had acquired ease in dealing with the public, and she was clearly enjoying her moment in the limelight. He, on the other hand, held back, maintaining a low-key presence, eyes glowing as he savored her triumph. Ricky had come a long way from the self-absorbed young man who had married my younger sister, just as Rae had come a long way from the insecure young woman whom I'd hired as my assistant at All Souls.

I felt someone tap me on the shoulder and turned. Greg Marcus, holding his copy of the book.

I motioned at it and said, "Hey, I didn't know you

cared." For some reason, Rae had always irritated Greg, and long ago he'd coined a nickname for her—"TPA," for "the pain in the ass."

He shrugged. "The kid's all right, and *Blue Lonesome* is one hell of an achievement." His gaze moved about the room. "Hy here?"

"Somewhere." I'd last seen him talking flying with one of the members of Ricky's band, who was also a pilot, hands swooping through the air as he described an aerobatic maneuver.

"Come outside with me," Greg said. "I'm feeling claustrophobic."

I followed as he shouldered his way through the crowd to the door and into the courtyard. The afternoon had been sunny and clear, but now a high fog was blowing in.

I said, "Nothing yet on that inquiry to the San Diego PD, I suppose?"

"No, not as of this morning."

I studied Greg, noting that his eyes were red-rimmed and deeply shadowed. Always a big man, he had put on weight since I'd last seen him, and his face was puffy, his blond hair streaked with gray.

I said, "I didn't want to ask the other day, because I was calling you at work, but how're you dealing with all the stuff that's been going down at the department?"

"Not very well. I wasn't directly involved in any of it, but SFPD isn't a good place for me anymore. I'm thinking of taking early retirement."

"Oh? What would you do?"

"A year ago I bought a place up in Amador County. Vineyard land that I lease to a winery. Small house, but we like it."

"We?"

He grinned shyly. "Yeah. I'm getting married again."

Now, that was a surprise. Greg's one and only marriage had been a somewhat tepid union that ended in divorce; since then he'd seemed content with bachelorhood. "Who is she?" I asked.

"Her name's Jo Martin. She's an illustrator of children's books. Pretty lady, about your age, great cook. You'd like her."

"Congratulations." I hugged him, then said, "How'd you decide to . . . you know . . . ?"

"Take a second chance? I don't know. One day you wake up, and it seems like a natural step."

Then how come I don't wake up and feel it's natural?

"Shar? What's the matter?"

"Nothing, really."

He put his index finger under my chin and tipped my face up so he could look into my eyes. "Hy wants to marry you, doesn't he?"

". . . Well, yes."

"And you . . . ?"

"It's not something I ever thought I'd do."

"Why not?"

"In case you haven't noticed, marriage isn't what the McCone family does best. My parents divorced; my brother John divorced; my brother Joey never even got close to marrying. Charlene and Ricky broke up; my youngest sister, Patsy, has three kids by three different fathers, none of whom she considered tying the knot with. Bad track record, all around."

"Your mother and Charlene and Patsy are happy with their present husbands, aren't they?"

"For now."

"And what about your birth parents?"

That gave me pause. "Saskia had a happy marriage. So did Elwood."

"Heredity's as important as environment. So what are you afraid of?"

"I don't know."

Greg patted my shoulder. "Well, think about it, Shar. You're pretty self-aware, when you allow yourself to be."

After Greg left me, I wandered back into the bookstore, spotted Hy, and was about to motion that it was time to leave when Mick came up, flanked by Lisa and Molly. The older Mick got, the more I was struck by his resemblance to his father; his hair was blond, while Ricky's was chestnut, but they had the same tall, strong build and handsome features. The major difference between them was in their abilities: Ricky couldn't have operated a computer to save his life, and Mick was tone-deaf.

He looked down at his sisters and said, "I need to talk to Aunt Shar for a few minutes. Why don't you guys check out the children's section."

Lisa nodded, but Molly, the elder, frowned and said, "*Young adult* section."

"Huh?"

"We're not babies, you know. Dad's even gonna let us read Rae's book, although he says there're parts we won't understand."

"*I'll* understand them." Lisa smiled smugly.

"She probably will, too," Mick said as the girls ran off through the crowd. "Kids grow up too fast nowadays."

"I can recall a time not too long ago when I was lecturing you about birth control, and you informed me you'd been sexually active and prepared since you were fourteen."

"That's different."

"Why? Because Lisa and Molly are girls?"

"No. Because . . . well, because they're my *sisters*."

"And you're a good big brother. So what d'you want to talk about?"

"That guy on Aguilar's staff, the one you nailed for leaking information from the mayor's office—Aguilar fired him two weeks ago, and he's moved to Seattle. Is it worth following up on?"

I considered. "Probably, at least to find out the circumstances of his being fired. What about Tony Kennett, the architect who tried to steal the disk containing my report?"

"He moved to Sacramento, got on as a draftsman with a firm there."

"Then I think we can discount him. Anything on this R.D.?"

"Not yet, but I'm pursuing it. And Sweet Charlotte said to tell you she's working the Tracy Escobar angle." Mick looked around the crowded bookstore. "I'd be enjoying this party a hell of a lot more if I wasn't worried about the loss of my livelihood."

"That isn't going to happen."

He raised a skeptical eyebrow.

"I promise you," I said with more confidence than I felt. "It will *not* happen."

Hy and I had planned a quiet dinner at a favorite neighborhood restaurant, but when we got back to my house, there was a message on the machine from Patrick Neilan. When I called him back, he said one of the tenants of his building had something to tell me and wanted to meet in person.

"Sorry," I said to Hy, who was coming back from moving his car so it wouldn't be ticketed in the morning, tomorrow being street-cleaning day. "I've got to go out, and I don't know how long it'll take, so dinner's probably off."

"Doesn't matter. I noshed plenty at the book signing, and I'm not very hungry. If you want, pick up some take-out on the way back."

"Are you sure it's okay? You look annoyed."

"At the goddamn Morgan, not you. It's crapped out again. Tomorrow I'm having it towed and sold for scrap."

"Too bad, but it really *is* in rotten shape. I'll be happy to give you a ride back to North Field afterward."

"Not necessary. I'm staying on for a while."

"Oh?"

"While we were at the bookstore, I had a call from Gage." Gage Renshaw, one of his partners in RKI. "A situation's heating up, and they may need me down south at world headquarters. Besides, I don't feel right, leaving you in the middle of this mess. I'm still hoping to come up with some angle that might be helpful." He held his hand up, forestalling discussion. "Remember what I said, McCone—no pressure on the personal front."

God, he was a good man! When I compared him to most of my much-loved but problematic relatives, I couldn't understand why I hesitated to allow him into my family.

Because you can't lose your family. Them, you're stuck with for life. But if a marriage doesn't work out, you could very well lose Hy.

Of course, you could very well lose him anyway. . . .

* * *

It was dark in Patrick Neilan's small apartment; a pillar-type candle flickered on the counter that separated the kitchen from the main room, and Angela Batista sat in shadow. When I suggested we turn on a light, she said, "No. I don't want you to see me like this. Sit down, please, and we'll talk."

I glanced at Neilan. He nodded, so I sat on the sofa; its fabric was shredded as if by cats' claws, and it smelled musty.

Batista said, "I didn't tell you everything about Alex Aguilar when you came to my apartment, but Patrick has convinced me I can trust you. And after what has happened to me, I want you to know everything."

"I promise you can trust me, Ms. Batista. What happened?"

"Back when that R.D. was staying in Aguilar's apartment, I looked over my lease, to see if there was a legal way to get him out of there. And there was—a clause prohibiting overnight guests for more than forty-eight hours, without written permission from the management company. I called Aguilar and told him he could either tell that R.D. to leave or I would report him. And he threatened me."

"With what?"

"He said he would send R.D. to see me; the two of us could settle the problem. Then he added, 'My friend has a temper. I can't be responsible for what he might do.' "

"Did you complain to the management company? Consult an attorney?"

"No."

"Why not?"

"I *knew* what kind of a temper that R.D. had. I'd heard

the arguments, the stuff breaking in that apartment. I was afraid, so I kept silent."

"And what happened to change your mind?"

"R.D. came back. Two nights ago. He waited for me in the hallway while I was taking down the garbage, and dragged me into my apartment. He said he knew I'd been talking to you about him and Aguilar. And then he"—her voice broke—"he beat me. Broke my nose, gave me two black eyes. Broke a rib, too. When he left, he said if I ever mentioned either him or Aguilar to anybody again, he'd kill me. I could tell he meant it."

The fear in her voice was palpable; it put a chill on me. "I'm so sorry. Did you call the police?"

"No. I had a friend drive me to the hospital. I said I was mugged and couldn't describe who did it. The police came and took a report, of course; they have to do that. But I didn't tell them anything, either."

"And R.D.? Where did he go afterward?"

"I don't know. He's not in that apartment, though." Angela Batista was crying softly now. "I can't go to work at my restaurant. I'm a mess, what would my customers think? I'm afraid to stay here; I haven't slept more than a few minutes at a time since it happened. I can't go to a motel, not looking like this; no respectable place would take me."

I thought for a moment. "I know a place—an apartment where you'll have twenty-four-hour security." Last year RKI had purchased a building on Twenty-eighth Avenue in the outer Sunset district, to house clients with serious safety issues; I'd stayed there myself one time. "If a unit is available, you can move in tonight."

"That's very kind of you. But why . . . ?"

"I'm glad to help. And you can help me. You've seen

this R.D. up close and personal. Maybe together we can identify him."

After Hy had okayed it for Angela Batista to stay at the RKI safe house, Patrick and I escorted her to her apartment so she could pack. In the light from the hallway fixtures, I glimpsed the extent of the damage R.D. had done. In addition to the fear she was experiencing, the pain must be severe. Psychological pain, too: her self-image as a strong, confident woman had been shattered as surely as her rib and nose, and would take much longer to heal.

I offered to help her gather her things, but she declined and told Patrick and me to be seated in the living room. After she left us, he said, "So what d'you think?"

"According to one of my operatives, Aguilar has a habit of sending thugs to intimidate people who oppose or threaten him. R.D.'s obviously one of them. He must've been hanging around the building the night I talked with Angela and—oh, God!"

"What?"

"You stay here with Angela. I've got to check on Vanessa Lu."

The preschool teacher didn't answer her bell. I knocked. Still no answer. No light shone from beneath the door, as it had the night I'd talked with her.

Maybe she simply wasn't home. Maybe.

I rushed back upstairs, confided my fears in Patrick. "What if R.D. got to her and she's lying in there dead or injured?"

He thought, raking his fingers through his curly red hair. "Angela said R.D. worked her over two nights ago—that was Friday. Around five o'clock that afternoon I saw Vanessa and her boyfriend getting into his car; she had an overnight bag. They must've gone away for the weekend, aren't back yet."

"Still, I should warn her about R.D."

"I'll wait around for her, take care of it. Once she knows to watch out, Vanessa'll be okay; she's into karate. And I may be skinny, but I'm tough enough to protect everybody in this building."

On the way to Twenty-eighth Avenue, Angela Batista and I exchanged only a few words.

"Ms. McCone, how do you think I can help you find out who that R.D. is?"

"I have a friend who's a graphic artist. I'm going to ask her to work with you on a picture of R.D. With Vanessa Lu and Patrick, as well."

"But I only saw him a few times, and when he was beating me I didn't notice anything but his fists."

"My friend will work on it with you, help you recall."

"Like the police, on the TV shows?"

"Yes."

"And when you know who he is, what will you do?"

"Nothing that will put you in any more danger."

"But you *will* do something?"

"Oh, yes, I'll do something. R.D. will never hurt anybody again."

Monday

·

JULY 21

By the time I poured my first cup of coffee, Hy was already on the phone to a towing company, arranging for them to remove the Morgan. Then he went outside and pushed it onto the sidewalk in front of the house so he wouldn't be ticketed for blocking the street cleaners. Because he also could be ticketed for parking on the sidewalk, he stuck a note of explanation under the windshield wiper.

When he came back to the kitchen, Michelle was with him. She prepared the syringe for Ralph, who was at his food bowl, and as she administered the shot, I heard the cat purr. This, from an animal that seemed determined to ignore me!

Maybe it was going to be another of those Mondays. . . .

Things began looking up, however, when I called my friend Daphne Ashford at her graphic arts studio.

"Yes," she said, "I've got software similar to what the police use to create a portrait of a suspect. The technology's very sophisticated—and accurate. I've used it to create images for posters and the like."

"I thought you'd mentioned that. Are you available to take on a job for me today?"

"You've caught me in a forty-eight-hour window between projects. I was planning to clean the flat, but what the hell. Clean flat? Make money? No contest."

"Is two o'clock okay?"

"Fine."

"I'll bring the first witness by the studio then."

Ted looked somber when he handed me my phone messages, and the top one told me why. Todd Baylis from DCA was requesting additional documents from the agency files and also wished to set up a meeting with Julia and me at our earliest convenience.

I thought for a moment, then said, "Okay, I'll phone him. And here's what I'd like you to do: give him everything he wants, and then some. Load him up with documents, relevant or irrelevant, so long as there's nothing sensitive in them. That'll buy us time while he reads them."

"Will do. How's the investigation coming?"

"I won't have a good handle on that till the staff meeting this afternoon. And yet . . ."

"Yet what?"

I shook my head, unwilling to get his hopes up. After all, it was just a feeling. But my feelings had usually stood me in good stead, and what I sensed now was that we were very close to a major break in the case.

"No trace of Dan Jeffers so far," Craig said, standing in the door of my office. "He's not driving that old van anymore—at least it wasn't reregistered when it was due in May, and there's no certificate of planned nonoperation or record of a sale on it. I know the highway patrol's been cracking down on people without current tags."

"He could've sold it, and the new owner hasn't gotten around to notifying the DMV."

"Lots of possibilities, I suppose, but there's the obvious."

"Meaning Jeffers has been killed by the person he saw at Olompali? Well, why don't you pursue that angle?"

"I'm already on it."

I picked up the phone, buzzed Charlotte. "Anything on Tracy Escobar?"

"A lot of background information, but nothing that seems relevant. Neighbors at her building say she stopped seeing Aguilar late last year, took up with him again late in June."

"After this credit-card business was set in motion. Revenge motive but wrong timing. For now, you'd better get back to your regular caseload."

"Okay." She sounded relieved. I understood why: earlier I'd reviewed my assignment log and found that Charlotte easily had the largest number of open files.

I set about doing my day's paperwork, and the morning sped by. My stomach was growling emphatically when I looked up and saw Hy standing in the doorway. His hazel eyes were shining in a manner usually reserved for fine aircraft.

"Come with me," he said.

I got up and followed him down the stairway to the floor of the pier. A silver-blue classic Ford Mustang with a white convertible top sat next to my MG.

Hy gestured at it. "Mine."

"Beautiful! But I thought you were going to buy a secondhand truck, and use a company car when you need a classier vehicle."

"That was the plan, but when I went down to the auto dealerships near Serramonte, this baby was sitting on one of the lots, just begging for me to buy her."

I walked around the car, studying it. It was in mint condition. "Well, how could you resist? What year is it?"

"Sixty-six. Fully rebuilt engine, new upholstery, new ragtop. Want to take a spin?"

"I shouldn't—"

"McCone, you're all stressed out. You need to be good to yourself. I'll treat you to lunch at that Singaporean place on Geary that you like so much. Besides, I want to talk with you; I've come up with an idea about this frame."

"You've had a busy morning—a new car *and* an idea."

"That's me—a regular dynamo."

We were sitting at a window table in the Straits Cafe, waiting for our samosas and sashimi salad, when he laid out his idea for me.

"Remember that time before we met, when you went up to the Delta to investigate some trouble your sister and her husband were having with their B and B?"

"Yes. Appleby Island."

"And when we did meet, you were at Tufa Lake, on loan from All Souls to Anne-Marie, who was temporary counsel for the Coalition for Environmental Preservation. Then, when I went missing down in Mexico, you cut loose of the co-op and came looking for me."

"So what're you getting at, Ripinsky?"

"You've always taken on cases that weren't officially

All Souls' or the agency's business. You ever consider that this harassment might stem from one of them?"

No, I hadn't. I'd been too focused on official files. "You may be onto something here."

"Okay, did you make notes on those investigations? Keep any records?"

"No."

"But you remember them."

"The significant ones, yes. But what's significant to me and what's significant to whoever's out to get me might be very different things."

"Well, let's go over them anyway. Start with the case in the Delta."

"It was a harassment situation, and the perp died accidentally."

"And we know about Mono County and Mexico. No possible threat from anyone connected with either." Our food came, and he refrained from speaking until the waiter had departed. "What about when you were searching for your birth parents? Step on any toes then?"

"Well, Jimmy D. Bearpaw didn't like me much, but it wasn't really personal. Besides, he's not smart enough to mastermind anything this complex. The technology would be totally beyond him."

Hy grinned wryly. He'd met Bearpaw, owner of a greasy spoon in Modoc County, who fancied himself a restaurateur and wit of the highest order. "Tell you what, McCone. Tonight we'll draw up a list and then brainstorm. Take you down memory lane, so to speak, until we've covered every possibility. Until then, bon appetit."

Daphne Ashford's studio was in a storefront on Stanyan Street across from the northern end of Golden

Gate Park, where she and her husband, Charlie, had operated a print shop until it was edged out by national chains and computerization. Charlie, a commercial photographer who was currently in great demand, occupied the floor above. When I arrived at two that afternoon with Angela Batista, Daphne's eyes quickly cataloged her facial injuries, but in a manner that Batista could scarcely have noticed. Then she served us tea and got us settled beside her oversize monitor.

Daphne, I reflected, was the perfect person to handle a sensitive interview like this. An artistocratic-looking blonde with manners to match, she was extremely tactful and could put the most uncomfortable individual at ease. As she began the session by explaining the process to Batista, I found my own stress level dropping.

"The first aspect of the person's appearance that we'll be concerned with is facial shape." She clicked on an icon, chose an option. "These are the standard shapes, but after you select the closest match, we'll refine it."

Batista studied the various choices, indicated an oval.

Daphne clicked on the oval prototype. "Now, what's wrong with this picture?"

". . . The chin. His is longer."

"Like this?"

"No, more . . ."

"Like this."

"Yes, but his face, it pooches out here and here."

"Around the cheekbones. Are there hollows underneath?"

"Yes."

"What's his skin tone? Pale? Medium? Dark?"

"Dark."

"This dark?"

"Darker."

"Good. Next, the hair."

"Black."

"And its length?"

"Short. Very short. Like a marine wears it."

"This way?"

"Yes." Batista was leaning forward in her chair, fascinated with the picture that was emerging.

"Okay, now the eyes. Shape?"

"They remind me of those nuts . . . almonds."

"Very good. Color?"

"Dark brown."

"This dark?"

"Yes."

"Now the nose. How's it shaped?"

"Long."

"Thin? Wide?"

"Thin, with a little hook."

"This way?"

"Yes. And maybe it was broken once."

"Why do you say that?"

"A bump in the middle. Here." Batista indicated a place on her own broken nose.

"Good." Daphne showed her different examples until she chose one that was the right size and shape. "Now his mouth."

"Thin. Very thin."

"Like this?"

"Smaller. Yes—that's it."

"Ears?"

"Big, but flat against his head."

"Facial hair?"

"None."

"Marks on his face? Moles? Pockmarks? Scars?"

Batista hesitated. "A scar. No, two or three."

"On his forehead? His cheeks?"

"Forehead, yes. Cheeks? There, too. Knife scars, or they could have been from acne. I don't know." Batista pressed her hand to her eyes. She was tiring, and the pain medication that she'd taken shortly before we left the RKI apartment was probably wearing off.

Daphne said, "You're doing really well. Don't worry about not remembering small details. The scar on the forehead—was it straight, jagged?"

". . . Jagged."

"Horizontal? Vertical?"

". . . Horizontal."

"Like this?"

"No, more on an angle."

"To the left? The right?"

Batista shook her head. "I'm sorry, I cannot—"

"That's okay. Show me where the marks on the cheeks are."

Batista indicated one place on the right cheek, two on the left.

Daphne asked, "Is there anything else you remember about his appearance?"

"There . . . there is something wrong with one of his hands."

"How so?"

"I don't know. I can't picture it. Just . . . something wrong."

"Which hand? Right? Left?"

"I can't recall." Batista slumped in the chair, clearly exhausted.

Daphne looked at me, and I nodded to indicate we

should end the session. She hit the print icon and swiveled away from the workstation. "You did really well, Ms. Batista. Can I get you some more tea, some cookies, perhaps?"

Batista glanced at her tea, which she hadn't touched. "No, no thank you. I would like to use the rest-room, and"—this to me—"maybe I can go back to the apartment?"

"Of course."

After Daphne had shown Batista to the restroom, she returned and handed me the composite sketch. "Will this help you?"

"Some. He looks vaguely familiar, but then, he's a type. He could be any one of the informants I've used in the Mission. And I'm not sure how reliable a witness Angela is. The guy beat her up, and trauma can affect memory and perception. There are two other people I'd like you to put through the process who may remember him more accurately."

"When're you bringing them by?"

"One at five this afternoon, if that's okay. And another some time tomorrow."

"Well, I'll be here. Actually, I'm excited about this. You've opened my eyes to a whole new service I can offer—plus, you've distracted me from my need to clean the flat."

At five o'clock I brought Vanessa Lu to the studio. The preschool teacher added significant detail to the image of R.D.: the shape of the two scars on his right cheek, and a small tattoo of a spider on his neck. She said he also had tattoos on his forearms, but she hadn't gotten close enough to him to identify what they represented.

After leaving Daphne's I dropped Lu off at home and went back to the pier. The agency staff meeting that afternoon had been largely unproductive, and I'd pulled everyone but Mick off the investigation so they would contend with their other assignments. Mick had wrapped up his inquiry into the circumstances under which Aguilar had fired his aide—he'd been accused of sexual harassment by a fellow staff member but had landed a better job in Seattle—and told me he'd be at home, working all night on tracing R.D., if necessary.

Hy had been called away to a meeting at RKI's world headquarters in La Jolla that afternoon, so our brainstorming session was off. I immersed myself in the rest of the day's paperwork, reluctant to return to an empty house and at least one surly cat. During recent years, I'd experienced greater and greater pangs of loneliness when Hy departed on one of his business trips or went alone to his ranch or our Mendocino County seaside retreat. Maybe it was time . . .

He'll still be going off on trips. He'll still need solitary time at the ranch or the coast. And so will you.

But somehow it would be different. We would have made a . . .

Commitment.

I hate that word.

Well, maybe not hate. Maybe fear.

It's such a risk, and I'm not sure I can afford that big a one.

Tuesday

·

JULY 22

"Shar," Ted said, "you remember Alison James." To my blank look he added, "She worked here for a while last month, and she'll be helping out again this week."

Alison had white-blond hair, sharp features, and was so short and slender that a stiff wind off the bay would have blown her halfway to Daly City. She didn't look at all familiar. So many of Ted's prospective assistants had passed through the offices during his search for the paragon of the paper clips that I hadn't noticed this woman.

I mumbled, "Of course," shook her fragile-looking hand, then turned to my office manager and snapped, "I thought you understood about the hiring freeze." I hadn't slept well in my empty bed the night before, and my voice reflected my generally bad disposition.

Ted frowned at me. "I said, *this week*. Alison's here on a temporary basis, to help me organize those files for the DCA investigator, as well as with cleaning the supply room." He smiled at her and, in what I supposed was an attempt to salvage the situation, added, "She's already proven herself invaluable. Come see what she found."

Ashamed of my surliness, I followed him into the supply room, where he showed me a file box labeled with dates from the year before we'd moved to the pier, when I'd still rented space in All Souls' Bernal Heights Victorian.

"Where was this?" I asked.

"Back of the closet, in with the outdated supplies like typewriter ribbons and carbon-paper sets. It must've been put there by mistake when we moved. I showed it to Mick, and he said he never got around to transferring those particular case files onto the computer. Maybe one of them will help you with this current investigation."

Alison had come into the room behind us. I turned to her and said, "Good work! Ted's told you about the problems we're having with the Department of Consumer Affairs?"

She nodded, looking nervous, hands clasped behind her. God, had I intimidated her that much with my snappishness? If so, she was not going to have a good week here.

I added, "I'm sorry I was rude before. I'm sure you'll be a great help to all of us."

"Thank you." To Ted she said, "I'll start printing out those files now."

After she fled the room, I said to him, "She seems efficient, if a trifle timid."

"Anybody'd be timid, the way you growled."

"I apologized, didn't I?"

Ted surveyed me sternly, then relented. "Okay, I had my doubts about her before, and I still do. She doesn't have a detectable sense of humor, and to survive around this place, that's a necessity. But what the hell am I supposed to do? I need somebody to help out."

"Well, let's not judge her yet. We can't afford to keep her for more than the week, anyway. What temp agency is she from?"

"None. She sent in her résumé in response to the ad I've been running in the *Chron,* and it looked good, so I asked her to come in last month on a trial basis. I can't believe you don't remember her."

"She probably hid every time she saw me coming."

"A wise move. Anyway, yesterday she made a follow-up call to see if the job had been filled, and I decided to give her another chance." His dark eyebrows drew together. "Shar, if money's that much of an issue, I'll pay her salary, and you can reimburse me later."

"Don't worry about that. The wolf's not at the door— yet. And the answer to our problems may very well lie in that file box. You want to haul it to my office for me?"

"Sure." He picked it up, balanced it on his shoulder, and we set off along the catwalk.

Dust and a faint smell of mildew rose from the box when I opened it. I leafed through the folders, noting the names on the labels, then began skimming them, bypassing the cases I clearly remembered. Again I was vaguely depressed by the ordinariness of their contents: a property-line dispute during which one neighbor repeatedly removed the surveyors' sticks and then claimed kids must have taken them; a battle between a landlord and a tenant, in which the tenant had moved to a new apartment, then attempted to hold up the landlord for thousands of dollars to relocate; a barking-dog episode that resulted in harassment on both sides and brought out the worst in all parties connected with it—including me.

And then my hand stopped at a file midway through the box: Winslip, Bryce and Mari.

Friends of my brother John. I'd taken on the case at his insistence. They were from Oregon, but their only child, Troy, had lived in San Diego. When Troy was stabbed to death in a field near the bull ring in Tijuana, the San Diego police received little cooperation from the Mexican authorities, so Troy's parents hired me to bring his killer to justice.

First I'd identified the man responsible for Troy's death, but turned up no hard evidence with which he could be charged. Then I found a message on Troy's answering machine, in which the killer had challenged him to a duel: "Knives at midnight, Winslip," the man's voice said, "Knives at midnight." The words were in a Spanish-accented falsetto, accompanied by weird, cackling laughter. Still not enough proof—at least not to charge him with murder—but perhaps there was some other crime that applied. I researched the state penal code, then advised my contact on the SDPD of a little-known 1872 statute that was still on the books—Chapter 225, Section 231:

Duels and challenges.
Defined: Combat with deadly weapons, fought be-
tween two or more persons, by private agreement.
Punishment when death ensues: state prison for
two, three, or four years.
Dueling beyond State: Every person who leaves
this State with intent to evade any provisions of
this chapter, and to commit any act out of the
State, which would be punishable by such provi-
sions if committed within this State, is punishable
in the same manner as he would have been in

case such act had been committed within this State.

I'd seen Troy Winslip's killer twice—in the murky light of a sleazy National City bar, some miles north of the Mexican border, and in a San Diego courtroom, where I'd testified against him. Reynaldo Dominguez, street name Renny D. An evil, sadistic drug distributor who controlled much of the traffic in the San Diego area. He'd been given the maximum sentence, and I'd given him little more thought.

Until now, when I remembered how his thin upper lip had curled and his dark, soulless eyes had stared me down as he was led from that courtroom.

Reynaldo Dominguez.

Renny D.

R.D.?

The man in the composite sketches Daphne had put together superficially resembled him, but there were significant differences. While the facial features were razor sharp, more *indio* than Mexican, Dominguez had no broken nose or scar on his forehead. He'd worn his black hair shoulder-length and pulled back in a tail, and half his left index finger was missing. He'd had no spider tattoo on his neck, but both forearms were entwined by sleek serpents.

But noses can be broken, foreheads scarred, tattoos acquired, hair cut. This afternoon I was meeting Patrick Neilan—a man who claimed to possess excellent powers of observation—at Daphne's studio. Maybe then I'd know more.

*   *   *

I studied the image on the oversize monitor. The sharp facial features were right, but the rest wasn't close enough to make a positive identification.

"You recognize him?" Patrick asked me.

"Can you describe the tattoos on his arms?"

"Better yet, I can draw them." He picked up a scratch pad and pencil from Daphne's desk and began sketching in swift, short strokes. When he held it out to me, I saw what could have been bulgy coils of rope. No sleek serpents. Unless . . .

"How tall is R.D.?"

"Six-two or -three."

"And his weight?"

"Around one-eighty, but he looks heavier. I'd guess he's into bodybuilding."

Then the sleek serpents could have been distorted by changes in the underlying muscle structure of his arms.

"One other thing," Patrick added. "Part of his left index finger is missing, down to the second knuckle."

"You *are* a good observer!" To Daphne I said, "Can you print this and then work with me for a while?"

"Sure." She hit the icon. "You want to make some alterations?"

"Yes. The hair—try shoulder-length."

"Like this?"

"No, pulled back straight and tight, bound at the nape of his neck."

"This way?"

"Yes. Now the scar on the forehead—remove it. Also the spider tattoo."

Both vanished, and my excitement intensified.

"His nose—make it straight and sharp but still slightly hooked."

"Give me a minute; that's a little more difficult."

She tried several options.

"How's that?"

"Great. Now, can you make him curl his lip?"

"Right or left side?"

". . . Right. And finally, can you make his eyes hard and kind of flat?"

Daphne did her magic, enlarged the image, and the malevolent face of Reynaldo Dominguez dominated the screen. Although it was only computer-generated, it radiated the same rage and hatred Dominguez had directed at me in that courtroom years before.

Got you, you bastard.

"Sharon McCone," Gary Viner of the San Diego PD homicide detail said. "It's been a long time. You still turning cartwheels?"

It was an old joke between us; Gary, a high school friend of my brother Joey, had been secretly enamored of me—and my lace-trimmed bikini panties—when I was a cheerleader.

"Better than ever."

"And I suppose you've still got that high-flying boyfriend."

"Sure do."

"My bad luck." His tone sobered. "Listen, I was real sorry to hear about Joey. He hadn't been in touch in a lot of years, but maybe if I'd made the effort—"

"Oh, Gary, nobody heard from him, and nobody could've helped, even if they had made the effort."

"You think so?"

"Yeah, I do. For a time there I beat myself up for not trying to save him, but now I realize that people who push everybody away can't be dragged back. They need to want to save themselves. Joey didn't."

Gary was silent. Then he asked, "You calling from down here?"

"No, San Francisco. D'you remember the Reynaldo Dominguez case?"

"Drug dealer you helped us nail with that antiquated section of the CPC? I sure do."

"Dominguez got the maximum sentence, and there was a sentence for dealing on top of it. He's out now, probably on parole. Could you find out who his P.O. is, get a current address?"

"Why? You think he's going to give you trouble?"

"He may already have." I explained briefly.

"The son of a bitch! Let me get in touch with the Department of Corrections. Call you back in, say, fifteen minutes."

I thanked him and broke the connection. Went to my armchair and watched the fog hover over the placid gray water while I remembered Gary and Joey in their teenaged years.

The two of them with their heads together under the hoods of the various clunker cars they'd owned. Joey pelting Gary with empty beer cans from the tree house that my father had built us kids in the finger canyon behind our house. Their hangdog expressions when the cops delivered them to our door minutes after they'd draped a curmudgeonly neighbor's trees with toilet paper. Their freshly scrubbed faces and wide grins as they'd pinned corsages to their dates' dresses before their senior prom—fingers straying dangerously close to the girls' breasts in spite of the prying lens of my father's Instamatic.

I was smiling at the memories. Smiling at something that had to do with Joey.

I was healing.

The phone buzzed. Gary on line one.

"Okay, about Dominguez," he said. "He was a model prisoner at the Men's Colony at San Luis Obispo, became something of a jailhouse lawyer."

"Studying up on the penal code so he wouldn't get caught the next time?"

"Maybe, but he also became well versed in the civil codes, advised other inmates on their divorces and so forth."

"And while he was at it, he probably stumbled across the Business and Professions Code, Sections seventy-five twelve to seventy-five seventy-three."

"Which is?"

"The Private Investigator Act. A study of it would tell him everything he needed to know about how to bring me down. So when was he paroled?"

"Last fall, October. Six months later he disappeared. Walked away from the janitorial job DOC had set him up in, and hasn't been seen since. If you've got information as to his whereabouts—"

"I don't. He's vanished again. Gary, will you do me another favor? A friend of mine on the SFPD has put in a request for information from your narcotics detail, but it hasn't come through yet. Would you expedite it?"

"Sure, what do you need?"

"Anything they've got on four people: Alex Aguilar, Johnny Duarte, Scott Wagner, and Dan Jeffers. Specifically, a connection with Dominguez."

"Spell the names, and give me the approximate dates you're looking at."

I did, and he said he'd get back to me before close of business.

I buzzed Ted and asked him to call a mandatory staff meeting for four o'clock, then, after a moment's consideration, phoned Patrick Neilan and asked him if he'd like to attend. As far as I was concerned, Neilan, with his business degree and keen powers of observation, was a natural for the position as one of Charlotte's assistants, and I wanted them to meet, as well as see how he interacted with the rest of the staff. When he accepted my invitation, he couldn't conceal his excitement.

Next I called Marguerite Hayley and Glenn Solomon. After I'd explained the situation to Hayley, she said she would meet with the people at BSIS and, as she phrased it, "thoroughly confuse them with the facts—which, you must admit, *are* confusing." Glenn told me he planned to sit down with the deputy D.A. who was to prosecute Julia and apprise him of the new developments. "I suspect they may want to back-burner the case until they see what else shakes out of the trees."

"I suppose I should inform the SFPD and DOC that Dominguez has been seen in the city."

"Wouldn't hurt, but I doubt they'll be of much help to you. The Department's on overload, and DOC isn't in much better shape. They both have bigger game to hunt than a so-called model prisoner who broke parole."

"But he's somewhere out there, and—"

"Nobody at SFPD or DOC is going to make much of an effort to locate him."

"Then who is?"

"Who do you think, my friend? Who do you think?"

*   *   *

When I entered the conference room, Charlotte and Patrick Neilan were chatting while nursing diet Cokes. He must have just told her a joke, because she threw her head back and exclaimed, "Oh, my *gawd*!" in the Texas accent that only surfaced when she was caught off guard. Mick glanced up from where he and Derek were going over a complicated-looking diagram, and frowned, then went back to tracing a line with his pencil. Craig lounged at the oak table, cross-trainers propped on its edge, while Ted paused in setting out bowls of pretzels to glare disapprovingly at him. Julia sat alone, slumped in her chair, staring down at her clasped hands.

I went over to her. "Good news. There's been a break in the case, and Glenn thinks he can get the D.A.'s office to back-burner their case against you."

She nodded listlessly, gave me a weak smile. "That's good."

Didn't she even want to know what the new evidence was? "Jules, you really look down. What's wrong?"

She shrugged.

"Okay," I said, "later on let's go down to Miranda's. I'll buy you a beer, and we'll talk."

"If you like."

"I like." I squeezed her shoulder. "Hang in there."

Before the meeting began, I taped both the past and present-day composites of Reynaldo Dominguez to the chalkboard. Then I introduced Patrick to the staff and explained the latest developments. "Apparently," I concluded, "it's up to us to locate Dominguez. The area we have to cover isn't a large one; he's somewhere in the Bay Area, more likely the city."

Charlotte asked, "Why d'you say that?"

"Because this is a guy who's hell-bent on revenge. He's not going to miss out on watching us crumble. He was at Aguilar's building as recently as Friday night, and I'm betting he's not far from there now." I turned to Craig. "I want you to go down to San Luis Obispo. Talk to the warden at the Men's Colony. Find out who Dominguez was close to while he was there. Interview them or, if they've been released, get their present addresses and track them down. The same with the places he was living and working while on parole. We need to know if anybody in this area may be sheltering him."

"I'll fly down tonight."

"Good. Charlotte, you're to work the financial angle. Credit cards, bank accounts. He's got to be getting money from somewhere. Coordinate with Mick, who will do background research on other friends and family. Derek, Craig's been working on locating that Dan Jeffers. Get the file from him and take over. And Julia, you and Patrick know the Mission better than any of us. The two of you will work with me. We're going to search every inch of the district for places where Dominguez may be hiding."

Julia nodded dutifully, but a wide smile spread across Patrick's freckled face.

"Welcome to McCone Investigations," I told him.

Gary Viner didn't get back to me till after nine o'clock. I'd spent the time since the staff meeting going over a detailed map of the Mission district with Julia and Patrick. We divided it into sectors and color-coded them: red for more affluent areas, where Dominguez's appearance would draw attention; yellow for those where he might go unnoticed; green for those where he'd fit right in. We discussed specific places within this "natural habitat" area that he might be frequenting, and decided to target them first.

After Patrick left for his security job, I suggested to Julia that we have dinner, and she volunteered to walk down to Miranda's and get us a table while I put in a call to Gary. I'd just picked up the receiver when the other line rang.

"Sorry it took so long to get back to you," Gary said. "Big narcotics bust here late this afternoon, and I had a hard time reaching anybody on that detail. But here's your information: we've got nothing on Alex Aguilar. He's that up-and-coming Hispanic on your board of supervisors that the papers have been profiling, right?"

"One and the same."

"Well, if there's a connection to Dominguez, it's buried deep. John Duarte, on the other hand, worked for Renny for years, but Narcotics never could gather enough evidence to charge him. When you helped us nail Dominguez, Duarte disappeared. Nobody looked very hard for him; he wasn't one of the hierarchy."

"Wonder how he managed to weigh in as a major distributor up here."

"Good connections or financing, I suppose. Guys like him, they always land on their feet."

"Until they land at the bottom of a cliff."

". . . Right. There's nothing on the third name you gave me, Scott Wagner, but Dan Jeffers—what a loser. Penny-ante dealer, always getting hauled in, did six months here, six months there. Finally left town in 'ninety-five."

"Would he have known Dominguez? Or Duarte?"

"Probably. Guys like Jeffers, they're hangers-on,

gofers. If either Duarte or Renny had a use for him, he'd've known them."

Gary and I chatted a few moments longer, and I promised to call him when I was next in San Diego, but I doubted I'd do so. The memories of Joey he'd evoked earlier had been pleasant enough, but there were others lurking in the backs of both our minds that were bound to be painful; I didn't care to entertain them, and I sensed Gary felt the same.

The fog outside the window was thick now, and night had fallen. Julia would be waiting for me at Miranda's, hungry but too polite to go ahead and order. I straightened the papers on my desk, grabbed a heavier sweater than the one I'd worn that morning, and tugged it over my head as I stepped out on the catwalk. Lights burned in the space Mick and Derek shared, and also in Charlotte's office. As I passed Ted's door, I saw him hunched over his keyboard.

When this situation was wrapped up, I would treat my staff to one hell of a celebration.

The wind that hit me when I stepped out onto the sidewalk was chilly. Summer in San Francisco. Pity the tourists from warmer climes who arrive with only shorts and tropical-weight clothing, thinking the city is like Southern California.

Feature films and television have created a patently false image of our state: L.A.-style congestion, high-rise cities. Rich people's palaces, endless suburban sprawl. Sand beaches sprinkled with surfers and bikini-clad babes, vineyards where nobody works particularly hard. Completely ignoring the wild northern coastline; the nearly inaccessible mountains; the deserts, both mile-high and below sea level; the wide agricultural valleys, where people *do* work hard, and often for little reward;

the small towns that are reminiscent of every small town in this country's heartland.

And then, of course, there's the fruits-and-nuts image: Yes, we're all weird, if not downright crazy. Sybaritic, immoral, and—probably—murderous. Set foot in the state and next thing you know, you'll be as wacko as the rest of us.

Well, maybe that isn't such a bad scenario. Keeps the riffraff out.

I turned south on the Embarcadero, pulling up the sweater's hood and stuffing my hands into its pockets. A tugboat's horn bleated out on the bay—a lonely sound. I hadn't heard from Hy all day, and I wondered if he was staying over in La Jolla. It would be a nice surprise if I went home and found him asleep in my bed—

A sound intruded, made me pause near a chain-link fence that stretched between Piers 28 and 36, where the intervening structures had been demolished. Faint, but attention-getting.

It came again. A whimper.

Something hurt. An animal?

A moan.

Not something. Some*one*.

I peered into the shadows. Called, "Hello?"

No response.

I took out my small flashlight, shone it around.

A figure lay crumpled against the fence. A figure in jeans and a leather bomber jacket. Like the jacket Julia had bought at a thrift shop for only ten dollars last month. She'd had it on today—

"Jesus!"

I rushed over, knelt down. Touched her neck, taking care not to move her.

Weak pulse. Her head flopped onto my extended arm. Her hot breath seared my cheek.

"Jules, it's Sharon. I'm here."

No response.

I fumbled in my bag for my phone. Damn it, why was the thing always hiding at the bottom when I needed it?

Julia whimpered again.

"I'm here. You'll be okay." I speed-dialed 911.

Her hand moved, caught my wrist, dropped away, but not before I saw that it was smeared with blood. Shot or stabbed.

"Nine-one-one," the emergency operator's voice said.

"Stabbing or shooting. Embarcadero, south of Pier Twenty-eight. Code three."

"Stay on the line, ma'am."

"Jules? Hang on." With my free hand I felt for the source of the blood. Her chest—her sweater was soaked.

"Help's on the way, ma'am. May I get your name, please?"

I gave it, fury at what had been done to Julia welling up inside me.

"Help's on the way. You stay on the line, ma'am."

"Will do. Jules, they're coming. You'll be okay."

Sophia Cruz, Julia's sister, clung to me, crying. We stood under the bright lights of the emergency waiting room at S.F. General Hospital. Julia was in surgery; she'd taken a bullet in the left side of her chest, which had narrowly missed her heart.

I stroked Sophia's thick, gray-streaked hair, stared helplessly over the top of her head at Mick, whom I'd summoned from the pier to the scene of the shooting. He frowned in sympathy, came over, and we guided her to a chair in a corner. Thank God tonight was a relatively quiet one at the city's trauma center.

I sat next to Sophia, took her work-roughened hand. "Jules will pull through," I said, wondering if the words sounded as baselessly optimistic to her as they did to me. "She's strong; she's a fighter."

"But if she doesn't, Tonio . . ." A fresh spate of sobs.

"She will."

"I feel so bad. This, after what I did to her."

I watched a doctor in greens emerge through the wide automatic doorway. He crossed to an anxious-looking Chinese couple on the other side of the room.

"It was so cruel, what I said," Sophia went on. "All this trouble she was in, but me, I couldn't keep my mouth shut. No, I had to go off on her about the drinking and the yelling at Tonio—"

"She's been drinking?"

"Yeah, real heavy, since this thing happened. And Tonio, he's just a little boy; he doesn't understand when she gets mad. This morning? I lost it. Told her to leave the apartment and not come back till she got her shit together. Said if she didn't, I'd claim abuse and sue for custody. That was why she was out there, walking alone in the dark. It's all my fault, and if she dies—"

"Sophia, she's not going to die. And she often walks along there at night. It was just her bad luck to be in the wrong place at the wrong time."

But I don't really believe that. She was a target, not a random victim.

Bad enough Dominguez framed her—and me. Now he's gone way over the line.

Sophia shook her head. "But if I hadn't thrown her out, she'd've been home with us."

"No, she wouldn't have. She was working late because there'd been a break in the case. When she was shot, she was on her way to Miranda's, where we were going to have dinner."

Sophia lifted her red, damp eyes to mine. Her mascara had run down her cheeks and into the creases around her mouth. "But she must have been careless because she was upset. I threw her out. Where would she sleep?"

"I knew she was upset, and we were going to talk about it at dinner. I'd've invited her to sleep at my house."

Sophia shook her head and looked down at her lap. At that moment she reminded me of Julia. It was a submissive, defeated response conditioned by a life filled with too much deprivation and too little hope. Sophia was determined to take the blame for Julia's being shot, and I knew I couldn't talk her out of it.

The door to the parking lot slid open, and Adah Joslyn strode inside. She glanced around the waiting room, then motioned for me to join her. Sophia had lapsed into a depressed, waiting silence, so I left her with Mick.

"You here officially?" I asked Adah.

"Yeah, I requested the assignment."

"It's not a homicide. Yet."

"No, but one of the guys on the crime scene unit knows Craig works for you and called me. I told my lieutenant I wanted in at the beginning, in case it becomes a homicide. What the hell happened, Shar?"

"She left the pier maybe fifteen minutes before I did, to get us a table at Miranda's. I was walking down there when I heard her moaning, found her crumpled on the ground."

"You hear the shot?"

"No. It must've happened while I was still at the office. I think she'd been there a while; she was soaked with blood. Are the uniforms canvassing the people in the nearby piers?"

"Sure, but I doubt they'll find anybody who heard anything. It was late for folks to be in their offices, and the traffic on the bridge and the Embarcadero overpowers most other sounds. The shooter picked an ideal spot; it's dark and deserted along that stretch." Adah's eyes rested on Mick and Sophia. "That the sister?"

"Yes. Sophia Cruz."

"How's she holding up?"

"She was pretty upset earlier; they had a bad argument this morning, and she feels guilty. Now she's gone into a holding pattern."

"Better that way. You think this has to do with what we discussed on Saturday?"

"I'm almost certain it does." I told her about my identification of Reynaldo Dominguez.

"Well, that makes my job easier. We'll put out a be-on-lookout order on him, ask some tough questions."

"I already contacted the department, as well as the Department of Corrections. Neither sounded particularly interested."

"That was before he came under suspicion of attempted homicide. You may not have concrete proof of his involvement, but I sure as hell want to talk to him."

"Well, good luck, but I don't think a BOLO will bring results. He's clever and probably has a number of places to hide."

"You know where any of those places might be?"

"If I did, I'd be hauling him out kicking and screaming right now."

Adah's eyes narrowed. "That the truth, McCone? You're not just saying that so you can go this alone?"

"I don't lie to you; you know that."

"Yeah, I do." She sighed. "And I know what's coming now: do I mind if you assist on this?"

"Do you?"

"Of course not. You've got a vested interest—first your career was on the line, now your employee's life. Just play it cautious and easy. Control those hotheaded impulses."

"Hotheaded impulses?"

"Let's face it, McCone: you can be damned angry and relentless when you're involved in something personal."

"I *feel* angry and relentless, but I'm not going to let my emotions rule me. There's too much at stake here."

Adah left to check with the other officers on the investigation, and I joined Mick and Sophia to wait for news of Julia. We sat mostly silent for over an hour, watching the room slowly empty, before a doctor came through the doors, spoke with the clerk on the desk, and approached us. Julia, he said, had survived surgery and would soon be moved from the recovery room to the intensive care unit. Her condition was critical, and they would know more in a few hours.

Sophia rose and grabbed his hands. "Critical—what does this really mean?"

The doctor's face was etched with weary lines, but he forced a kindly smile and said, "Why don't we talk about that on the way to the ICU? You'll want to see your sister. And even though she's not conscious, your presence may help her."

I watched them go, the doctor putting his arm around

her shoulders to guide her. "Jesus," I said to Mick, "people like him are the real heroes."

"People like Jules, too. She made it through."

"So far."

"So far."

"Listen, Mick, I've got to get out of here. Will you wait for Sophia, take her home?"

"Sure."

"Find out what the doctor said, and leave a message on my machine at home."

"Will do. But where're you going?"

"I've got a few places to check out."

"Shar, not alone. Not at this time of night."

"I'm not alone." I patted my bag, where my .357 Magnum rested. I'd never gotten around to returning it to the office safe after I'd taken it along on my aborted appointment with Johnny Duarte.

Wednesday

·

JULY 23

One twenty-five in the morning. Smack in the middle of the dangerous hour. Smack in the middle of a dangerous place.

A dark, half-block-long Mission-district alley that, so far as I knew, didn't have a name. Near the projects, where men loitered on the sidewalks doing drugs and drinking from bottles in paper bags. Sirens wailing in the background—police cars and ambulances speeding toward S.F. General. Busy night in the Mission, and by now the emergency room I'd left earlier would be filling up with its victims. But here in the narrow space between two old warehouses silence prevailed.

I walked along, hand on the .357 Magnum in the outside compartment of my bag. Listened to the crunch of my shoes on gravel and broken glass. The cold wind whipped down the alley and blew the hood of my sweater off my head, bringing with it the smell of garbage, urine, and feces. On the street behind me tires screeched, there was a thin crash, and then the vehicle sped away.

Halfway down the block on my right a row of rundown clapboard cottages abutted the warehouse, and in the street-level window of one glowed the name "Sam's." I went down three steps to the door and pushed through. Inside was a bar fronted by old chrome-and-vinyl stools and backed by a smeared and cracked mirror. The only light in the small room was cast by a half-dozen beer signs and a bulb above the cash register. A few tables and chairs of the same vintage as the stools, a jukebox with an Out of Order sign taped to its glass, worn and curling linoleum floor—your extremely basic watering hole, designed for serious drinking and drug-taking in the restrooms.

At one of the tables I spotted the individual I was looking for: a short man wearing jeans and a denim jacket, pointy-toed boots, and a Stetson hat much too large for his small head—Claude Cardenas, street name Cowboy, although the closest he'd ever been to a ranch was a state work farm. Claude was a petty thief, sometime drug dealer, sometime pimp, and all-around loser. He was also one of my best informers.

He glanced at me, registered surprise, then looked away. I turned and went back outside. After a few minutes he came through the door and started down the alley; I followed him into the shelter of a Dumpster behind the warehouse. Claude lighted a cigarette, cupping his hands around his Bic, then pulled up his collar against the wind.

"Long time, McCone." His voice was rough from decades of chain smoking.

"It's been a while."

"But now you need the Cowboy."

"Yes, Claude, I do." From my bag I took a copy of the composite of Reynaldo Dominguez. "You seen this guy?"

He held up his lighter and squinted at it through the smoke. "Looks familiar. I might've seen him in one of the joints the other side of Army. The Viper? Sharl's? Nah, haven't been over there in more'n a month, and this was recent. Where've I been this past week? Dude's. La Cucaracha."

"What, you were disloyal to Sam's?"

"That dump's my office. For pleasure I hang at the better joints. Your guy, I don't think he was in a bar. So where else've I been? The bank. Mike's Burgers. The BART station. Ngoc's Grocery. Wait a minute, I got it. The Cash Cow."

"That pawnshop near the Mission Street Safeway?"

"Yeah. I was there talking with Darrin Boydston last week, and your guy came in, asked to look at guns."

I knew Darrin Boydston. The pawnbroker had been an All Souls client, and I'd once assigned Rae to conduct an investigation for him. In many ways he was a decent man, but he wasn't above breaking the law, provided the price was right. The Cowboy had probably been talking to him about fencing stolen goods.

I said, "Will you ask around, see what you can find out about the guy?"

"Sure. Can I have this picture?"

"I'd rather you just described him. He's not to know I'm looking for him."

Cardenas nodded and scanned it once more. Drug-and-alcohol-saturated though his mind must be, he had good recall.

I took the composite back and handed him forty dollars—our usual upfront arrangement. He nodded his thanks and stuffed the bills in his pocket.

"McCone," he said, "this have to do with the hit that was supposed to come down tonight?"

"What hit?"

He dropped his cigarette to the ground, crushed it out with the toe of his boot, looking uneasy. "I don't know the details, but word was out on the street some woman was gonna die. Surprised me to see you come into the bar, because what I heard sounded a lot like you."

The little bastard! All these years I've put money in his pocket, treated him like a human being. He hears there's a contract out, suspects it's on me, and doesn't give warning.

Well, what do you expect from a scumbag paid informer? Loyalty?

"So what did you hear? And where?" I asked him.

"Where, I can't tell you. Just on the street. They said she was young, a private detective, and had been mixed up with a drug dealer."

"And you thought that sounded like me?"

He shrugged. "I'm sixty-six years old, McCone. You look young to me. As to who you get mixed up with, I don't know. I'll be in touch." He turned and started back toward Sam's.

So Dominguez had been in the Cash Cow looking at guns—probably because he'd heard that Darrin Boydston occasionally sold untraceable weapons without complying with the state licensing procedures. And the word was out on the street that a young female detective who had been involved with a drug dealer was going to die.

But why kill Julia? She'd never laid eyes on Dominguez, couldn't connect him with either Aguilar or Johnny Duarte.

The answer was obvious: Dominguez wanted me to pay big time for what I'd done to him years ago in San Diego. Killing one of my employees was part of that payback.

Another obvious realization shook me. What about the rest of my employees? The other people I cared about?

For a moment I pushed the panicky thought aside, because there was something wrong with the picture: Why had he talked about the shooting beforehand? While a great many women now worked in my profession, Julia was a Mission-district resident and had been in the news recently; surely Dominguez must have realized someone would have recognized her as his target and warned her.

The answer to that was obvious, too: he didn't care.

I thought back to the man I'd glimpsed in the National City barroom, holding court to a circle of admirers, openly bragging about killing Troy Winslip. And then there was his voice on the answering-machine tape that had cinched the case against him: "Knives at midnight," interspersed with crazy laughter. This was more of the same: Catch me if you can.

He brought himself down then. I'll bring him down now.

I was stopped at the light at Mission and Army Street—the latter now called Cesar Chavez Boulevard, but we longtime residents had yet to make the mental transition—when, on impulse, I turned right. The first few blocks of Mission were reasonably quiet at this hour, the stores dark, iron gates locked across their doors and windows, but soon the street exploded into a kaleidoscope of light and motion. People entered and exited all-night groceries; the bridge-and-tunnel crowd filtered out of the clubs on the first leg of their journey home to the suburbs; muggers eyed them, assessing targets; working girls and junkies prowled, looking to score; the sound of police radio calls and music filled the air. Near the Sixteenth Street BART station a ragged man kept up a persistent, spine-chilling howl; a black-and-white turned on its flashers and pulled to the curb beside him.

I drove a couple more blocks, turned right, and right again into Minna Street, between Mission and South Van Ness. Drove half a block more and stopped behind the building that housed Trabajo por Todos. Darkness there, except for an occasional fog-hazed streetlamp and lighted window. I edged the MG next to the fence around the building's parking lot and got out. Silence, until I stood still and strained to hear. Then there were faint rustling noises as rats or stray cats moved through the night.

Or as a stealthy human moved.

The gate in the fence was closed and padlocked, but it was old, its frame bent, the chain that wound around its supports loose. I bent it some more and squeezed through, catching it so it wouldn't clang.

Criminal trespass, McCone. You get caught, you'll be in even more trouble.

Then I won't get caught.

Only one vehicle was parked there, close to the wall, a shabby white Datsun. Dim light shone through the glass door leading into the building. I moved toward the steps, then stopped in the shadows, feeling a chill.

Someone watching.

But from where?

I closed my eyes, focused on the sensation.

Not behind me. Not to either side. Not ahead—that

hallway's well lighted. Above? Maybe, but there aren't many windows.

All right. Chalk it up to nerves, too much imagination.

I climbed the steps, tried the door, expecting it would be locked, but it was open. Why . . . ?

Then I heard the whirr of the sewing machines from the downstairs clothing manufacturer's space. Of course—companies like that maintained around-the-clock shifts. Fortunately for me, the door must've been left open to comply with fire regulations.

I slipped inside, moved along the hall, and peered into the sewing room. A dozen or so women, heads bent over their machines, expertly guiding fabric. I darted past the door and headed for the staircase next to the elevator.

The second floor lay in darkness, except for dim lights in the hallway. I followed its jogs and turns to the job-training center, found one side of the double doors ajar. My hand on my gun, I slipped inside and waited, listening. No sound, and the place had a vacant feel. Even so, I remained there a few minutes more before proceeding.

I moved through room after room: physical fitness, day care center, language lab, classrooms, lunchroom. All were dark and silent. But in the cubicle next to Gene Santamaria's a light glowed. I stopped, drew back around the corner, and listened.

Some sound must have given me away. A voice called, "R.D., is that you?"

A voice I remembered from my initial interview when he hired us to investigate the thefts here. Alex Aguilar was back in town.

"Look, R.D.," he added, footsteps coming toward the cubicle's entrance, "this vendetta has got to stop. Johnny Duarte's dead. Harriet Leonard has run off with the cash and merchandise he had on hand in his condo. Tracy blames me for everything and is threatening to go to the cops. And now my contact at SFPD tells me Julia Rafael's been taken out. You've got to stop!"

What now? Hide?

No way.

Confront him.

I came around the corner, gun extended in both hands. "You bet it's got to stop."

Aguilar's face contorted in surprise, then paled. He took a few steps backward. "Christ, what're you doing? Have you gone crazy?"

I motioned him back into the office, indicated he should sit at the desk, stopped a safe distance from him. The chair was adjusted too high, and his feet didn't quite reach the floor; he pointed his toes and they slid around, struggling for purchase. No charismatic smile now—his mouth pulled down, and his eyes were wide with fear.

I said, "So you're planning to meet your friend R.D. here tonight."

"He is not my friend."

"But he is coming here."

". . . Yes. But he's late."

"Why the meeting?"

No reply. His eyes moved from side to side, looking for a way out.

"Why?"

"He . . . All right, he needs money."

"And even though he isn't your friend, you're going to give it to him?"

Silence.

"Okay, if you won't tell me, I can reconstruct what

went on between you two. Reynaldo Dominguez—yes, I know his name and why he's out to ruin me—Dominguez has something on you. I assume it's that you were dealing for him when you lived in San Diego."

Aguilar looked away from me, staring at the wall of the cubicle.

I went on, "You were a pretty minor figure in the scheme of things down there, and my guess is that your dealing was simply a more lucrative means to earn tuition money than your restaurant jobs. And because you were minor, when Dominguez went to prison, you were able to escape, move to L.A., and take up a legitimate career in social work. Quite a switch, wasn't it?"

Silence.

"I admit, some of my theory is guesswork. For instance, I believe that you genuinely care about furthering the lot of your people. This job-training center is testimony to that. But somewhere along the line you got seduced into gaining political power, and when the publicity machine about your future mayoral candidacy got going, your old boss Reynaldo Dominguez must've seen one of the articles and decided to come up here from San Luis Obispo to put the bite on you. And your old associate Johnny Duarte was already doing that."

Aguilar shook his head, lips compressed.

"It's tough being squeezed from two sides, isn't it? Duarte forcing you into importing his drugs through your shop in Ghirardelli. And Dominguez demanding money and shelter. And when he found out you'd employed my agency to investigate the thefts here, Dominguez saw another way to use you."

More head shaking.

"You helped Dominguez by setting up Julia Rafael, ordering all that merchandise in her name, using your own credit card and the center's computers. But now you're afraid, because Dominguez is out of control. He's left a long string of casualties behind him: Johnny Duarte. Dominguez probably killed him so he could take control of his drug business—and exercise greater control over you. Dan Jeffers, one of your fellow dealers in San Diego. He's missing, probably dead. Angela Batista, your neighbor. He beat her up last Friday. And now Julia. He didn't take her out, but she may not live. And then there's Scott Wagner, your former partner."

"Scott's death was an accident. He fell—"

"You don't really believe that, and neither do I. According to Dan Jeffers, Scott was beaten to death and pushed into the ravine at Olompali by someone he— Dan—recognized. Now, who do you suppose that was?"

Aguilar's toes again strained to reach the floor, but they slipped and slammed the desk chair backwards into the workstation. His white-knuckled hands clenched the chair's arms. "Why would R.D. kill Scott?"

"My guess is, Scott somehow found out about his plans and decided to put a stop to them. I gather he was the kind of man who wouldn't be afraid to stand up to Dominguez."

Momentarily, the fear in his eyes was overshadowed by anguish. "Scott," he said, "oh, Jesus . . ."

"What about Gene Santamaria?" I asked. "Is he aware of what's been going on?"

"Gene? No, he couldn't suspect—"

"Better be sure. You don't want to lose another good administrator to Dominguez's violence."

Aguilar's head drooped, and he let his hands slip from the chair arms in a gesture of surrender. "All right, I'll warn Gene. But I must know—what are you going to do about all this?"

"Me? Nothing—yet. You, on the other hand, will go to Inspector Adah Joslyn at SFPD Homicide and tell her the full story. You will cooperate with the police investigation in every way you can."

"That's impossible. My position, my career—"

"You don't get it, do you, Aguilar? All that is over. It was over from the minute Duarte and Dominguez walked back into your life. Write these numbers down." I recited Adah's home, office, and cell, watched him shakily scribble them onto a pad. "I'll give you an hour to contact Inspector Joslyn. After that, I'll go to her and then to the press."

I made him read the numbers back to me, then left the cubicle but not the center. When Dominguez showed, I'd be waiting for him.

I positioned myself down the hall, in an alcove that led to the restrooms. Sound echoed off the unadorned walls and uncarpeted floors, and after a while I heard Aguilar dialing a number. The receiver slammed into the cradle; then he dialed again.

"Is he there?" he asked the party who'd answered. "This is . . . a friend. He was supposed to meet with me at eleven. . . . Well, where the hell is he? . . . Great, just great! Shouldn't the ball game be over by now? All right, listen, you tell him this when he gets home: call Alex, no matter what time it is. Tell him we've got serious trouble."

Aguilar again slammed down the receiver. After a few minutes I heard him leave the cubicle.

So had Dominguez shot Julia, then casually strolled down the Embarcadero to Pac Bell Park? Or was the claim of taking in a Giants game an alibi to cover up for the shooting? And to whom had Aguilar been speaking?

As soon as the sound of the supervisor's steps faded, I came out of my hiding place and followed him. I'd felt as if I was being watched when I entered the building; possibly Dominguez was lying in wait outside, to ambush either Aguilar or me. But the supervisor moved safely from the steps to the fence, unlocked the gate, and drove the old white Datsun that was pulled close to the wall from the lot, relocking the gate behind him.

I went back upstairs, located a window with a view of the parking area, and surveyed the scene below. Nothing moved down there except a ragged man who was picking through the trash bins on the opposite side of the street.

I waited for what seemed a lot more than an hour. No Dominguez. By then it was obvious he wasn't coming. Had he given up on extorting money from Aguilar and fled the city? Or had the supervisor's phone call been a veiled warning?

Either way, I was considerably more cautious than Aguilar had been when I finally left the building.

My house was dark when I returned, and neither cat greeted me. No Hy, but the answering machine indicator was flashing. Seven messages. I bypassed it, went into the kitchen, and turned on the lights. A box labeled "Glucometer Elite" sat in the center of the table—the device for measuring Ralph's blood-sugar levels. Michelle had attached a Post-it note to the box; she'd gotten the meter for half price from the pet-sitting client on Chenery Street, whose cat had just died. Great—shades of the future.

I poured a glass of wine, went to listen to my messages.

Hang-up. Probably telemarketing.

Mother One: "You never called back like Ted promised you would. Is everything all right?"

No, Ma.

Brother John: "Ma's pissed because you forgot my birthday. I'm not, but just thought I should warn you."

Thanks, John.

Ted: "My God, Shar, I just caught the late news. Is Jules going to be okay?"

I honestly don't know, Ted.

Hy: "Hey, McCone, I'm wrapping things up here. Be back tomorrow."

Thank God, Ripinsky. I need you.

Mick: "The doctor said they won't know anything conclusive about Jules's prognosis for hours. Sophia doesn't want to leave the hospital, so I'm gonna stay with her. I'll let you know more when I hear."

Please do, Mick, and let it be something good.

Heavy breathing, and then a crazy, cackling laugh. Same laughter as on the answering-machine tape that had convinced the San Diego jury to convict Dominguez of staging an out-of-state duel resulting in a death.

I was right: he didn't care if I identified him.

I looked at my watch. Well past the deadline I'd given Aguilar to contact Adah. I phoned her at home, got her out of bed.

Aguilar hadn't been in touch with her.

"I gave him an hour," I said. "I told him if he didn't call you, I would, and then I'd go to the press."

"Kind of late to be calling a hardworking member of

the third estate, don't you think? Hardworking cop, for that matter." Adah yawned loudly.

"So what're you going to do?"

"Give him till noon tomorrow. He's probably trying to contact his attorney, get advice on how to handle this. And if I were you, I wouldn't go to the papers or the TV stations yet—it's premature, could be actionable. You've got enough trouble as is."

"Tell me about it."

"McCone."

"What!" I came fully awake from a bad dream where I was running through a labyrinth of dark alleyways in pursuit of a faceless man in a top hat and jogging suit. Flailed around and felt my elbow connect solidly with something.

"Ow! Break my jaw, why don't you?"

The bedside table lamp flashed on, momentarily blinding me. Hy stood by the bed, rubbing his chin. I glanced at the clock: 4:15.

He added, "You were lying spread out in the middle, and I was trying to move you over. Feeling romantic, till you bashed me."

"Sorry. Oh, God . . ." I flopped back against the pillows, covering my eyes with my forearm.

He turned off the light, took off his clothes, and slipped in beside me. "What's wrong?"

"Give me a minute. How'd you get here? There aren't any commercial flights at this hour."

"Buddy down at Lindbergh Field was ferrying a guy's private jet to Seattle. He invited me along for the ride, provided I'd pay the landing fee at SFO."

"I swear you've got a buddy at every airport in the world."

"Most of them, anyway. Comes in handy. So you want to tell me about it?"

I did, beginning with my identification of Reynaldo Dominguez and ending with the crazy laughter on the answering machine.

"You know," Hy said when I finished, "I've arranged to take some more time off from work. Back when we were on high alert against terrorism, I felt I ought to make myself available, but now I find I'm just playing shrink to a bunch of paranoid clients."

"Isn't that part of the job?"

"Part of the service we provide, yeah, but I'm not good at it. I told Dave and Gage that they should assign operatives who employ more tact and suffer fools better to the TLC detail. They agreed. If there's a genuine crisis, I'll be there, but otherwise . . ." I felt him shrug.

"So I guess you'll be off to the ranch or Touchstone."

"No way. I'm staying right here, with you. We'll deal with this Dominguez character together, starting a few hours from now."

The Cash Cow, sandwiched between a Filipino travel agency and a Thai restaurant, had all the earmarks of its proprietor's eccentricities. Red neon tubing spelled out the name, but the animal depicted beneath it was a bull. To further complicate matters, during business hours Darrin Boydston had taken to rolling out onto the sidewalk a stuffed camel and grizzly bear he'd accepted in some dubious transaction. The camel leered at me as I went inside.

The pawnshop was also a curious hybrid: Boydston

possessed possibly the largest stock of used vacuum cleaners in North America. Their sheer number was rivaled only by exercise equipment, VCRs, obsolete computers, and TVs. Every other imaginable type of merchandise was crammed into the small space, and guitars, bicycles, chandeliers, and chairs hung from the low ceiling. This morning Tommy Jones, a Eurasian boy whom Boydston had rescued from the streets, was in the process of hoisting a surfboard up there while his mother, Mae, dusted the jewelry case. She smiled when she saw me, and said the boss was in his office.

The office was small, and Boydston, a chunky, bald man dressed in electric blue polyester, seemed to fill the space. He looked up from his cluttered desk as I came in, and said, "Hey, how ya doin', little lady?"

Boydston was an old-school Texan and, unlike Charlotte Keim, had never lost the accent—or his antiquated attitudes. Years before, when I'd given him a ride because his car had broken down and he told me I drove "right good, for a girl," I'd decided it was useless to go on resenting his genial sexism.

I removed a stack of files from the other chair and sat. "Not so good, Darrin."

His weathered face creased with concern. "I can make you a nice loan—"

"It's not about money." I took the composite of Dominguez from my bag. "You know this man?"

He squinted at it. "Looks familiar, but I see lots of people every day."

"Try last week. The Cowboy was here when this guy came in, asking about guns. Did he buy one?"

"Give me his name, I'll check my records. The application should still be pending."

"He wasn't looking for a legal deal."

Boydston tried to act offended, then must have decided it was too much effort. He knew I was well aware of the illicit side of his operation. "Afraid I can't comment on that, little lady."

"Darrin, I like you—in spite of the 'little lady' shit. I like what you've done for Tommy and Mae, and a lot of other folks in the neighborhood. But this is serious stuff. The gun you sold this man was probably used to shoot my employee Julia Rafael last night."

He blinked. "Little Jules? God*damn*! She's not . . . ?"

"As of a couple of hours ago, they say she's going to make it." Mick had called from the hospital at around seven o'clock. "But she almost didn't, and she's going to have one long recovery."

"Damn! I've known that little girl since she was turning tricks on Sixteenth Street. Not a bad girl, just poor and rebellious, and the Youth Authority turned her around. Folks in the neighborhood are proud of her, don't believe any of this nonsense about the supervisor's credit card. What's this asshole"—he jabbed his finger at the composite—"got against her?"

I played on his fondness for Julia, said, "I don't know. But this is personal for me, and it should be for you, too. Tell me about the gun."

"Okay, but it goes no further. If it does, I'll deny you ever talked with me, and Mae and Tommy'll back me up. Was a Saturday night special I took off a young punk who came in here a couple of months ago, all drugged up and stupid, thinking to make a big score. What he got for his pains was a busted arm."

"And you didn't turn the piece over to the cops."

"No cops involved. He split, yowlin' for his mama—no harm done, except to him."

"The guy who bought the piece is Reynaldo Dominguez. You know anything about him?"

"Never seen him before or since. Never heard the name."

"I'm going to leave this drawing with you. Show it to people you trust. Ask around about him—discreetly. Let me know if you hear anything, no matter how insignificant it may seem."

Boydston nodded and fingered the composite. "I'll do it for little Jules. You, too. That law cooperative you used to work for, they were good to me over the years. By the by, how's little Miss Kelleher?"

"Rae's fine."

"I sure do like her hubby's music."

"And now she's an artist in her own right—just published a novel."

"A novel. You don't say." Boydston shook his head. "Women these days—ain't it amazin'."

Half an hour later I found Ted at his desk, staring morosely at several tall stacks of files. "What's this, the stuff for Todd Baylis?" I asked.

"Yes, except now his superior's told him to put the investigation on hold."

Marguerite Hayley must have already laid out the facts for BSIS. "Well, that's good, isn't it?"

"It's good, until you consider that we've used up reams of paper and four ink cartridges creating duplicate files that we'll probably end up shredding. And they're taking up my whole goddamn desk."

"So ask Alison to find a temporary place for them."

"Alison quit."

"She was only here one day!"

"There was an unfortunate incident this morning. What happened—"

"I don't want to know. Any messages?"

"Claude Cardenas called with a couple of leads on places Dominguez has been frequenting. He said to tell you that you owe him another forty bucks."

I took the message slip he held out. On it Ted had scribbled an address on Nineteenth Street and the name of a bar on Mission, the Remedy Lounge. I knew the Remedy well; it was at the foot of Bernal Heights and had once been All Souls' tavern of choice. I'd heard it had gone downhill in recent years, and the rumors must be true if the likes of Reynaldo Dominguez were hanging out there.

"Anything from Craig?" I asked.

"Nothing. But you've gotta hear this. What happened was, Alison came in this morning, and . . . Well, you know those wharf rats have been getting awfully bold, even though I've set out traps—"

"I don't want to know!" I left his office.

After I'd glanced through the papers in my in-box, I called Adah at SFPD. Still nothing from Aguilar, and she said she hadn't been able to reach him at his home or office numbers. "You should've brought him in yourself, looks like."

She was right. I should have.

"I'll give him another hour," Adah added, "then issue a be-on-lookout order."

"Let me check something and get back to you." I broke the connection and dialed Patrick Neilan's number.

"Hey," he said, "I just got off my security-job shift and was about to call you. Aguilar's back in town, but it looks like he's leaving again. I ran into him on my way into the building; he was loading a bunch of suitcases into his car."

"How long ago?"

"Maybe ten minutes."

"Thanks. Why don't you come by the pier after you've slept."

"I've already slept. It was an easy shift."

"Then come ahead. And by the way, I think you'll be able to quit that job, once the agency's status is resolved."

"I can't tell you how much I'd like that."

I called Adah back, explained the situation. "Sounds like Aguilar's on the run."

"Then I'd better put out that BOLO. Talk to you when I know more. And please, hold off on going to the press. Any more news about Julia?"

"As of seven this morning it looks as if she'll make it."

Calls to Marguerite Hayley and Glenn Solomon confirmed that the case against Julia and the BSIS investigation had been put on hold, pending future developments. I'd just called the hospital and learned that Julia's condition was unchanged, when Hy arrived, followed by Patrick. I introduced them and brought them up to date.

"My informant in the Mission has come up with two leads that may be worth pursuing," I finished. "Patrick, are you familiar with the Remedy Lounge?"

"I know where it is, yes."

"Well, both Ripinsky and I are known there, so why don't you check it out, see if Dominguez has been frequenting the place. And you," I added to Hy, "can run a surveillance on the Nineteenth Street address, if you'd like."

"Sure. Where'll you be?"

"Right here, catching up on paperwork and waiting for you guys to report in."

The hours dragged by. Neither Hy nor Patrick called or returned. There was nothing from Craig, and when I tried his cell phone, it was out of range. None of my other operatives had anything to report. Julia's condition remained the same. I immersed myself in paperwork, asked Ted to bring me a sandwich when he went out for lunch, and fended off yet another offer of an explanation about Alison and the wharf rat.

The sandwich was something chopped and pressed that pretended to be chicken, loaded with sprouts and tomatoes because, as Ted claimed, I looked "peaked" and needed my veggies. I ate the sourdough roll, picked at the rest.

Patrick returned shortly after two. He'd sat at the bar at the Remedy, nursing a couple of beers for hours, but saw no one remotely resembling Dominguez. When Brian, the owner, came on shift, Patrick noticed him casting covert glances, so he decided to leave and come back that evening. But as he paid up, Brian handed him an envelope and said, "The guy you're looking for asked me to make sure McCone gets this."

Now, *that* was interesting. How had Brian known Patrick was working for me? I'd only hired him the previous afternoon.

The envelope was a standard type that can be found in any supermarket or drugstore; my name was written on it in a childish scrawl. I stared at it, holding it by the edges.

Not likely there'd be any identifiable fingerprints, since it had passed through both Brian's and Patrick's hands, but—

"I handled it so I wouldn't smudge anything," Patrick said.

Good man. I slid my finger under the flap, carefully took out and unfolded a single sheet of paper. Taped to it was a newspaper clipping that looked to be from one of the Macy's ads that make up the bulk of the Sunday *Chronicle*.

Wusthoff knives. Set of five.

Knives.

I laid the paper on the desk, turned it around so Patrick could see it. He frowned. "What does it mean?"

I explained about the duel in Tijuana, and Dominguez's taped dare: "Knives at midnight."

"What else did Brian say?" I asked.

"He didn't know Dominguez's full name, only heard him called R.D. He's been coming in there off and on for a month, hangs with a group of four or five guys Brian would just as soon not have as customers, but tolerates on account of business being so bad. Dominguez talks a lot, but Brian doesn't listen, because he doesn't want to know what he's into."

"Who are the guys he hangs with, and what're they into?"

"Brian doesn't know their names, but he says they're small-time dealers, petty thieves. One's a pimp; another's done time for armed robbery."

The Remedy *had* gone downhill; in the old days Brian would have kicked such characters out onto the sidewalk.

"Dominguez is playing games," I said. "He's been following me, watching my moves. He may even have planted those leads with the Cowboy. He knows you from your building, and he described you to Brian, but I don't understand how he found out you're working for me."

"If he's been watching you, he's probably watching the pier. He could've seen me come here yesterday."

"Yes, but it doesn't naturally follow that you're anything more than a witness. Unless he's had someone spying on us . . . Oh, my God . . ." I picked up the phone, buzzed Ted. "What's Alison James's address?"

"If you're looking to rehire her, I wouldn't try. That rat was one big mother—"

"This is important."

"I'm checking." He was silent for a moment. Then, "I'll be damned. No wonder the address Claude Cardenas phoned in sounded familiar. They're one and the same."

No wonder Alison was so nervous around me.

"Thanks," I said to Ted, and replaced the receiver. From my file cabinet I took a Ziploc bag, deposited the note and envelope inside, and handed it to Patrick. "Will you take this over to Richman Labs for fingerprinting, please? We have an account with them, and Ted'll give you the address."

He nodded and left the office.

I dialed Hy's cellular number.

Alison's apartment was on Nineteenth Street in the Mission, over a store that sold soap, bath oils, sponges, candles, and sex toys. In the window, a pair of handcuffs hung from a wire basket full of colorful towels, and a pyramid of boxes containing anatomically correct blow-up items—including one labeled "Edna the Party Sheep"—was positioned below it. Hy met me on the sidewalk, indicated a door to the right of the shop, and went back to his Mustang. I climbed a narrow stairway that smelled of mildew and other things I didn't care to contemplate.

When Alison opened the door, she paled, then backed up, raising her hand to her left cheek in an attempt to cover a nasty bruise that hadn't been there the day before.

I shut the door behind me. "R.D. do that to you?"

Tears filled her eyes, and she turned away, moved along a narrow hallway.

I followed her into a tiny, sparsely furnished room. "He's gone, isn't he?" I asked.

She nodded, her back to me.

"You want to tell me about it?"

"I don't have to tell you anything."

"No, you don't. But you might prefer speaking with me to speaking with the police."

"The police!" She turned, throwing up her hands in a panic.

"Think about it, Alison. You took a job at my agency under false pretenses. You stole and copied the key to the mail room, as well as Julia Rafael's key to the storage unit at her apartment building. Did you remove the packages from the mail room and place them in Julia's storage space, or was it Dominguez?"

Silence.

"Do you really want a face-to-face with my friends at the police department? Or with the FBI? Tampering with mail is a federal offense, you know."

She bit her lip, shook her head.

"Then answer my questions. How long has R.D. been staying here?"

". . . About a month."

"Did you know from the first you were giving shelter to a man who's broken parole?"

Her eyes widened. "He said he'd done his time and been released."

"But only on parole."

"Oh, God, I knew he lied about a lot of things, but . . . Okay, I can't afford any trouble. I had an alcohol problem, and my ex-husband got custody of our kid. I'm trying to straighten out my life so I can get her back. What d'you want to know?"

"All of it, from the beginning."

"I met R.D. at this mail-drop place on outer Mission where I work part-time. He has a box there. We went out for coffee a couple of times, then some drinks." She saw my frown and added, "Yeah, I know what you're thinking. But it's not so easy to get your life together, not when you're lonely and nobody gives a shit about you. Anyway, we shared our troubles. He said he'd gotten kicked out of this friend's apartment and needed a place to stay. So I took him home with me."

"And?"

"We did some coke, sat up all night, talked. He told me about you. Said you'd had him falsely imprisoned, and now that he was out, he'd heard you still had it in for him. He'd seen an ad for an assistant office manager at your agency and asked, since I have office skills, if there was any way I could get on with you. So I sent in a kind of puffed-up résumé. I guess Ted was getting desperate, because he didn't check it very carefully, just said come in on a trial basis. And I did all the things you said, except R.D. was the one who put the packages in Julia Rafael's storage locker. Then, after everything was set up, I told Ted I didn't think it was working out, and he agreed."

"But then Dominguez wanted you back there."

"He said the scheme wasn't working. You'd caught onto him, and he needed to find out how close you were getting."

"And you told R.D. everything you overheard there yesterday. Probably snooped through our files, too."

She hung her head. "Yeah. You must hate me."

Hate you? No. Think you're pathetic? Yes.

I asked, "What happened between you and Dominguez today?"

"There was this rat in the supply room at the pier. . . . Anyway, I couldn't deal with it, so I quit and came home. R.D. was furious, said he needed me there. When I refused to go back, he smacked me. I ran into the bathroom and locked the door. He stayed out here a long time, talking to himself and laughing. He sounded crazy, and I was really scared. There's no window in the bathroom, so I was trapped. After a while I heard him come to the door. I thought he'd break it down and kill me. Instead, all he said was that he'd left an envelope for you on the table, that you'd be around and I should give it to you. Then he left."

More game playing.

"Where's the envelope?" I asked.

She motioned toward a table by the front window.

The envelope was the same kind as the one Patrick had brought me. I handled it with care, took out the message. A single word:

AT

Knives at . . .

"Alison, you say you work at a mail drop where R.D. has a box?"

"Yes."

"Let's go there, take a look at what's in it."

"I can't do that! Opening mail that's addressed to somebody else is a crime. I could get fired."

"I'm not saying we'll open it. You sort the mail, put it in the boxes, right?"

"Uh-huh."

"Is it a crime to notice what the return addresses are?"

". . . I guess not."

"Then let's go."

Alison came up to the counter in the dingy storefront on outer Mission Street and extended an envelope to me. "That's all there is."

My name was printed on it in the same childish scrawl as Dominguez's other communications. Again I handled it carefully, took out the folded sheet of paper. Again, a single word:

MIDNIGHT

Knives . . . at . . . midnight.
Not this time, Dominguez.

The dangerous hour isn't always late at night. During the day, in unfamiliar territory, you're exposed and vulnerable. Particularly when you're tracking a man who's intent on destroying you. When you don't know if you're the predator or the prey. . . .

I was parked on Regis Avenue on the backside of Bernal Heights, close to the site of the Farmers' Market on Alemany Boulevard, and the intricate maze where the 280 and 101 freeways intertwine, then split off again. Following up on a lead Craig had provided me: one of Dominguez's prison buddies, Sly Rawson, lived in the shabby blue frame cottage down the block. Hy and Patrick were elsewhere, pursuing other leads Mick had turned up on R.D.'s friends in the city. Charlotte had discovered nothing on the financial angle, and Derek had found only that there was no record of Dan Jeffers's death.

No activity here. A quiet afternoon in a quiet neighborhood, or so it would seem, but I knew better. Numbers 313 and 444 were infamous crack joints. The boarded-up house at the corner had been the scene of a drug bust gone wrong, where two cops were killed and the residents had subsequently been taken out by police firepower. Apparently the house's history didn't intimidate the squatters; I'd been watching them enter and leave through a side door for the better part of an hour. An old woman came along the sidewalk pulling a shopping cart full of recyclables; she entered a fenced yard that at first I thought was her own; then I realized she'd gone into the shrubbery to relieve herself. After a few minutes she shuffled on.

I looked at my watch. After six. Still nothing happening at the blue house, but this was a neighborhood where most people only emerged after dark. Craig had little information on Dominguez's friend; he'd completed parole six months ago, was no longer required to report his job status or whereabouts, but a former cellmate claimed he still lived at this address.

My cellular rang. Adah.

"They've located Aguilar's car," she said. "It was

abandoned at a rest stop off Two-eighty, the one with the statue of Father Serra that looks like he's holding a football for the kicker. No suitcases. Somebody must've met him there."

"Try this somebody: Tracy Escobar, his girlfriend and an employee at the job-training center." I explained her history.

"I'll get on it."

I returned to watching the blue house. Thought long and hard about Reynaldo Dominguez. Began to reconstruct the chain of events since he came to town.

He'd moved in with Aguilar. It hadn't been a harmonious living arrangement. Then he'd found out that Aguilar had hired the agency to investigate the thefts at the job-training center, and blackmailed him into taking part in his scheme to bring me down. Somehow Scott Wagner found out about the scheme, and Dominguez killed him. Probably caught up with Dan Jeffers and killed him, too. Just because there wasn't a death record for the former Deadhead didn't mean Dominguez hadn't disposed of him; the wilderness areas of this country are full of unidentified bones.

Julia was arrested. I began investigating. Dominguez was already watching me, saw me paying visits to Aguilar's building. So he stole the case file from my car to find out what I knew. He probably saw me with Johnny Duarte, too, so he paid Duarte a visit and found out what he'd told me. Then Duarte went off the cliff at Devil's Slide.

I could understand the twisted rationale behind killing Wagner and Jeffers, but why kill Duarte? He'd told me nothing about Dominguez. As I'd speculated before,

Dominguez might have wanted in on the drug operation, but there were easier ways to accomplish that than by throwing someone off Devil's Slide. Duarte's murder didn't seem logical to me, but then, guys like Dominguez don't need a good reason to kill. He'd enjoyed staging the knife duel in which he carved up Troy Winslip. He'd probably enjoyed doing Johnny as well.

Since then he'd been busy, trying to find out all he could about my activities, and taunting me with those notes. He knew I'd identified him and was closing in, but did he realize how quickly? And if he realized, what would he do next? Not run away; he was having too much crazy fun. Most likely he'd go after another one of my people, or force a confrontation with me, depending on how long he wanted to continue the game.

Neither possibility was a good one, but I favored a face-to-face between Dominguez and me over anyone else getting hurt or killed. Somehow I had to bring him out into the open. Until then, no one—my employees, friends, or associates—was safe.

The thought chilled me. What could I do? Ask for police protection for everyone I knew or cared about? Yeah, sure. Well, there was one thing, and I could accomplish it right here in the car.

I picked up the cell and called Ted. Explained the situation and asked him to caution the staff. Then I started from the top of my automatic-dial address book, leaving warnings with people and answering machines.

Dusk now, and still no activity at the blue house. I'd moved the car twice when residents who emerged from the shadows gave me suspicious glances. Nothing from Hy or Patrick. Nothing more from Craig. Mick had called from S.F. General to say Julia had been moved from the intensive care unit to a semiprivate room and was asking for me. I explained I was on a surveillance, gave him a message to pass along.

I was stiff and cramped from sitting still for hours. Thirsty, too, but I'd had to leave off drinking bottled water; I really didn't want to resort to the bushes, like the old woman I'd seen earlier. Finally I got out of the car and walked slowly along the block toward the blue house.

Faint light behind sheets that were draped across the front window. Yard so overgrown that if I hunched down, the weeds would hide me. I hunched, slipped into a clump of them. And stifled a sneeze just in time.

I froze, waiting, listening. And stifled another.

Damn it, I've never had allergies! Why does my body pick this time to develop them?

There was no reaction from anyone inside the house. Maybe my snorts only sounded loud to me. After a few minutes I moved forward, slipped along the house's side. The windows were dark there, but at the back, light glowed.

More high weeds, and a half-collapsed fence. The house had once had a service porch, but now two of its three walls were caved in. The floor was rotted out, but I balanced on a beam and peered through the crack-webbed window in the back door.

A kitchen. Unused. Nothing on the countertops, mismatched dishes in the glass-fronted cabinets.

I listened. Quiet in there. Nobody home. I took out my gun and then grasped the doorknob. It moved easily, and the door swung open.

You're committing criminal trespass again.

No, I'm assisting in a police investigation.

The voice of my conscience fell silent.

I moved slowly across the kitchen. Stopped at a short hallway where a door opened to either side. Ahead was an archway leading into the front room; light shone through it, laying a path on the linoleum floor.

Steady and quiet, now.

Down the hallway. Bathroom to the right, empty. Bedroom to the left, same.

Pause. Listen.

Nothing. Move on.

Next to the archway, I flattened against the wall, then peered around its edge.

Empty room. Minimal furnishings.

But ample signs of a struggle.

A lamp lay smashed on the floor, its bulb flickering. A rocking chair was overturned, a bookcase tipped, paperbacks scattered. The jagged neck of a broken beer bottle shone in the light from the overhead fixture, and the rest of it lay in puddled shards.

I stepped into the room, sweeping it with my gun while searching for a closet or anyplace else someone might be hiding. Then I lowered the weapon and took in the scene in segments, as if I were photographing it. Not much to see: a scarred fake-leather sofa, an end table covered with burns and stains, a TV, a rotary phone that had been ripped from the wall.

Possible crime scene—don't disturb it.

I went back down the hall to the small bedroom, turned on the overhead. Double bed with rumpled sheets, bureau, men's clothing hanging from pegs on the wall. Nothing more. On the bureau was a pile of change and a wallet. I went over there and, using a Kleenex, flipped open the wallet.

Cash—fives and ones mostly. No credit cards. A single photograph of a young woman with a teased hairstyle that dated from the sixties. Driver's license made out to Dan Jeffers. The photograph showed a narrow-faced man with a wispy beard and receding hairline; the license had expired two years ago.

Jeffers, living here, in a house belonging to Dominguez's prison buddy?

I set down the wallet, went through the bureau drawers. Standard clothing, inexpensive and serviceable. In the bathroom I found the usual items, plus a prescription vial half full of Xanax tablets, filled in May at the Los Alegres pharmacy I'd visited. One refill left.

I held the vial in my hand, shaking the pills around. Something wrong here. There was no trace of Dominguez's prison buddy in this house. But Dan Jeffers? Had he also been in prison with Dominguez and Sly Rawson? If so—

Muffled ringing in my purse. I put the vial back in the medicine cabinet, pulled the phone from my bag, and answered.

"Shar?" Charlotte's voice, shaky and high-pitched, betraying her west Texas origins, as it always did when she was excited or upset. "Somebody took a shot at Mick outside the pier. He's okay, but I think you'd better get over here right away."

Flashing lights, police lines, traffic slowing as drivers rubbernecked. A Channel 7 news van. I pulled the MG onto the sidewalk in front of the adjacent pier, ran down there. Adah was standing near our entrance, talking with a pair of plainclothesmen; a technician was perched on a ladder, digging with a knife at the stucco wall—removing the bullet that could have killed my nephew. I stepped over the yellow tape, went up to Adah.

"Where's Mick?"

"Inside. He's okay, McCone. Shaken, but just fine. That shot"—she waved her hand at the wall—"wasn't intended to hit him. It's way high and to the right."

"Maybe Dominguez is a bad marksman."

She took my arm, walked me away from the other detectives. "You don't know it was Dominguez."

"Of course it was Dominguez! Who else?"

"Could've been random."

"Come on, Adah. Two shootings, both my employees, same general location. Not random."

"Give me some proof."

"I gave you proof: Alex Aguilar, who admitted helping to set up the scheme to bring me down."

"Your word against his. And we don't have the witness; he's vanished."

"Then try Dominguez buying an illegal gun."

"You said the pawnbroker won't corroborate what he told you."

"Well, what about Dominguez leaving crazy messages for me all over town?" I took the last two from my bag, handed them to her, along with one of the composites. "The first note, which is at Richman Labs, was a picture of knives. 'Knives at midnight'—get it?"

She examined the notes as I explained how I'd gotten them. I asked, "Isn't that enough proof to put out an APB, bring Dominguez in?"

She sighed wearily. "Not my call. I've been removed from the investigation."

"Why?"

"Phrases such as 'too close to the victims' and 'special treatment' were tossed around."

"Jesus Christ, the fucking department—"

"Lower your voice." She jerked her chin at the plain-clothesmen, who were watching us. "Those guys'll be working the case. The last thing you need is for them to overhear you dissing our little fraternity."

She sounded as bitter and tired as Greg Marcus had at the book signing last Sunday. How long before she got fed up and quit? But what would she do then? I couldn't imagine Adah as anything other than a cop, and in any department other than San Francisco's. She was a native of the city, one of the "red-diaper babies" of Bernal Heights, which had once been considered a hotbed of Communism.

"Okay," I said, "sorry." For a moment I considered telling her about what I'd found at the house on Regis Street, but decided against it. Adah would bend the rules when it suited her, but she wouldn't take kindly to me committing criminal trespass.

"Look," she said, "I'll show them these notes. Maybe then they'll take the investigation more seriously. But if I were you, I wouldn't hold my breath: those guys are old guard, and over the years, neither of us has racked up too many points with that crowd. Where'll you be if they want to talk with you?"

"The pier, with Mick." I moved away, turned. "And thanks, Adah."

She nodded and went back to her colleagues.

The floor of the pier was deserted when I entered, but voices echoed from upstairs.

Mick: "I'm fine, goddamn it! I don't need to go to the

hospital. I told the cops I was fine; I'm telling you I'm fine. *I'm fine!*"

Strident, Texas-accented words that I couldn't understand.

Mick: "Stop fussing! You remind me of my grandmother!"

Charlotte: "Maybe your grandmother could talk some sense into you. Obviously, I can't!"

Ted: "Why don't we all take a deep breath and calm down now."

Silence as I took the stairs.

They were in Ted's office: Mick seated in the chair, his face red; Charlotte pacing, hands clasped behind her; Ted perched on the edge of the desk, frowning. As I came in, Mick glared at me and said, "Don't *you* start!"

It was his typical defensive reaction when he was scared but felt he needed to appear strong—bred into him during a childhood when his father was almost always gone and his mother depended on her oldest son for emotional support and help with his siblings. Lots of hard times, and then the big time, when the money gushed in and none of the Savages knew how to cope with sudden affluence. All things considered, it was a wonder Mick had turned into such a level-headed man.

I said to him, "Why don't we talk in my office?" To Charlotte and Ted I added, "Will you excuse us for a while?"

Ted nodded, relieved that I'd defused the situation. Charlotte thrust out her lower lip, then apparently reminded herself that a grown woman shouldn't pout.

I didn't speak until we were in my office and seated by the window, the door closed. Mick slouched in my desk chair, which he'd rolled next to the ratty old relic under the schefflera plant, staring grimly at his reflection in the glass.

"Rough evening," I said.

"Yeah." He paused. "Shar, d'you mind if we turn off the lights? I feel like . . ."

"I know, a target." I got up, switched off the overheads. It was more pleasant in the darkness, and when I returned to my chair, I sensed him relaxing. After a moment I reached for his hand. He didn't pull away.

"You want to talk about it?" I asked.

"I do, and I don't, but I'd better. Okay, after I left the hospital—Jules is doing well, by the way. She got to see Tonio for a while, and Sophia's with her tonight. Anyway, after I left them, I started back here, and wouldn't you know it, my bike ran out of gas a few blocks from our condo. I only filled it a couple of days ago, and haven't driven it very far. I don't know how that could've happened."

"You have a lock on the gas cap?"

"It's busted—oh."

"Right."

"So it was Dominguez, and he *planned* to pick me off."

"Planned to scare you. And me. What next?"

"I pushed the bike over to our building, left it there. Then I walked down here."

"You hear anybody following you?"

"No, and I'm pretty streetwise."

"Yes, you are. He must've been waiting outside the pier. He has an uncanny way of knowing what people will do, and he's probably been studying all of us for some time now. Go on."

"I was crossing the sidewalk toward the pier. This

skiptrace on Dan Jeffers has been frustrating Derek, so I sent him home at five—no sense abusing a new employee—but I decided to do some more digging. Next thing I knew, there was this loud noise. I've fired guns; I know a shot when I hear one, so I dived for the sidewalk, flattened, and covered my head. A car peeled away; I guess it was the shooter."

"You get a look at it?"

"No. I stayed down, wasn't taking any chances."

"I'd've done the same."

"Well, a couple of guys came running across the Embarcadero and helped me up. They didn't see the shooter, either. And as soon as I was on my feet, there was sweet Charlotte, screaming and grabbing at me. Nearly knocked me down again. If I'd've been wounded, she'd've probably finished me off. Shar, does she remind you of Grandma?"

"Let's not go there now."

"Because if she's going to turn out like that, I'd just as soon not marry her. I love Grandma, but . . ."

Marry Charlotte? Marry anyone*? My God, you're so young!*

He's older than both his parents were when they married.

I asked, "Have the two of you been talking about marriage?"

"Off and on. But now I'm not so sure we should."

"I don't think life's major decisions should be made when you've just been shot at."

"You *do* think she's like Grandma."

"I don't know what I think. Wait and ask me a week after this nightmare is over."

He squeezed my hand. "Sorry. I'm only thinking about

me, when I should be . . ." He put his other hand to his eyes.

"Of course you're thinking about you. You've had a bad scare; it makes you question everything. But you shouldn't judge Charlotte by one Grandma-esque performance. If anything, it proves she loves you."

He was silent for a moment, except for faint snuffles, which he tried to disguise. When he spoke again, he sounded drained. "So what do we do now?"

"I want you and Charlotte to spend the night at your dad's. He has a security man and an excellent alarm system. You'll both get a good night's sleep there."

"But I want to help. I won't be able to sleep, anyway."

"Take your laptop, then. Here's something you can look into." I explained about the blue house on Regis Street and what I'd found there.

"Dan Jeffers, Sly Rawson. Two-oh-one Regis Street." He reached for a scratch pad and wrote down the names, proving how shaken he was. Mick had a sharp memory and seldom made notes.

I said, "Promise me this: don't stay up all night."

"Jeez, now *you're* sounding like Grandma."

"Say that again, and I'll truss you up, drive you to San Diego, and make you spend a week with her."

After Mick left, I buzzed Ted and told him to go home. He refused, said he'd already called Neal, explained the situation, and told him he'd stay at the pier overnight. "Frankly, I feel safer here than I would driving back to the apartment," he added. "There's that blow-up bed in the conference room. Unless you're planning to use it."

"No. I'm living on pure adrenaline. I may never sleep again."

After Ted went off to inflate the bed, I called Hy's cell. He was still running a surveillance at a house on Potrero Hill where Dominguez might be staying.

After I explained about the shooting and reassured him that Mick was all right, he said, "The time frame fits. Subject who's built like Dominguez left here and gave me the slip in time to get to S.F. General, siphon off most of Mick's gas, and position himself at the pier. Hasn't returned yet, but when he does, I'll be waiting for him."

"You can't make a positive ID?"

"Too dark for that. But if he comes back, I will."

"Let me know what happens."

I replaced the receiver, only moderately optimistic. Dominguez was sly and moved through the city with a slippery ease. What were the chances that he'd return to the same place after the shooting? He seemed to have an inexhaustible supply of places to hide.

The afternoon and early evening had been clear, but tonight the fog had returned. I switched off the office lights again and went to my armchair, stared out at the shifting white wall. The plainclothesmen to whom Adah had said she would show the notes and composite hadn't bothered to talk with me. Patrick hadn't called to report the results of his surveillance, and by now he'd be on his shift at his security job. As far as I knew, Craig was still in San Luis Obispo.

And here I was, at close to eleven. Waiting.

I got up, began pacing. I was exhausted but wired. Wanted to be doing something, needed motion, action.

I paced some more. Returned to the armchair. Stared at the fog. Again went over the details of what had happened from the day Reynaldo Dominguez had arrived in town to the events of a few hours ago. He was out there somewhere, and I—

Sudden jolting thought. I grabbed my bag and jacket and ran for the MG.

It was just what I'd feared: something had happened at my house. Every window was lit, and a car from Hollister Security sat in my driveway. On the sidewalk, two men in the company's dark blue uniforms stood, talking with Michelle, who was tightly cradling Ralph.

I pulled up, blocking the driveway, jumped out of the MG, and hurried toward them. Michelle didn't look upset, but the cat had his head burrowed into the crook of her elbow—the position he usually assumed when at the vet's. Michelle waved to me, and the security men turned.

"I'm Sharon McCone, the owner," I called. "What's going on?"

"Prowler or Peeping Tom," the older man said. "Your neighbor was inside feeding the cat and set off the panic button. We've checked the premises, and everything's secure."

Prowler or Peeping Tom, my ass. Reynaldo Dominguez.

I said to Michelle, "You see this prowler?"

"Yeah. Ugly dude. Scars, weird eyes, nose that looked like somebody'd taken an Allen wrench to it. He was staring in the kitchen window at me. Started laughing in this totally insane way when I shut off the lights and ran out of the room. You really should think of putting up curtains in there."

"Probably." Motion at the window of a house across the street caught my eye. Mr. Winter, whose interest in what went on with the rest of us was enough for an entire neighborhood watch force. At least the silent alarm hadn't alerted anyone else in the immediate vicinity.

The security man asked, "Do you want us to check around the neighborhood for him, Ms. McCone?"

"No, thank you. I'm sure he's long gone by now."

"We'll say good night, then."

They started back to their car, and I realized I'd have to move mine to let them out. That accomplished, I pulled into the drive and went over to where Michelle still stood.

"Are you all right?" I asked.

"Of course. It takes more than a face at the window to scare me." She thrust out her chin defensively, but her lips quivered. I let her maintain the fiction; she wouldn't want to know that her tough-kid facade was showing a few cracks.

When I patted Ralph's side, I felt him trembling. "Why were you feeding him so late?" I asked.

"I wasn't. I've been working on this term paper, and when my eyes started crossing, I took a break, saw you still hadn't come home, and decided to come over and check on Ralphie. Thought I'd take a blood-sugar reading, and while I was getting set up, the dude appeared in the window."

"Your parents know you're out?"

The corner of her mouth twitched in annoyance. "No, Shar. I'm old enough to walk a few feet down the sidewalk by myself at night. My folks're at a City Arts lecture."

"Well, maybe you'd better stay with me till they get back. Just in case the guy's still around. I could use the company."

Now she grinned, seeing through my feeble attempt not to seem overprotective. "You'll have Ralph's company, and Allie's—she's under the sofa in the parlor. I need to get back to the paper I'm writing." She handed me the cat and walked toward her house.

I waited till she was safely inside, then went up my front steps. Bolted the door and reactivated the alarm. And stood in the dark hallway until Ralph stopped trembling.

Dominguez wants a confrontation. Soon. He may be back.

No, he won't. He doesn't want it now. Or here.

Clicking of claws on the hardwood floor. Alice meowed and brushed against my legs. I switched on the hallway lights and set Ralph down. Both cats headed toward the kitchen and their food bowls.

In the sitting room, the light on the answering machine was blinking. Four calls.

Mother One: "Sharon, please call me. I'm worried about you."

Me, too, Ma.

Half sister Robin: "Hey, I'm gonna be out there next month, looking for a place to rent in Berkeley. Would it be an imposition if I stayed with you?"

None at all, Robbie.

Patrick: "I couldn't get through to the office before, so I thought I'd better call you at home. I kept the house on Precita Street under surveillance for most of the evening, and then the family that lives there came home. Dominguez's friend sublet it to them nine months ago, didn't leave a forwarding. I'll check in tomorrow."

Thanks, Patrick.

Hy: "That situation with RKI's client is heating up again, and I'm off to La Jolla. Nothing at the place where I was maintaining the surveillance for you, and I doubt there will be. Sorry to cut out on you at a time like this, McCone. We'll talk when I get back."

Hurry home, Ripinsky. I need you.

Close to midnight now, but I didn't want to sleep; Mick or Craig might contact me with a fresh lead anytime now. I went to the kitchen, contemplated a glass of wine, rejected the idea. I was so tired that even the smallest amount of alcohol would put me under. Finally I sat down at the table and began to play my own brand of solitaire.

A few years before, one of the witnesses in an investigation had showed me how to play the game backwards and incorporate a few rules that made it more a contest of skill than chance. Since then I'd invented a few rules of my own that made it even more enjoyable.

I must confess, I win a lot.

Shuffle, cut, deal. Red on black, ten on nine, king to the top . . . The rhythm relaxed me, and my mind began to wander. Would anyone really turn up valuable information at this time of night? Maybe I should try for a few hours' sleep—

The phone rang. I dropped the portion of the deck I was holding, scattered the cards across the table. Went to the sitting room and snatched up the receiver.

"Sharon? Ray Rios, at Olompali State Park."

"Yes, Ray. What's happening?"

He spoke, but between his accent and a bad connection I could barely understand him. "Would you say that again, please?"

"Sorry—I'm on my cell, and it don't work so good here. I wouldn't've called you this late, but I knew you'd want to know. I found Dan Jeffers hiding in one of the cold rooms off the dairy barn. He's real scared. The guy who killed Scott Wagner, he found Dan at some house in the city and beat the shit out of him."

"Are you with him now?"

"Outside. I don't want him to hear me, 'cause he might split again."

"Stay with him. I'll come up there."

"Okay. The bar gate across the access road is locked at sundown. What you do is pull your car off to the right of it. Nobody patrols after midnight. Just walk in to the barn."

"I'm on my way."

Backup. I need backup. Dan Jeffers is a used-up old druggie, probably not dangerous to anyone but himself, but that's an isolated place, and I've only met Ray Rios once. Can I trust him?

I tried Adah and Craig's place. Got the machine and left a message for either of them to meet me at Olompali as soon as possible. Tried Craig's cellular, too; still out of range. SFPD said Adah was off duty.

I considered calling Mick and Charlotte but decided against it. They were both overemotional tonight, and besides, he was family and she might as well be—the reason I'd so far confined them, in spite of much chafing on their parts, to safe fieldwork and desk jobs.

Patrick Neilan didn't have a cellular and hadn't told me where his security gig was taking him tonight. On the off chance he'd get home soon, I left a message on his machine.

Then I headed for Marin County.

Thursday

·

JULY 24

The fog massed heavily through the Golden Gate but dwindled to wisps by the time I passed Sausalito. Traffic moved at a steady pace, and I sped along, keeping an eye out for highway patrol cars. North of San Rafael I rolled down the window. Sweet-smelling warm summer night.

Some fifteen minutes later I spotted the park entrance, drove on, and U-turned. Followed the access road to the bar gate and parked to its right. Another vehicle was pulled into the weeds there, an antiquated VW van. I got out of the MG, taking my flashlight, and checked the van's plates; it was the one that Jeffers had failed to reregister this year.

I checked my watch by the light of the flash. One-seventeen, and no sign of Craig or Adah. I tried their apartment and again reached only the machine. Called the pier with the same results.

Craig was probably still down south in San Luis, but where was Adah this long after midnight on a Thursday? Not on official business, or the officer who'd caught my call would've said—oh, right, now I remembered: the bachelor party for another inspector who was getting married on Saturday. That could go on till dawn. Patrick? If he was on the same schedule as the day before, he wouldn't be home till midmorning. I could call the security company and ask where he was working, but by the time I got hold of him . . .

Okay, I was on my own. I'd been on my own plenty of times before.

And I needed to get to Dan Jeffers before he disappeared again.

The sky was star-shot, with a sliver of new moon— not much light pollution this far from the towns that lined the 101 corridor. The temperature was lower here, chilled by the wind blowing across a maze of waterways and tule marshes that extended east to San Pablo Bay. The "dreaded crosswind," area pilots called it; on a breezy day, landings at nearby Gnoss Field were a test of one's skill.

I zipped my jacket, turned up its collar, and skirted the iron gate. Walked swiftly along the pavement, shining the flash downward. The road split around a tree at the edge of the formal garden, one branch leading to the visitors' lot, the other into the park proper. I followed the latter, then picked my way down the slope into the garden. There I moved slowly, avoiding gopher holes and fallen branches. The trees rustled above me, and a night creature ran off through the brush. I caught the scent of bay laurel and something more pungent.

A small plane droned on its climb-out from Gnoss. I looked up, spotted red and white lights blinking through the palm fronds. Its sound diminished in the distance, and then all I heard was a murmuring and whispering like the waves in the cove at Touchstone. The tires of cars on the highway, muted by distance. If I closed my eyes, I would have believed I was near the sea.

I walked the length of the garden, passing the stone steps and the dark, craggy shape of the dry fountain, and scrambled up the slope near the bridge that spanned the stream. Hurried across the trail and into the shelter of the trees, where a bird's shrill cry gave me a brief start.

Behind me small security spots shone down from the old adobe, but the yellow house beyond it was dark. Although Ray Rios had said the rangers didn't patrol after midnight, someone might come looking if he saw my light, so I shaded it and kept well into the underbrush. After I passed the horse barn, I spotted the road leading to the staff housing at least a quarter mile away. A faint glow showed there, and I caught the glint of headlight beams on the highway beyond.

I rounded a curve and saw the outline of the sagging dairy barn, flanked by the cold rooms. Darkness enveloped it. I stopped for a moment, searching for signs of occupancy; thought I saw a red ember fall to the ground and disappear as someone extinguished a cigarette. Did Rios smoke? I didn't remember. But Jeffers did.

If it was Jeffers, I couldn't risk calling out and scaring him off, so I approached slowly and in a roundabout way, the high grass rustling and thistles catching at the legs of my jeans. Dust rose, and I sneezed—into my forearm, to muffle the sound.

Jesus, what is it all of a sudden with me and weeds?

As I neared the cold rooms, I spied another glimmer of light—yellowish this time. When I moved closer, I saw that plywood had been placed over the high windows of the front room. The light came from the rear. A stack of lumber blocked the steps that led there, so I went around the structure to the narrow passageway between it and the barn and peered into the front room. Dark there, but flickering light outlined the interior doorway.

Something wrong here.

I slid the flashlight into my jacket pocket, drew the Magnum from my bag. Stood very still, listening for movement, a breath, anything. Total silence. Then a scurrying sound as some small creature ran into the weeds.

Definitely something wrong. Should've waited for backup—

A rushing noise close behind me. Before I could turn, a strong arm gripped me around the neck; another chopped at my right hand. I felt a slash of pain, couldn't hold the gun after the second fierce chop. Then my assailant spun me around and dragged me backwards through the door to the cold rooms.

I struggled against him, trying to back-kick his shins. He laughed—a familiar insane cackle that put a chill on my spine and made me struggle harder. I kicked again, tried to bite his arm. Futile. He dragged me into the second room, where an oil lamp sat in the middle of the floor. Slammed me so hard against the far wall that I bounced off and sprawled onto the old metal desk next to the leaning stack of plywood, breath forced from my lungs, my vision blurring.

Gasping, I pushed up on my elbows. My eyes focused again. Dominguez was standing several feet away, on the far side of the oil lamp, a gun—a .45, not the Saturday night special Darrin Boydston had sold him—aimed at me.

"No knives," he said, "and it's not midnight, but you

fell for it. 'Ray Rios at Olompali State Park,'" he added in imitation of what I now realized was his earlier phone call. "'I found Dan Jeffers hiding in one of the cold rooms.'"

I fell for it, all right. Stupid!

Anger with myself allowed me to regain control. I took a couple of breaths and lowered my feet to the floor, watching Dominguez closely. The lamp's glow highlighted the sharp planes of his narrow face. Highlighted his scars, twisted lips, and dead eyes. He'd aged markedly since I'd last seen him, but those eyes were the same. They had probably been the same on the day he was born.

He said, "Don't know one spic accent from another, do you? Can't tell us apart."

I measured the distance between us, the distance to both exits.

"Am I right?" he asked.

"It was a bad connection. A deliberately bad one, I suppose. And you're a good mimic. When did you talk to Ray?"

I can't run out the way he dragged me in — he's blocking the door. Maybe I can edge over, dodge through the door to the right, but then there's that stack of lumber, and his damn gun.

Neither way's good.

Dominguez said, "I followed you the day you came up here to ask about Scott Wagner. Talked up old Ray, told him I thought you were a fox, asked what you were doing here. Guy had serious diarrhea of the mouth."

"What've you done to him?"

"Nothin'. I ain't even seen him. He's probably snuggled up in bed by now. Nobody knows we're here."

"What about Dan Jeffers? Where is he?"

He made an offhand gesture. That and his expression said the same thing: *dead.*

"Did you kill him down at Sly Rawson's house?"

"Nah. Sly went back inside last week on a trumped-up rap, said I could use the place till the lease ran out. I figured you might catch on to it and bust in, so I set it up good. Don't you worry about Dan; he's long gone. I kept his wallet, pills, van. It's just me and you now, *puta.*" He took a step toward me.

I held my ground. There was a pronounced twitch at the corner of his mouth, and his eyes moved erratically. The hand that held the gun jerked. Drugged up, overconfident, and out of control.

"Just me and you," he repeated.

All in one motion I pushed off the desk and kicked out, toppling the oil lamp. Glass shattered, and a line of flame shot across the floor.

Dominguez fired wildly, a deafening roar in the small space. The bullet hit the wall above me, sending down a shower of concrete chips. Then the firelight sputtered out and the room went dark.

I was out the side door before he could fire again. I tripped on the top step, fell onto the stack of lumber. Cascading boards carried me down onto the hard ground. My left side throbbed from the impact, but I pushed myself up and scrambled through the high grass. Behind me I heard Dominguez crashing around in the lumber, cursing.

I headed for the road to the staff housing, hoping someone there had heard the shot. No more lights there, no motion. Of course—the thick walls of the cold room had muffled the sound; at a distance of half a mile, it would have sounded like a car backfiring on the highway.

I had perhaps a thirty-second lead on Dominguez, but he could probably run faster than I. The staff quarters were too far away, over more or less open ground, where I'd be a clear target. My side felt on fire now. I'd never make it there before he overtook me.

Misdirect him.

I slipped between two of the old ranch buildings on the far side of the trail. The flashlight was still in my jacket pocket; I shielded the lens and briefly shone it around. A pile of miscellaneous junk lay behind the blacksmith's shed—chunks of concrete, wood scraps, twisted iron. I tried to pocket the flash again, dropped it, and it bounced away and went out. I couldn't find it.

I did find a large piece of concrete, and hefted it, further wrenching my side and gritting my teeth against the pain. Some yards away I could make out the giant bay laurel tree in the declivity. I toted the chunk of concrete over to the edge of the shed, raised and hurled it. It thumped, breaking off a tree branch as it rolled into the declivity. Then I screamed.

Dominguez's footsteps pounded that way. I slipped around the cottage behind the blacksmith's shed and moved swiftly across the road and around the horse barn, toward the ruins of the garden. It would be a while before Dominguez realized I wasn't in the declivity. I dug into my bag, pulled out my cellular, hit the auto-dial for 911. The display showed I was out of range. Damn!

Okay, I wouldn't panic. The night was clear enough, and the security spots on the old adobe guided me. Soon I'd get to my car and drive to a place where the cell worked. Or find that dinosaur of the communications in- dustry—a pay phone.

I slipped along to the side of the trail, trying to blend into the shadows. All the while I was beating myself up for falling for Dominguez's ruse. Chalk it up to impa- tience, a desperate desire to bring the matter to a conclu- sion before anybody else got hurt. But I'd been damned stupid, and it could still get me killed.

When I reached the bridge by the garden, I slid down the slope and began walking swiftly back the way I'd come. Branches and leaves littered the ground; they crackled and snapped under foot. Several times I paused, listening for footsteps. Checked the cell again, but found it still nonfuctional. I was skirting the far side of the stone fountain when I heard him whisper from somewhere close by. Too close.

"Where are you, *puta*?"

I fought off a surge of panic, ducked down behind the fountain's wall. When I peered over it, I saw his figure silhouetted at the top of the steps. He hadn't fallen for my ruse with the concrete. Had anticipated the direction I'd take. . . .

I'd never make it to the parking lot and my car. Like the road to the staff housing, the public access road was too long and exposed.

Hide someplace.

Hide!

Dominguez was between me and the adobe and other buildings—the logical place to take shelter. I looked up at the towering fountain. Some of the cavelike spaces be- tween the rocks were large enough for a person my size to conceal herself. I spotted one halfway up—some ten or twelve feet—that would also give an advantage over Dominguez on the ground.

I rolled over the wall, quietly let myself down into the dry pool. Leaves crunched under my feet as as I moved toward the dark, craggy mass. When I reached it, I grabbed the rough rocks, dug my toes in, and started up toward the opening I'd pinpointed. The pain in my side flared white-hot. The rocks ripped at my hands, tearing a nail to the quick. My foot slipped, then found a toehold again. Finally I reached the ledge above, slipped through the opening.

Safe. For the moment.

Dominguez was closer now. I could hear branches snapping under his feet. I crouched at the mouth of the little cave, watching.

After a moment his footsteps stopped. Then they started up again. He was coming closer, circling the fountain.

I held my breath, listened to him as he prowled. He was so close, I could hear him panting. He circled the fountain twice, then started away, toward the access road.

I leaned out, looking after him, and my foot dislodged a loose stone. Shit! It rolled through the opening and clattered to the fountain's floor.

Dominguez's footsteps halted, then returned.

Again I held my breath.

"I know you're in there," he whispered. "Come on out!"

He was below me now. I could make out the outlines of his angular figure as he leaned across the wall, but he couldn't see me in the deep shadow. Then he swung over it and lowered himself down to the fountain's floor.

"Stop playing games with me, *puta*!"

He staggered through the branches and leaves, whispering epithets in Spanish.

This could go on all night, unless I took the offensive. I waited until he was below me, then deliberately scraped my foot across the cave's pebbled floor.

Dominguez stopped, uttering a small sound of surprise. Then I heard him scrambling and grunting as he started to climb.

I braced myself, hands flat on either side of the opening.

"Game's over, *puta*," he said.

Your game, not mine.

His head appeared above the ledge in front of the opening. I raised my legs and kicked out. Caught him smack in the middle of the forehead.

He yelled, driven backward, and then went tumbling to the concrete floor below. There was a bone-cracking sound as he hit.

I crouched, panting, on the floor of the little cave. The pain in my side radiated out and engulfed my entire body. I shuddered, fighting against it. When it subsided some, I edged forward and peered over the ledge. Dominguez lay on his back, motionless.

I climbed down to the fountain's floor and edged toward him. He was breathing, but just barely. I hesitated a bit, then knelt and felt his neck for a pulse. Found a weak one.

I turned away, climbed out of the fountain, and breathed deeply of the crisp air. Massaged my side, dropped my head back, and looked up at the star-shot sky. Then I started for the staff housing, to rouse someone who would call 911.

Sunday

·

AUGUST 3

At five in the afternoon, my house teemed with people. At first I'd envisioned the agency's celebratory party as an elegant catered dinner for staff members only, but then there was the problem of Hy, who was still in town. How could I include my man while excluding the others' men or women? But if I did include them, there wouldn't be enough space at the table for everybody.

So finally I said the hell with it, come one, come all. I'd make a few of my special sourdough loaves—hollowed out and filled with every imaginable cheese and deli meat, then baked to perfection—a big salad, and a sinful dessert. We'd eat outside, weather permitting, or all over the house if the fog rolled in.

Then Rae called, lonesome because Ricky was on an out-of-state concert tour, and I invited her. She asked if she could bring Molly and Lisa and their older sister, Jamie, who were up from L.A., and volunteered to supply hot dogs and burgers and tend the grill. Next Hank Zahn called to say he and Anne-Marie Altman and their adopted daughter, Habiba Hamid, were back from vacation, so I invited them. He said they'd bring three different kinds of salsa from Trader Joe's, and both yellow and blue corn tortilla chips. The Curleys volunteered potato salad. The Halls, next door on the other side, offered up three-bean salad. Glenn Solomon and his wife, Bette Silver, supplied a case of wine. Maggie Hayley augmented it with champagne. My half sister Robin, who had arrived early to look for an apartment in Berkeley, made a special trip to my favorite bakery for a tray of pastries.

Party quietly out of hand. The best kind.

I put the sourdough loaves in to bake, then went out on the deck. People lounged in chairs or perched on the railing, noshing and drinking soda and beer and wine; Rae was tending the Weber with an intense expression usually seen on the faces of male barbecue fanatics; the smell of charcoal set off my hungry button, and I looked at my watch. Twenty-five minutes to go.

Even Julia was there, still uncomfortable from her chest wound, and being fussed over by everyone, including her sister, Sophia. In the yard, Tonio and the other kids ran around, tossing a Frisbee and screaming. Jamie, almost grown now, was sitting on the steps leading down there, in earnest conversation with Derek Ford. Now, that would be an interesting match. . . . I caught Hy's eye and smiled.

Adah came up to me. "Let's go inside and talk."

We went to the kitchen, got glasses of wine, then moved to the sitting room.

She said, "Given everybody's good mood, I guess BSIS isn't pursuing the complaint against you."

"As Marguerite Hayley puts it, the paperwork is lost at

the bottom of a pile on a low-level bureaucrat's desk and will stay there."

"That's good, because Dominguez is still stonewalling it. I've got a feeling the shrinks're starting to believe him."

Since his release from Marin General Hospital, where he'd been treated for a concussion, ruptured spleen, and other injuries sustained in his fall, Dominguez had staged a very convincing insanity act at the county jail. A court-appointed psychiatrist, as well as those hired by the prosecution and defense, were holding interviews with him to determine the extent of his mental disorder. Adah and I, as well as investigating officers in Marin, Sonoma, and San Francisco Counties, were in agreement that he was crazy like a fox.

"Damn it!" I exclaimed. "Can't the shrinks see through him? This guy was a jailhouse lawyer; he knows if he gets put away on an insanity plea, he'll eventually be back on the street."

"Yeah, after killing three people. But the Marin County people have to go through the process, and if the shrinks aren't perceptive, and they get a sympathetic judge—"

"I wish Marin didn't have jurisdiction. There's no strong case for him having killed Scott Wagner."

"But there is for his attack on you. You ought to know; you signed the complaint."

"But Dan Jeffers—they turned up evidence that he was killed in that little house in Los Alegres. That's Sonoma County, and it's a capital charge."

"A weak case, though. The evidence only shows that somebody of Jeffers's blood type was injured or killed there. And they've got no body."

"It's probably hidden in one of those canyons up on Sonoma Mountain, where it won't be discovered for years, if ever. But down here—there's Johnny Duarte. Alex Aguilar as good as admitted to me that Dominguez killed him."

" 'As good as' isn't good enough. And we haven't been able to locate Alex."

"The assault on Angela Batista or Alison James?"

"Neither'll press charges. Batista claims it would damage her reputation and her business. The other one's worried about her child-custody case."

"Julia's shooting, and the attempt on Mick . . . the gun . . . Oh, hell. Dominguez didn't have it at the park— that one was a forty-five. He probably tossed the Saturday night special into the bay right after he fired on Mick. Nobody has anything on Dominguez, unless you find Aguilar and persuade him it's in his best interests to turn state's evidence. Or if Dominguez makes a slip of the tongue to those shrinks, and they realize he's not only sane but guilty."

Adah was silent, her face still, her eyes thoughtful. "You know," she said, "nobody here or in Marin and Sonoma Counties wants to see this guy get a vacation in a mental hospital. Even his public defender doesn't seem too keen on the idea. Maybe—"

"McCone!" Hy called from the kitchen. "These loaves're ready. What d'you want me to do with them?"

"Maybe what?" I asked.

Adah shrugged. "I'm not promising anything, but I'm thinking the other investigators and I might be able to work out an interagency deal. We'll talk more tomorrow."

Tuesday

·

AUGUST 5

Reynaldo Dominguez and I were seated across from each other at a table in an interview room at the Marin County Jail, near the sprawling, blue-roofed civic center designed by Frank Lloyd Wright. Behind the one-way window overlooking the room were the three psychologists assigned to evaluate him, his public defender, the Marin investigating officers, Adah, and other investigators from the San Francisco and Los Alegres police departments.

Like any good jailhouse lawyer, Dominguez knew we were being watched, probably videotaped. And he was putting on a good act: he mumbled to himself and laughed, his gaze roving aimlessly around the room, never meeting my eyes. When the sheriff's investigator who was in charge of the case brought him in, he'd asked if Dominguez wanted his court-appointed attorney present. Dominguez shook his head, said, "Fuck my lawyer," and began talking to himself in Spanish. He hadn't yet stopped.

Yesterday evening, after this meeting was finally arranged, Adah and I had drawn up a list of questions for me to ask Dominguez. The idea was to take him through the chronology of what he'd done since coming to San Francisco and attempt to provoke a reaction or outburst that would prove he was in full possession of his faculties. So far, I might as well have been talking to a Spanish-speaking magpie.

For all his babbling, though, I could tell Dominguez was faking. A satisfied light flickered beneath the cold, flat surface of his eyes. He knew exactly what I was trying to do, and once again he was taking pleasure in taunting and defeating me. Before, a gun had been his weapon; now it was inane mutterings.

I glanced at my watch. They'd allowed me an hour, and time was growing short. The hell with this, I thought, and deviated from the scripted questions.

"Tell me, Dominguez," I said, "what did you plan to do to me that night at Olompali?"

His eyes flickered, not enough for those on the other side of the glass to see, but I knew I had his full attention.

"You want to tell me," I added. "You know you do."

He laughed, muttered in Spanish. Something involving the word *coño*—"cunt."

I scribbled the word on the legal pad in front of me, shielded what I'd written with my hand.

Dominguez's eyes narrowed, and he shifted, trying to see the pad. I made another note, just scribbles. The corner of his mouth twitched.

I said, "Well, I can guess your plans for me. At first it was enough to ruin me professionally, but when you realized I'd identified you, it turned into something different. You wanted me to die, but first you wanted me to suffer."

"Vete al carajo, coño."

He'd told me to get fucked, but the light in his eyes confirmed my assumption.

"You don't like women, do you, Dominguez?"

"No me jodas."

Don't fuck with me.

"You like that kind of word, don't you? *Puta. Coño. Carajo.* They're obscene, degrade the woman whom they're directed at. Let's talk about other words—or actions—you like. *Humiliación. Torturo. Violación. Homicidio.* Humiliation. Torture. Rape. Murder. Acts of a coward who's really afraid of women."

His eyes came alive with rage, but he didn't move or speak.

Keep pushing him.

"So that was what you had planned for me. I don't know how you thought you'd get away with it, though. If I were dead, everybody at my agency would've known you killed me. And they could've proved it. We have testimony from witnesses, composite sketches. A homicide inspector on the SFPD has been monitoring our progress the whole time we've been looking for you.

"You made a lot of mistakes, Dominguez. You involved Alex Aguilar—a weak man. The police are going to find him sooner or later, and he'll break easily. You used scare tactics—like beating up Angela Batista and firing a shot at Mick Savage—that called attention to yourself. You killed three people, and attempted to kill one more. You're faking this insanity business, but not very well, and the shrinks are going to see through you. And eventually the authorities will uncover compelling evidence to link you to all those crimes. Then you're going away for the rest of your miserable life. Or maybe they'll give you a lethal injection."

His hands tensed on the edge of the table.

"When you take a good, hard look at what you've done, you've got to admit you've been downright stupid. Or maybe you really are crazy."

His nostrils flared, and he made a growling sound deep in his throat.

Got him.

I stood up, leaned over the table toward him, and said softly, " 'Knives at midnight.' You left those words as a message on Troy Winslip's answering-machine tape. 'Knives at midnight.' You spelled them out in the notes you left for me. You really must be crazy to make a mistake like that twice. Crazy and stupid. A stupid, stupid man—"

Dominguez sprang from his chair, grabbed me by the throat, dragged me halfway across the table. I grasped his fingers, trying to break his grip.

"*¡Coño!*" he screamed. "You don't talk to me that way! I am not stupid! I am not crazy! I planned; I acted—"

The door crashed open behind me, and two sheriff's deputies ran in, pried his hands off me, and subdued him. I pushed off the table and reeled backwards, clutching at my throat, struggling for breath. One of the psychologists appeared and took hold of my arm, guided me to a chair.

"Are you okay?" she asked.

I nodded, watching Dominguez being dragged from the room. The look he shot me over his shoulder was the same as in the San Diego courtroom. I supposed I'd see it again when he was finally convicted of one or another of his current crimes.

"Do you want to talk about it?" the psychologist asked.

I shook my head.

"That's all right, dear. You've been through a trau-matic event, and sometimes it's difficult to articulate your feelings. If in the future you'd like to discuss it . . ." She was fishing around in her purse.

Good God, she's going to give me her business card! If I start talking to a shrink about all the trauma I've en-dured over all the years, I'll be on the couch for the rest of my life!

"Thank you," I said, "but what I'd really like is a glass of water."

Saturday

·

AUGUST 9

Hy put Two-five-two-seven-Tango into a loop high above the tule marshes south of Los Alegres. I closed my eyes and savored the disorientation that flying blind imparts. No matter how often you've experienced it, you're sure you know your altitude, attitude, and direction—and then it's a surprise when you open your eyes and discover you're totally wrong.

Disorientation aloft is pleasurable. It's on the ground that it's tricky.

Fortunately, my life was more or less on an even keel again. Reynaldo Dominguez had been found sane and bound over for trial for assaulting me. Alex Aguilar was finally located in a suburb of San Diego, and his lawyer had negotiated a plea bargain in exchange for his testimony in the various other cases pending against Dominguez. The attractiveness of pleading out was greatly enhanced when Aguilar learned that Harriet Leonard had revealed to the authorities that Johnny

Duarte had coerced him into importing his drugs through the shop in Ghirardelli Square.

Julia was fully in the clear and working overtime to accumulate the hours that would qualify her to take the exam for her license. I'd put Derek Ford on salary and hired Patrick Neilan full-time. Ted was still searching for the paragon of the paper clips. BSIS had removed the complaint against me from the pile on the low-level bureaucrat's desk and torn it up. Life was good. Even Ralph's health had improved. The vet had told me the cat's recent glucose curve indicated he was responding to the insulin.

But now Hy and I were flying off for a weekend at Touchstone, during which I was sure he would once again bring up the subject of marriage. I still hadn't a clue to what answer I'd give him.

I opened my eyes. We were in a climbing turn now, spiraling out of the airspace designated as an aerobatic box, on our way northwest after we'd both given the plane a good workout. Since I'd been with Hy, he'd enriched my life in so many ways: with the flying we loved; the remote and beautiful places he'd shown me; but mostly with his love, support, and understanding. So why was I afraid—?

"McCone," he said through our linked headsets, "I can't think of a better place to do this than at a mile high in our airplane. Maybe it'll bring me luck. For what seems like the hundredth time: Will you marry me?"

You've risked your safety time and again. You've risked your life, too.

Why not risk happiness?

The word was out of my mouth before I had time to argue with myself: "Yes."

Disorientation in the air. A splendid thing.

Hy didn't say anything—probably he was as shocked as I—but he reached over and squeezed my knee. Then he waggled the plane's wings exuberantly, and put it into a steeply banked right turn.

"Why're you changing course?" I asked. "Where're we going?"

"Reno, before you change your mind."

About the Author

MARCIA MULLER has written more than thirty novels and many short stories. Her novel *Wolf in the Shadows* won the Anthony Boucher Award. A recipient of the Private Eye Writers of America's Lifetime Achievement Award, she lives in Northern California with her husband, mystery writer Bill Pronzini. Please visit her Web site at www.MarciaMuller.com.

More
Marcia Muller!

Please turn this page
for a preview of

Cape Perdido

available in hardcover.

Friday

•

FEBRUARY 20

Jessie Domingo

"Three-three-Sierra, turning final."

Jessie gripped the seat with both hands and stared at the back of the charter pilot's head, hoping he was as calm and capable as he sounded. Through the tiny plane's window she saw nothing but pine trees stretching toward the placid gray sea.

Where the hell was the runway?

"Make sure your seatbelts're fastened tight, folks. We'll be on the ground in a couple of minutes."

Thank God!

She yanked on the end of the belt so hard that it all but forced the air from her lungs, then glanced at her traveling companion, Fitch Collier, for reassurance. Wouldn't you know it? The lawyer was sprawled out in his seat, sound asleep.

What an asshole!

First he'd upgraded to business class on their flight from New York, leaving her with her knees pressed against her nose in coach. Then he'd proceeded to wander back and forth between their seats the whole time, bringing her documents he'd finished reading and annoying the other two passengers in the cramped row by leaning across them to issue comments and instructions. And now he was comotose, just as the pilot of the little four-seater got set to plunge them into a thick forest in the wilds of northern California!

Where the hell *is that runway?*

The tops of the trees came level with the window. Jessie felt as if she were being sucked down a steep green chute. She closed her eyes, her ears popped, and then the plane thumped onto the ground so hard that pain shot up her spine. She tried to remember if her health plan paid for chiropractic treatment.

When the pain cleared and she opened her eyes, the plane was turning toward a low brown prefab terminal where two figures stood in a patch of pale winter sunlight. The welcoming committee from the Friends of the Perdido River. An ancient, mud-splattered white van was the only vehicle in sight. If this was to be their ground transportation, Jessie hoped it had good suspension.

Beside her, Fitch stretched and yawned—a honking sound that reminded her of a recent *National Geographic* special on Canadian geese. She glared at him before she felt around at her feet for her briefcase. Predictably, he didn't notice.

She'd met Fitch Collier, as prearranged by her employer, in the boarding area at Kennedy a long ten hours before. Already she was beginning to loathe him. Besides the upgrading and the kibitzing from the aisle, he'd spent their entire layover in San Francisco on his cellular, talking to more people than Jessie even knew about a variety of subjects designed to impress anyone within the Greater Bay Area. From these conversations Jessie had learned, among other things, that Fitch expected to make a small fortune on the upcoming IPO of SoftTech; that the 'Benz was being repainted; that he was still searching for a good deal on a time share on St. Bart's; that "the babe" couldn't get enough of him.

In short, that Fitch was an ostentatious, inconsiderate jerk—all the more so because he made her feel mean spirited for disliking him so much on so short an acquaintance.

When she'd drawn this assignment, Jessie had been excited—what community liaison specialist at Environmental Consultants Clearinghouse wouldn't've been? An opportunity to work with Fitch, one of the best water-rights attorneys in the country. A trip to a remote part of the northern California coast. A complex and potentially precedent-setting case that, should they win it, would earn them front-page coverage in newspapers across the country.

Jessie Domingo, in the *New York Times!*

Jessie Domingo, on "Sixty Minutes"!

Jessie Domingo, stuck at the end of nowhere with an egomaniacal, dictatorial lawyer who clearly considered her a mere flunky. And who, should they succeed, would end up taking all the credit for their joint efforts.

Reality strikes. Jessie strikes out—again.

The pilot shut down the plane, and Jessie peered out at the pair by the terminal. The stocky woman in the voluminous multi-colored skirt and cape would be

Bernina Tobin, and the lanky denim-clad man with the cloud of silver-gray curls, Joseph Openshaw. From both her reading of the foundation's research files and phone conversations with Bernina, Jessie knew that she was a Maine transplant and had led the Friends of the Perdido River in their year-long battle against a water grab by Aqueduct Systems, Inc., a North Carolina corporation. Openshaw had been one of Jessie's heroes ever since she became interested in ecology; a nationally known environmental activist and author, and native of the Cape Perdido area, he'd returned from the state capital early in the fight to lend his support, and had done much to turn public opinion against the waterbaggers, as the locals called them.

Jessie and Fitch had been sent by ECC to Cape Perdido in order to familiarize themselves firsthand with the situation; they would consult with local experts in hydrology and ecosystems, as well as with the leaders of the protests and other residents of the area. Next week they would journey to Sacramento, where Fitch would argue their case before the state water resources control board. If all went well, they would score a major coup for pro-environmental groups; if not, the board would rule to allow a pumping station to be built upstream on the Perdido, and pipe laid across a defunct lumber company's mill site, where the river's waters would be sucked into massive rubberized bags moored offshore, to be towed south and sold to drought-starved southern California municipalities such as San Diego.

Leaving the community with no recompense for its loss.

Leaving the ecology of the Perdido permanently damaged, and a visual blight on what was now a pristine and beautiful coastline.

Leaving the door open for violence in a place where the citizens had long embraced the tradition of taking the law into their own hands when the law didn't suit them.

The challenge was clear. Jessie stepped down from the plane, prepared to embrace it.

Joseph Openshaw

"Here come the New Yorkers."

Joseph ignored Bernina Tobin's comment and folded his arms across his chest, squinting at the luggage-laden pair moving toward them. What in God's name did they have in those suitcases?

The woman was very attractive, tall and slender, with straight light brown hair that swirled about her shoulders in the strong breeze. The man was also tall, and very thin, with silver-rimmed glasses and blond hair that was styled in casual disarray. They were dressed in what city dwellers always assumed was proper attire for the wilderness: pressed jeans, stylish sweaters, brand-new down jackets, designer walking shoes. Within a week, the jeans would be rumpled, the sweaters in need of dry cleaning, the jackets mud-stained, and the shoes replaced by sturdy boots from Perdido Feed and Surplus.

Thanks for coming all this way, strangers. And welcome to a world you can't begin to understand. No offense, but I doubt there's anything you can do for us.

Joseph unfolded his arms and, nudging Bernina foward, went to greet the visitors.

"You must be Ms. Tobin," the young woman said, extending her hand to Bernina. The heavy bag she had slung over her left shoulder slipped free and landed in the crook of her elbow. Momentarily she was thrown off balance and bumped against her traveling companion, who frowned in annoyance.

"Call me Bernina," Tobin told her. "You're Jessie, of course, and you're Fitch." She nodded at the man. "And this is Joseph."

Joseph relieved Jessie Domingo of the uncooperative bag and returned Fitch Collier's stiff nod with a smile.

"This all your stuff?" Bernina asked.

"Pilot's unloading the rest." Collier gestured at the plane.

Joseph glanced over there, saw Al Raymond, the regular on the charter flights from San Francisco to Soledad County, dragging two more bags from the luggage compartment. Jesus, they really didn't travel light! Each had gotten off the plane with a briefcase and a large duffel, plus Collier carried a hanging bag. Maybe it contained his golfing clothes—or his formal attire?

Joseph went to help Al load the luggage into the back of his van, while Bernina got the delegation from ECC settled inside.

When the offer of assistance in the Friends of the Perdido's opposition to the waterbaggers had come from Environmental Consultants Clearinghouse's executive director, Joseph had felt uneasy. Not that ECC didn't have an excellent track record. A nonprofit foundation funded by grants from corporations and wealthy philanthropists, it employed a full-time administrative staff and called upon a large panel of attorneys and other professionals specializing in a wide spectrum of environmental issues. When the foundation took on a cause, it would pair the various experts—such as Fitch Collier—with an on-staff community liaison specialist—in this case, Jessie Domingo—and send them into the field to gather information. This method created a picture of the situation which encompassed the legal, technical, and sociological issues. More often than not, ECC was able to work out environmentally favorable solutions through the appropriate legal channels.

Now, viewing the pair that had been sent west, Joseph's unease returned. In spite of her confident manner, the woman couldn't be much more than twenty-five, and the man, while closer to his own age, reminded him of the fresh-faced fraternity boys he'd known at U.C. Berkeley, who laughed and played their way through the world, oblivious to the fact that it was swiftly going to hell. Neither of these people seemed capable of dealing with the volatile situation that was shaping up at Cape Perdido.

But it was Eldon Whitesides, ECC's director, who really raised the level of Joseph's discomfort. He and Whitesides had come up together in the environmental wars of the eighties at Berkeley, but had long since followed divergent paths. Whitesides' route led him into the rarefied realm of important political connections and substantial philanthropical backing, while Joseph's led to the grassroots, poorly financed ghetto. While Whitesides made compromises and hammered out agreements in well-appointed parlors and boardrooms, Joseph held to a hard line in storefronts and on the streets. Not once in the year that the Friends of the Perdido had opposed the North Carolina water-exporting firm's proposed project had Eldon Whitesides taken notice of the battle raging in Soledad County—a battle whose outcome might very well determine the way water rights were handled throughout the state, and perhaps the country, for decades to come.

So why, when the hearings before the state water resources control board were so near, had Whitesides surfaced with his offer to help?

Joseph slammed the van's back doors, mock-saluted Al, and went around to the driver's side. Bernina sat half turned in the passenger's seat, chattering at the newcomers in her Down East accent. Something flattering about the Shorebird Motel and the Blue Moon Cafe, obviously trying to paint an appealing picture of what to outsiders would seem a pretty drab coastal outpost on an overcast winter day. He started the van, only half listening, and drove down the access road of the small airport. At least Tobin wasn't getting dogmatic on them just yet.

He didn't dislike Bernina, but an uneasy and sometimes prickly philosophical truce existed between them. She embraced the principles of feminist ecology—which Joseph, in an admittedly paranoid and simplistic fashion, interpreted as the view that everything wrong with the natural world was the direct result of men's piggish behavior toward it. Although he didn't like to think in terms of labels, if he had to characterize himself according to the currently accepted guidelines, Joseph would say he was a social ecologist.

Which, once the fancy rhetoric was stripped away, meant a practical person who believed there were ways for humans and nature to coexist in health and harmony. Throughout the six months since his return to Cape Perdido, Bernina—who was also his landlady— had spiritedly lectured him about the wrongness of his beliefs, insisting that if he'd only admit that a patriarchical society had fucked up the earth, he'd be on his way to enlightenment.

To Joseph, she sounded like the missionaries who used to come around to convert the coastal Pomos, a tribe with whom he had blood ties: Cast off your heathen religion, accept our teachings, repent your sins, and the kingdom of heaven is yours.

From the corner of his eye he saw Bernina glance at him, a frown that said she thought he was being inhospitable knitting her thick eyebrows. "Oilville coming up," he said, too heartily.

Jessie Domingo asked, "Why's it called that? I don't recall from my reading."

Bernina said, "It's the site of one of the first oil fields in California. Most people think all the state's oil wells are in southern California, but there was a short-lived boom here in the mid eighteen sixties. After the wells dried up, so did the town. Now, that's what's left." She motioned at the lone gas station and convenience store, the scattering of small frame houses that nestled in a clearing upon which the thick forest was slowly encroaching.

The lawyer, Fitch Collier, hadn't spoken or moved since they left the airport. With some concern, Joseph glanced into the rearview mirror. No, not dead, just sleeping.

Bernina went on, "Cape Perdido is a different story. The lumber mill, first called Breyer's, and then McNear's, was built there in eighteen sixty-three. The Cape became a doghole port, where schooners would take on lumber for transport south to San Francisco. Generation after generation worked that mill, but the decline in the lumbering industry forced its owner to shut it down five years ago, and now—well, you know from the press coverage about Timothy McNear offering to let Aqueduct Systems lay the pipe for their operation across the site. Anyway, the Cape's managed to hang on economically because of tourism and recreational opportunities. And people like me, who enjoy the small-town atmosphere and natural beauty, are still moving there—although there's no telling what'll happen if those waterbaggers succeed in raping our river. And rape is the right word for it. I can draw a lot of parallels between a violent sex crime and what that man, Gregory Erickson, wants to do here."

Please don't start, Joseph thought. Not now. Let these tired people get settled in before you try to indoctrinate them.

To turn the conversation in another direction, he said, "Bernina's a real authority on our little piece of the earth, even though she only came out from Maine three years ago."

Immediately he regretted the way it sounded. Bernina's eyes narrowed and she glared at him. "I suppose *you're* an authority, even though you abandoned this 'little piece of the earth' twenty years ago?"

He was not going to argue with her in front of strangers. "Oh, look, folks!" he exclaimed, pointing skyward. "There's a golden eagle!"

As they craned their necks to spot the nonexistent bird, he accelerated toward the turnoff for Cape Perdido.